Dear Reader,

Twenty years ago I began my career by writing romances under several pseudonyms. These were stories of women and men who meet, fall in love despite the odds against them, and endure the heartache and joy that is unique to that experience.

This story reflects those classic themes that have engaged and entertained audiences since storytelling first became a popular pastime. It has been reissued at your request and for your enjoyment. I hope you have as much fun reading it as I did writing it.

As in all romance novels, expect a happy ending. . . .

Sandra Brown

Tiger Prince

SANDRA BROWN

Previously published under the pseudonym Erin St. Claire

ISBN 1-55166-531-X

TIGER PRINCE

Copyright © 1985 by Sandra Brown.

Visit us at www.mirabooks.com

Printed in U.S.A.

Tiger Prince

One

"How could this have happened?"

"I've told you, I don't know. I'm sorry. It was a mistake, a human error. That's the only explanation I have."

"I think that's what the lookout at Pearl Harbor said," the man remarked dryly. He tossed the manila envelope down on his desk in disgust.

"You don't have to resort to sarcasm, Larry. I get your point." Caren Blakemore slumped wearily in her chair. This is just great, she thought. Just what I needed. She had been called in on the carpet because of one measly letter that contained nothing but a friendly hello from an official of one government to an official of another. You'd think she'd sold missile blueprints to the Russians.

"Good, but I'll reiterate it anyway. The wrong document got placed in that diplomatic pouch. It wasn't serious this time, but mistakes made on any level in the State Department can have grave repercussions. Next time you could pass on classified information.''

"Oh, come on!'' she cried, leaving her chair. She began to pace angrily. "I realize this office handles classified documents. I know I had to get clearance from the day I was born to work here. I made one mistake, Larry. I was momentarily distracted and slipped the wrong letter into a pouch. I'm sorry. Can I expect to be interrogated by the CIA?''

"Now who's being sarcastic?''

"So lay off.'' She returned to her chair, anger spent. An exhausting feeling of defeat pressed her into the cushions. That depression had lived with her for a year. It seemed to ride on her shoulders as though strapped there. In stressful situations like this one, it seemed to grow heavier.

Larry Watson tapped a ballpoint pen against the leather desk mat his wife had given him the Christmas before. He looked the part of under secretary to an under secretary to the Secretary of State of the United States. He had close-cropped hair, wore the correct charcoal-gray suits, white shirts, dark ties, wing-tip shoes. But his expression wasn't regulation. It was compassionate as he looked at his secretary.

"I'm sorry I came down hard on you, Caren. It's for your own good.''

"That's what my mother used to say every time I got a spanking. I didn't believe it then and I don't now.'' When she glanced up at him, he was smiling ruefully.

"That did sound rather trite, didn't it?'' Propping

his arms on his desk, he leaned forward. "But I meant it. Much as I'd hate losing you as my secretary, I know you need that promotion."

"Yes, I do. For many reasons."

"Money?"

"That's one. Kristin's school is expensive."

"She could go to public school," he reminded her.

"I promised Mother before she died that I'd give my sister the best possible education. In D.C., that means private school."

"She doesn't have to board there."

Caren was already shaking her head. "Trying to coordinate schedules would be impossible. I'd worry about her getting home safely every day and…" She waved her hand to encompass all the other trials. "It's so much better this way."

"You could have taken that cash settlement Wade offered." This suggestion was spoken even more softly. Larry knew it might have the impetus of a lit match held to gunpowder. It did. She flew out of the chair once again.

"Wade's way of buying himself a free conscience for leaving me for another woman? No way. I wasn't about to let him off that easy. Besides, when the divorce was final, it was final. I wanted nothing of his. He certainly wanted no part of me."

After thirteen months and twenty-two days, it still hurt to think about the rejection. When was this purgatory going to end? She had hoped the promotion to a higher-level job in the State Department would give her a new focus on her life. Now, she'd more than likely blown that. Just as she had her marriage.

Stop blaming yourself, Caren! she admonished. It wasn't your fault the rat walked.

Or was it?

"You want some sound advice?" Larry asked her.

"Do I have a choice?"

"None."

"Shoot," she said smiling at him. Usually they got along famously. Today had been a rare exception.

"You made the mistake with the pouches because you're tired. Worn out. At the end of your rope. On the brink of physical and mental collapse."

"Gee, this is just the pep talk I need."

"Caren," he said, coming from around the desk to sit on its corner. "Isn't that altar of martyrdom getting uncomfortable? A real louse of a husband leaves you for no apparent reason—"

"A girlfriend," she interrupted. "A blond bombshell with bazoomas out to here," she said, gesturing with her hands.

"Still, that's no *real* reason."

"I agree. I doubt if they're real."

"Will you let me get serious for a minute?"

"Sorry."

"It's been a tough year. You've had to make the psychological adjustment to the divorce as well as cope with the responsibility of supporting you and Kristin on your salary alone. I think you need to treat yourself to a week of R and R."

"I can't right now. I—"

"I insist."

"Insist?"

"Either take the vacation willingly, or I'll suspend you without pay for a week."

"You can't do that!"

"I can, as disciplinary action for getting those documents mixed up." She stared at him speechlessly. "Either a week's paid vacation or suspension without pay. Which is it going to be?"

Put like that, what choice did she have?

On the way home, as she fought with the killer instincts of a gladiator to survive Washington D.C.'s rush hour, the idea of getting away from it all began to appeal to her more and more.

She had felt nothing but utter dejection this past year. When your husband left after seven years of what you thought was a happy marriage, your ego became bruised to a point of never healing. At least Caren Blakemore's hadn't yet.

Outwardly she had shed the accoutrements of married life, but adjusting to the "singles scene" had been impossible for her. Her self-esteem was at its lowest ebb. She had never been a mixer anyway. How could she change now?

But maybe she could. Maybe she should. Maybe she should force herself to.

She had no social life. Work had gone sour. By the time she reached her small apartment in Georgetown, Larry's idea had taken root. Rushing through the door and dropping her purse into the nearest chair, she scrambled toward the desk tucked under the window. Several drawers were pillaged before she found what she was looking for.

Kicking off her shoes, she stretched across her bed and spread the colorful brochures in front of her. Endless stretches of sugary sand. Crystal-blue waters. Fern-banked lagoons. Bubbling waterfalls. Tropical sunsets. Moonlit horizons.

All were pictured in a photographic layout that would have appealed to the most jaded hedonist's senses. Fun, frolic, and food. Laziness. Blissful irresponsibility. Only a few hours' flight away.

She picked up the phone and dialed a familiar number.

"Hello."

"Hi, Kristin."

"Hi, Sis! I'm cramming for an algebra test. Really the pits. I'm not even going down for dinner. My roommie's bringing me a tray. What's going on in your life?"

"I screwed up at work."

"Was it a bad screwup?"

"Hardly. The Portuguese consul got a letter of congratulations on his daughter's wedding. He doesn't have a daughter. The letter was intended for the Peruvian consul. Well, they both start with P."

Kristin giggled, and Caren marveled over how nice and infectious the sound of her sixteen-year-old laughter was.

"Was Larry upset?"

"He chewed me out."

"He's a stuffed shirt, all government protocol."

"He was entitled. It was a mistake, and in my work there's no room for them. Especially if I want that new job."

"You'll get it."

Caren twisted the telephone cord. "Kristin, what would you think of my taking a week's vacation?" Hastily she explained, as though their roles were reversed, as though she were asking permission, as though she wanted to justify it before Kristin could ask her if she'd lost her mind.

"I think it's a really bitchin' idea."

"Is that good or bad?"

"That's good. I hope you meet some terrific guy. Those resorts always attract tanned, athletic, European types in string bikinis."

"Only in the white rum ads," Caren remarked with a wry smile. "You approve?"

"Absolutely. Go and have a blast."

"You'll have to spend the weekend at school."

"I'll wangle an invitation out of someone. Don't worry. Go. Have a ball. You've earned it."

"It'll take a big bite out of our savings."

"You'll replace it when you get that promotion."

Caren held her breath, closed her eyes, and clutched the telephone receiver. "All right, I'll go," she said on a gust of air before she could change her mind.

"Eat, drink, and be merry!"

"I will."

"Meet a wonderful guy. Someone between Richard Gere and Robert Redford with a little of Burt Reynolds's humor thrown in.''

"I'll try." Would she? Well, why not? If she were going to spread her wings and fly, she might just as well shoot for the moon. Of course, she wouldn't go down there *looking,* sniffing out all the eligible men the way prowlers in the singles bars did, but if the opportunity presented itself...

"I'll call you before I leave and give you all the details on where to reach me in case of an emergency and—''

"Have a good time. For once think of yourself and don't worry about anything."

They said their goodbyes. Caren pressed down the button on the phone rather than hanging up the receiver. She was afraid if she put it down, she'd change her mind and never pick it up again. There were a million reasons why she shouldn't go. And one pertinent reason why she should—

To save her life.

When a woman had to cope with the adversity Caren had been faced with this year, when she'd been rejected by her husband in favor of another woman, she had two choices. She could either succumb to the depression until she withered up, or she could go on living.

This afternoon marked Caren's decision. She had opted for the latter.

Consulting the telephone number on the brochure, she dialed it and then counted three rings before a cordial voice answered.

"Hello," she said with only a trace of hesitancy in her voice, "I'd like to go to Jamaica."

He stared at the amber contents of the brandy snifter and analyzed why he didn't want it. It had been poured from an expensive, vintage bottle. Its color was as clear and pure as a dark Mexican topaz. The bouquet was intoxicating.

He sipped. It was tasteless. He couldn't appreciate it any more than he appreciated the seductive efforts of his hostess. Clad now in a diaphanous peignoir designed to arouse any human male, she adjusted herself in the opposite corner of the short sofa and smiled at him over the rim of her snifter.

"You're not very talkative, darling. Did the play leave you meditative?"

They had just returned from the Kennedy Center, where a new play about the Vietnam War had premiered for a black-tie, by-invitation-only audience.

The man shot her a sardonic look. He doubted that the subtleties of the play had registered on her, much less evoked an emotional response. It might, however, have dampened the party mood they had been in. They had left the pre-theater dinner accompanied by a crowd of Washington's glittering social personalities. He had been as happy as the rest. It was no surprise his date wondered at his dour mood now.

"It was rather sobering."

She shifted impatiently, but not so casually as to miss the opportunity to let the robe slide away from a long, shapely thigh. "I don't like to think about things like that. They depress me.'' Her pout was intended to entice. Instead, he set his snifter on the glass coffee table and stood. Only inbred good manners kept him from showing his disgust over her shallowness as he crossed to the wide windows. He gazed out over the Tidal Basin, where city lights flickered in wavering lines.

He crammed his hands into his pockets, irritated with himself. What the hell was wrong? Why this sad-sack mood? Why this dissatisfaction with everything, his life, himself?

He had no problems. Ask any man on the street what kind of life he'd like to lead and the average guy would describe his. He had money. Clothes. Cars. Women. His date tonight had the best body and the worst reputation in the city. And he wanted her no more than he wanted her brandy.

He was sick to death of it all, the glamour, the blasé attitude of his friends. What sickened him most was the pretense that he was enjoying it.

''What's wrong, Derek?''

He heard the peignoir rustle as she crossed the thick plush carpet on bare feet. Her arms came around him and her hands slid beneath his tuxedo jacket. Laying them on his chest, she began to rub in slow circles. She knew her stuff. Her thumbs must have had the sensitivity of radar, because they found his nipples under the starched shirt and stroked them to respond.

She was a product market-tested for consumption. Lotioned and creamed and plucked and scented and shaped. Her career was to have a good time, to spend Daddy's money, to live life in the fast lane, to take as many lovers as possible until she eventually made a "good" marriage.

"I'll bet I can get you out of your bad mood," she purred as she moved closer to him, pressing her body against his back. Coming up on tiptoes, she gently blew in his ear. Her hands slid down the pleats of his shirt, over the black satin cummerbund to the fly of his pants.

Normally her talented hands could stir him to passion in seconds. Tonight they only served to heighten his vexation. He turned abruptly, clasped her shoulders harder than he intended to, and pushed her away. "I'm sorry," he said quickly when he noted the startled look on her face. Immediately he released his grip on her shoulders. He tried to smile. "I guess I'm just not in the mood tonight."

She tossed back a mane of hair that a highly paid, flamboyant hairdresser kept in perfect condition. "Well, that's a switch," she said scathingly.

He laughed shortly. "I guess it is."

"Usually I wonder if you even remember my name. You come here. We strip. We make love. You say thanks and leave. What's different about tonight?"

"I'm tired, have a lot on my mind." He was gradually making his way toward the front door. He didn't want it to appear that he was escaping, but that was exactly what he was doing.

She laid a restraining hand on his arm. After all,

Derek Allen was a good catch in more ways than one. Even a woman like her who usually didn't cater to men was willing to swallow a little pride for Derek.

"I can take your mind off anything," she promised with well-glossed lips. Like coiling snakes, her arms wound around his neck and pulled his head down for her kiss. She made her body an open invitation. She used her tongue.

He felt nothing. Not a glimmer, not a spark of desire. Only that bitter dissatisfaction that was like a bad taste in his mouth.

Reaching up, he pried her arms away from him. "Sorry. Not tonight," he said with a tilting grin.

"If you leave now, don't bother calling again." She wasn't accustomed to being the one left wanting. "You son of a bitch. Who do you think you are?"

At the door, he glanced back at her. Her fists were digging into her hips and her ample breasts were heaving as she glared at him malevolently. At least this loss of control was something different, something unrehearsed. For the first time that night, he thought she looked beautiful, because for the first time she was genuine, real. But he still didn't want her.

"Good night," he said softly as he pulled the door open.

"Go to hell," she screamed as he closed it behind him.

"It might be a pleasant change," he mumbled with dry humor. Her obscene epithets followed him down the corridor to the elevator. Only its closing door si-

lenced her piercing voice. At the first floor he crossed
the lobby of the high-rise apartment building, anxious
to breathe the open air and clear his head of her heavy
perfume. He nodded to the doorman, who held the
door for him.

"Good night, Mr. Allen," he said respectfully.

As soon as he stepped outside, a flashbulb ex-
ploded in his face. Automatically his arm went up to
protect himself from being photographed again, but
to little avail. Motor-driven cameras continued to
snap one picture after another as a group of paparazzi
converged on him, surrounding him on the sidewalk.

"Give me a break, you guys," he said resignedly
as he tried to wade through them. "Didn't you get
enough pictures at the premiere?"

"We'll never get enough of you, Allen. You're too
hot, especially with your papa coming to town this
week."

Derek's rushed footsteps came to an abrupt halt,
and he whirled around to face the reporter who had
mentioned his father. "Who told you that?"

"Wouldn't you like to know?"

Derek faced Speck Daniels. He should have
known. He was looking into the corpulent countenance of one of the most obnoxious and dogged
members of the "press." Speck worked freelance,
but his pieces usually showed up in the tabloids that
printed scandalous and damaging stories, whether
they were true or not.

The photographer was incredibly unattractive. His
potbelly strained the buttons of his none too clean

white oxford-cloth shirt. His legs were squat and short and seemed continually planted wide apart in a belligerent stance. Oiled, thinning, black hair was plastered to his pale, perspiring scalp. Derek knew there was a naked woman of awesome proportions tattooed on the photographer's forearm. It was Speck's most prized possession, and he never failed to show it off. His camera dangled from his thick, bullish neck by a sweat-stained strap.

"Oh, I know your pop's visit was a big hush-hush secret and all," he was saying. "But hell, you know this town. No secret can be kept for long."

"How do you feel about your father's visit?" another reporter asked Derek.

"No comment," he said. "Now, if you'll excuse me—"

"You must have something to say." Speck Daniels barred his path. Derek thought, unkindly, that for a fat man he moved with remarkable agility. "How long's it been since you saw your old man?"

"No comment." Derek spoke through his teeth. "Please get out of my way."

"What would he think of that young lady you were squiring around tonight? Is she someone special?" Speck asked.

"Have you been seeing her for long?" someone else butted in. "Are there any marriage plans?"

"Oh, for God's sake," Derek said angrily. Another camera took a picture of his profile. He pushed one photographer aside only to be blocked again by Speck's girth.

"Let's have one more picture for your old man's scrapbook," Speck said as he raised his camera.

The flashing blue-white light blasted Derek's eyes, momentarily blinding him. It was unfortunate for Speck that Derek's vision cleared seconds later. Derek yanked on the strap of the camera and pulled it from around Speck's neck. Why the vicious jerking motion didn't snap the photographer's neck was something to be marveled over for weeks by those who witnessed it.

Derek dashed the camera against the brick wall of the building, then threw it to the sidewalk. The others, murmuring, moved back. Derek, with his chest heaving and fists working at his sides, faced Speck. "If you ever harass me again, I'll see to it you never work. You won't be able to get a paper route. Got it? Now get out of my way."

Speck's bravado disappeared. He stepped aside and let Derek pass. Over his shoulder the tall receding figure called back, "I'll send a check to cover the camera tomorrow."

Then he disappeared around the corner of the building, vaulted into the driver's seat of the Excalibur convertible he had irresponsibly left unlocked on the city street, and ground the engine into life. The remarkably subdued group of reporters were still collected in a small huddle when he sped by seconds later.

Some of his temper had cooled by the time Derek reached his own apartment building and turned the car into its designated place in the underground garage. In the elevator he leaned back against the wall and drew in long draughts of air.

Why hadn't he handled it better? Why hadn't he let them take his picture all they wanted? But as long as he had gone to the trouble to get angry, why hadn't he wrapped his hands around Speck Daniels's neck and strangled him until his piggish eyes popped out? He was slime, and he represented the worst of those who constantly hounded Derek.

It was the unexpected question about his father that had gotten to him. He hadn't known the public was aware of his father's visit to D.C. Well, by morning they would know. And Daniels would see to it they knew his son's reaction to the visit. He would be made out a hothead. Somehow Daniels would twist it to look as if it was his father's visit that had provoked his anger. Hell. Why hadn't he stayed home with a cold can of beer tonight?

He let himself into the penthouse. It was sterile. Dark and cool, the only sound the purr of the air conditioner. It reminded him of the reception room at a funeral home. He stayed there only frequently enough to justify holding onto the apartment.

He dropped pieces of clothing as he took them off, letting them fall where they might, knowing that a maid service would clean the apartment the next day. He was naked by the time he reached his bathroom and turned on the cold tap in the shower.

The water pounded him, stung his skin, punished him for his behavior tonight, both with the woman and with the paparazzi.

They weren't to blame. He was. He was only taking his restlessness out on them. He gripped the gold-plated handles hard as he turned off the water and let his head fall forward wearily. Water dripped from the points his hair made around his face.

"I've got to get away."

He didn't even know he'd spoken the words aloud until he heard them echoing off the marble walls of the shower stall. Stepping from the shower, disregarding his wet nakedness, he padded into the bedroom and switched on the bedside lamp. In the drawer of the table he found a telephone directory and began flipping through its pages.

He had to get out of Washington. Even the farm wouldn't be far enough away while his father was in town. The press would be crawling over him like ants, watching his every move, recording every word he said, misquoting his opinion on matters that didn't concern him in the least and that he didn't want to be concerned about. He would do something that would make his father angry, embarrass his mother, alienate the press even more.

No, he couldn't afford to stay in town this week. For everyone's sake, he would clear out.

The voice that answered his call was friendly and feminine.

"I want to take a trip," he said bluntly. "I want to leave tomorrow. Can you arrange it?"

The woman laughed, instinctively knowing she was talking to an extraordinarily attractive male. "I hope so. There's only one tiny problem, sir."

"What's that?"

"Where do you want to go?"

"Oh." He raked a hand through his dripping hair. Where did he want to go? Where hadn't he been in a long time? Somewhere sunny, laid back. Not too far. "Jamaica," he said for lack of any other inspiration.

The sun had never seen her breasts before.

She had never had occasion to bare them to the sun. If she had, no doubt she would have lacked the nerve. But she had to start somewhere if she was going to have a fling.

Feeling totally out of character, Caren Blakemore lay on the beach towel in nothing more than her bikini bottom and three applications of suntan gel.

Lying beside her was the fire-breathing dragon she'd spent the early hours of the morning sculpting out of sand. More than six feet long, his humped back periodically arching out of the sand, the dragon was a masterpiece of scaly perfection. She fancied him as her protector against intruders.

Admittedly, there wasn't that much risk of her privacy being interrupted. She was lying on her private stretch of beach, which sloped down from the bungalow she had rented for the week. She had opted for the bungalow in favor of staying in the central hotel of the resort. Somehow an ordinary hotel room lacked the romance of the secluded bungalow tucked away in its private tropical garden.

No one could see her here. She would spy the boats

out in the bay long before they saw her, and she could reach for cover should they cruise too close to shore. If this trip proved to be uneventful except for the rest and relaxation it promised, she would at least have a spectacular tan to boast about when she got home.

And lying topless really was a glorious sensation. A bit pagan. A tad naughty. Certainly brazen. All of which only heightened the pleasure of it. She emptied her mind of troublesome thoughts and let her senses take over.

The sun was a warm caress on her skin. The sand was a soft pallet. The scents that wafted on the cooling Caribbean breeze were of flowers and sea and sun-baked earth. The sounds were those of wind soughing through the palm fronds overhead and water gently lapping at the shore, and—

Another sound she couldn't instantly name. But it sounded like a small cyclone bearing down on her with thudding footsteps.

He was there before she knew it. He came sailing over the dragon's head, breathing like a locomotive and running pell-mell.

"God*damn!*" he shouted when he spotted her. The words were spoken in two precise syllables, as though the first was an exclamation over the situation and the second was an assessment of it.

He extended his leg in an attempt to keep his Nike-shod foot from landing square between her ribs. That movement broke his stride, and his foot landed wrong in the giving sand. Cursing again, he lost his balance and went tumbling, all naked limbs and sweat-beaded skin. The dragon's long-reaching forked tongue was squashed between the runner's shoulder blades and one fire-emitting nostril was irreparably damaged.

He rolled over to face her. Like an Olympian athlete about to begin a race, he stopped with one knee bent, the other leg stretched out behind him. He was supported by arms that Tarzan would have envied as his fist dug craters into the sand. He was taut, tense, poised. Sinews were stretched. Sleek muscles were contracted. His breathing was hard. His eyes glowed. Had he not been a perfect specimen of a man, Caren would have thought she was about to be pounced upon by a great jungle cat.

Two

Those eyes! Green and gold and agate swirled together in a most unusual harmony—both dangerous and captivating. She seemed to be swallowed whole by the deep blackness of the pupils in their centers.

And his hair. Brown. A rich brown, but striped with golden strands as evenly spaced as those on a tiger's pelt. It was longish, but not unattractively so. It suited him and matched the wildness about him. Naked as he was, save for a pair of blue running shorts and the Nikes, he appeared savage, primitive. His grin was slow, devilish, sultry.

"Hello." His voice was as smooth as his sweat-bathed tanned skin and just as sinfully appealing.

"Hello," Caren squeaked stupidly.

"Did I manage to avoid tromping on you?" The tiger eyes prowled over her body. When they stopped at her breasts and widened with interest, Caren became aware that she was no more clothed than he. She grabbed up a towel and clutched it in front of her.

"Yes. Just barely," she said breathlessly. Good Lord! She had wanted adventure, new experiences. But...*this?*

"I'm sorry. I didn't see you until I was right on top of you." He smiled again, suggestively, and she was certain his choice of words had been no accident. "You're lying behind the only dune on the beach."

"It's not a dune, it's a dragon." He cocked his head to one side as though trying to envision a dragon in the mashed lumps of sand. "Or it *was,*" she said with asperity. "This is supposed to be my private beach." She sounded like an old-maid schoolteacher. No doubt he would be dazzled.

"Sorry about the dragon," he said with a smile that could melt an iceberg. He raised his eyes to the top of the slope. "That's your bungalow?"

"Yes."

The smile broadened. "I'm your next-door neighbor. Derek Allen." He stuck out his hand, and she jumped. Cursing herself for acting like such an idiot, she reached for his hand, anchoring the towel across her breasts with the other arm.

"Caren Blakemore." When she tried to withdraw her hand, he kept it snugly clasped in his.

"You really shouldn't bother covering up with that towel."

"Yes," she said, licking her lips quickly, "I really should. Please let go of my hand."

"Your breasts are beautiful."

Fevered blood rushed to her cheeks and infused them with color. "Thank you."

"You're welcome."

Suddenly she dropped her chin against her chest. "I don't believe this conversation."

"Why?"

"If you knew me, you'd know why." She tugged on her hand in earnest, and he finally relinquished it. "I've had enough sun for today. My goodness, look at my arm. It's already pink. Tropical sun. I'm not used to it, and I don't want to burn on my first day."

She rattled on as she awkwardly stuffed her belongings in the large straw bag. When she had collected everything with one hand, she struggled to her feet with all the grace of a knock-kneed ostrich. He placed a hand under her elbow and assisted her.

"Goodbye, Mr....uh..."

"Allen."

"Goodbye, Mr. Allen. Have a nice vacation."

With what shreds of dignity were left her, she turned around and started up the slope. "You forgot something," he called.

"Oh!" was her startled cry when she saw her bikini top dangling from his outstretched fingertips. Retracing her steps, she snatched it from him. "Thank you."

"Would you like to put it on?"

"No."

"Sure? I'll be glad to help you."

"*No!* No, thanks, I mean," she muttered as she gave him her back again. "Goodbye."

With each retreating footstep she could feel his eyes boring into her back. Hoping that her suit bottom was modestly pulled down over her derrière, she all but ran the rest of the way until she was safely behind the wall surrounding her private terrace.

She was shaking from head to toe by the time she slid the glass door closed behind her. Going into the small kitchen alcove, she reached into the tiny refrigerator for the jar of water she had placed there the night before and took a long, jarringly cold drink. Perhaps it would relieve that cottony dryness in her mouth.

Not until she was in the bedroom of the bungalow did she drop the towel from her breasts. Then she collapsed onto the bed. So much for the swinging singles life. So much for adventure and going with the flow. She had behaved like a blithering idiot. He was probably still down there on the beach, convulsed with laughter.

Damn! This ruined everything. She'd never be able to look that man in the eye again. Would she have to spend the remainder of her vacation cooped up inside the bungalow for fear of running into him?

No. She wouldn't. She refused to. She'd go right back down to the beach.

Her mind made up, she strode militantly through the bungalow. She even made it as far as the glass door to the terrace. Then she stopped and reconsidered. There was a perfectly comfortable chaise on the terrace. It was private. Quiet. At this time of day, it was sunny. Why not just stay here?

Coward! her mind screamed.

Even so, before she went onto the terrace she put on her bikini top.

She could be married.

Probably to a linebacker for the Pittsburgh Steelers. That's it. She's married to this fiercely jealous husband who...

No, he didn't think she was married. She had been scared, but of *him*, not of a jealous husband. Or had it been him? Was it merely the situation? Or a combination of the two. Whatever had caused her nervousness, it had endeared her to him.

Derek stood at the window and gazed at the roof of the neighboring bungalow as he sipped a bottle of chilled Perrier. He chuckled softly as he remembered her startled expression. She had sprung bolt upright as though hinged at the waist. Her eyes had been as wide and round as saucers and as softly brown as velvet. The honey-colored hair had been tied up in a ponytail, but he guessed that when let down it would fall to her shoulders.

He should have been gentlemanly enough to offer her the towel right away and spare her that flush of embarrassment. But *damn*, that shy blush had been enchanting. When had he last seen a woman blush? Had he ever?

Any woman he knew would have leaned back, stretched languorously, and offered him an unrestricted view, striking a pose and smiling a smile calculated to tantalize and excite.

He'd been tantalized and excited all right. Her

body was compact and slender, but achingly soft and feminine. If that weren't enough to lure him, her timid awkwardness and her discomfort with the situation had intrigued him.

He wanted to see her again. How would he ever know if she had a husband or a traveling companion if he didn't try? Derek Allen had never refused a challenge in his life, especially where a woman was concerned.

He dropped his shorts where he stood and strode into the shower.

Caren came out of the shower and surveyed her body in the mirror. Her tan was coming along nicely. Not bad at all for the first day. To protect against peeling, she smoothed on a flower-scented lotion. Taking the towel from her head, she shook out her wet hair and ran her fingers through it. She was just reaching for the hairbrush when a knock sounded at the front door.

Stepping into a strapless terry cloth jumpsuit, she tiptoed through the bungalow and peeped through the sheer drapes. "Oh, no," she whispered when she saw him standing on the small porch. Was he going to be a pest?

She would wait him out. He would eventually tire of the game and go away. On the other hand, she had come down here to learn to assert herself, hadn't she? If she were going to welcome the advances of some men, she had better learn how to discourage the others. Garnering all her courage and putting a haughty,

I've-got-your-number-Mr. expression on her face, she pulled open the door.

"Hi."

His first hello on the beach had been formal. This greeting was intimate, spoken as much with his eyes as with his voice. She could almost swear those golden-green eyes had the power to stroke her, for she felt their warm gaze pouring over her dishabille and liking it. They coaxed responses from her body that were mortifying and embarrassing.

Pressing her thighs tightly together, she propped one bare foot on top of the other. Nervously, she crossed her arms at her waist, noting that her palms had suddenly gone damp. She prayed he couldn't see what her breasts were doing, but feared that he could. His grin was lazy and more than a little arrogant.

"Can I do something for you, Mr. Allen?" Oh, that was good, Caren. If she had been auditioning for the role of straight man, she couldn't have asked a more leading question. It had been used in every B-grade movie ever produced. Would he think she was being deliberately provocative? God forbid. This man didn't need any encouragement.

"Yes, you can, Caren." Her stomach turned over as her name came sliding through his lips. "You can loan me a cup of sugar."

"P-pardon?" What had she expected, an invitation to his bed? Yes. The very innocence of his request surprised her.

"A cup of sugar," he repeated, wedging himself inside the door. "No sense in letting the cool air out," he remarked casually as he closed it behind him. "Do you like your bungalow? I find mine quite comfortable."

A million gruesome possibilities ran through her mind. She hadn't read *Looking for Mr. Goodbar* for nothing. He was too smooth. Too polished. She imagined that invading a woman's space was nothing new to him, but it sure as hell was out of the ordinary for Caren Blakemore.

"Mr. Allen—"

"Please call me Derek. If we're going to be 'borrowing' neighbors, don't you think we should be on a first-name basis?"

His insouciance miffed her, and her chin went up a notch. "Were you planning on doing some baking while you're here?" she asked tartly.

"Baking?"

"The sugar. What did you want with a cup of sugar?"

"Oh, the sugar. Let's see." He made no pretense of the fact that he was constructing a lie. "I brought tea bags and was in the process of making myself a pitcher of iced tea." His mouth tilted down sulkily. "I hate unsweetened iced tea."

Because the lie was so unapologetically made, she laughed. She bit her lower lip, trying to keep the laughter inside, but it wouldn't be contained. "I'm sorry. I don't have any sugar. I have Sweet'N Low."

He made a face. "No sugar?"

"No sugar. I can't help you, Mr....Derek," she said hastily when his brows veed into a frown.

"Do you have a soft drink?"

She let out an exasperated sigh. "I'm not exactly up to playing hostess right now. My hair is wet. I don't have any makeup on. I'm not dressed properly." She pulled in another deep breath. "And I didn't invite you."

"Why didn't you come back to the beach? I waited a long time."

"I sunbathed on my own terrace so I could have some *privacy*." She emphasized the last word. He only grinned.

"Topless?"

"What?" she asked, momentarily dazed by the white sparkle of his teeth.

"Topless. Did you sunbathe topless?"

"No, not topless."

"Why? Afraid of Peeping Toms?"

"No. Of pesky neighbors."

He laughed out loud then, a deep, rolling laugh that vibrated through his wide chest. She remembered how it looked bare. Dark skin. Sun-gilded hair, damply curled with perspiration. Flat, brown nipples nestled— My Lord! Would you listen to yourself! She brought her eyes away from that impressive chest, which was now covered with a loose cotton pullover.

"Are you here alone?" he asked suddenly.

"Uh…sort of…I—"

"How can you be 'sort of' alone? Do you have a husband?"

"No, but—"

"A lover?"

"*No.*" Then, when his brows shot up in query at her emphatic answer, she said evenly, "Not with me."

"Great! I'm alone too. We can do things together. It'll be much more fun."

Crossing her arms over her chest, not out of nervousness now, but aggravation, she tapped her foot impatiently. "What could we do together?" When she heard her own words, her faced paled. Terrific, Caren. So far you're doing just great.

"Something immediately comes to my mind." He took the steps necessary to bring them toe to toe.

He was wearing shorts. She could feel the crinkly hairs on his legs against her. "What?" she asked in a voice that sounded like sandpaper.

"Something it takes two to do."

"What?"

"Tennis."

Her head snapped up to meet his teasing grin. *"Tennis?"*

"Yes, why? Were you thinking of something else?"

She blushed hotly. "No. Of course not," she lied.

"You play, don't you?"

"Play tennis?"

"Isn't that what we're talking about?" He had seen straight through her lie.

"Sure I play. Some. What grade are you?"

"A-plus. What about you?"

"B at best. See? It would be no fun for you."

"Better than the other way around. If you were the better player my male ego would never survive it."

She seriously doubted that. Any man who was so audacious as to let his eyes roam at will over a half-clad woman he'd met only a few hours before wouldn't have to worry over the mortality of his ego.

"How do you feel about snorkeling?"

"I'm afraid of sharks." She shot him a meaningful look, and he laughed again.

"Is there a double meaning hiding in there?"

"If the shoe fits—"

Her comeback was bit off abruptly as he raised his hands and threaded his fingers through her hair. He combed them through the thick, wavy strands on either side of her head. "Your hair is a beautiful color," he remarked candidly. He studied each damp strand as it slid through his widespread fingers.

"Thank you."

"I couldn't tell how long it was when it was in the ponytail. I guessed about here." His hands paused at her shoulders before moving down onto her chest, measuring the hair as he went. "I was wrong. It's longer. It comes to…" His fingers ran out of hair and touched her skin. Lightly, lightly, he caressed the rising curves. "…Here," he finished on a whisper.

Resting his fingertips against the top swell of her breasts, he captured her eyes with his. For a long moment they stared, barely breathing, still but for the chaos going on inside them. He wanted to touch her, sample the sweetness of her mouth, lose himself in her scent. But her wide-eyed gaze and the slight trembling of her body told him she wasn't ready. He didn't want to frighten her off again.

He stepped back, and she shook herself out of the trance his lulling voice had induced.

"What are you doing for dinner tonight?" he asked.

"I'm not sure."

"When will you be sure?"

She tried to avoid his eyes. They had some mystical power. When she looked directly into them, she seemed to give herself over to his will. "I really don't want to make any plans," she hedged. "That's what this week of vacation is for. To rest, relax, do things when I please."

"I see." When he had come in, he hadn't had any idea of how it would go. They could have been in bed by now, or the linebacker could have tossed him out on his ear. He assessed his actual position as somewhere in between.

She obviously wasn't accustomed to having casual affairs. But she wasn't made of wood, either. Derek knew his way around a woman's body, a woman's mind. He knew the signs. She was interested, but cautious.

It was a foregone conclusion that he would have her in bed. He'd decided that on the beach. But for now, it was time to retreat and regroup.

Flashing his most irresistible smile, he asked, "You're sure you don't have any sugar?"

Her spontaneous laugh was encouraging. When she

did let her guard down she was going to be fabulous.
"'Bye. I'll catch you later.''

"Goodbye."

She showed him out, and as soon as the door closed behind him, she slumped against it, feeling as though she'd just run a marathon.

She muttered every curse she could think of as she softly thumped her fists against the door. Why was this so difficult for her? Had Wade destroyed every molecule of confidence she had? What had made her think she would be good at the games modern singles played? She, who hadn't been able to keep her husband interested, couldn't possibly compete with the sexual piranhas who had this temporary mating game down to an art.

Yes, she had considered having a vacation affair. Something sweet and swift. Here today, gone tomorrow. Something to be reviewed with fond memories when she got home, rather like vacation snapshots. Yes, she had hoped to meet a man.

But not one like this. She had hoped to meet someone as lonely as she, someone as unsure of himself as she, someone just as nervous about embarking on a brief, finite love affair.

She certainly didn't want a man with Derek Allen's suavity. He was too handsome, too glib, too virile. And too sure of his virility. He teased too easily, making naughty remarks but keeping them inoffensive. His technique was too cool and his eyes were too hot. No, he wasn't the one.

On the outside chance that he would return before

dinner and catch her alone in the bungalow, she planned to make herself scarce.

Maybe this wasn't a good idea after all, Caren thought dismally. The open-air dining pavilion was designed with even-numbered parties in mind. She sat alone at a table for two surrounded by couples absorbed with each other, or by groups of four laughing and joking. She felt alien, lost, and conspicuous.

Last summer's backless sundress seemed downright dowdy compared to the airy wisps women were wearing this season. Tomorrow she would go shopping and spend the last of her savings on something frothy and bare. And she was going to discard panty hose until she returned home. No one wore stockings in the tropics.

A sextet was playing soft dinner music under a thatched gazebo. The sun had set only minutes before, painting on the sky and sea a rainbow of vibrant colors from the softest peach to the most brilliant indigo. Fresh flowers decorated the center of each table. Hurricane lamps flickered in the sea breeze. The whole concept behind this resort was romance. What was she doing here?

"Have you been waiting long?"

She looked up from her morose musings. Derek was smiling down at her. Like a moron, she glanced around to verify that he was speaking to her. Without waiting for her to answer, he slid into the chair across the table. "I'm sorry I'm late."

She folded her arms on the table and tried to appear

vexed. In fact, she was immensely pleased. "You have a remarkable amount of gall, Mr. Allen."

"And you have remarkable eyes and beautiful breasts." Her mouth fell open slightly. "You look shocked. Did you think I had forgotten?" His eyes skimmed her front and his voice lowered an octave. "I remember them in vivid detail. Soft, round, pink—"

"Can we talk about something else?"

"Certainly." He reached across the table and took her hand, pressing it between his. "What shall we talk about? How about French-kissing? Do you French-kiss on the first date?"

Too rattled to speak, she stared at him mutely.

"Would you care to order wine with dinner?" The wine steward had appeared from out of nowhere. Or was she so caught up in the audacity of the man sitting across from her that everything else in the world seemed to have vanished?

"No, thank you—"

"Yes, please." They answered at the same time.

The steward's hesitant eyes bounced between them until Derek took charge. He ordered a vintage Caren couldn't even pronounce. It sounded incredibly rare and expensive. The steward was impressed. He began snapping his fingers at subordinates, who rushed to carry out his commands.

"I hope that's agreeable with you," Derek said to her.

Her lips felt rubbery as she tried to fashion a blithe

smile. "Of course." I'm out of my league. Far out of my league.

"Do you want to go through the buffet or eat à la carte?"

"The fresh fruit on the buffet looks scrumptious."

"Then the buffet it is." Smoothly he got up and helped her from her chair. She noted the envious and speculative looks of other women as she and Derek wended their way through the candlelit tables.

Derek was easily the best-looking man she had ever seen, and apparently the rest of the female population wasn't immune to him either. He had on cream-colored trousers, a double-breasted navy blazer with brass buttons, and a cream-colored silk shirt. No tie. There was a jaunty red handkerchief in his breast pocket.

The deep, open V of his shirt gave only a hint of the male beauty of his torso, which Caren knew firsthand was broad at the shoulders and chest and tapered to a hard, flat stomach and abdomen. It was all covered with taut, deeply tanned skin and a forest of soft, tawny hair. The rising moon and the hurricane lamps picked up the gold streaks in his hair and made them shine.

They had similar tastes in food. They selected fresh fruits, vegetables, and lean meat, but little starch or bread.

"Open up." She turned. Derek was holding a ruby-red, succulent strawberry for her. She hesitated. Had she ever eaten out of a man's hand before? Literally? She never remembered sharing that particular intimacy with Wade. But then, gazing into Derek's exotic face, she could barely remember what Wade looked like.

Of their own accord her lips opened. He placed the tip of the strawberry in the narrow opening, forcing her lips to work up and over it until they touched his fingertips where they held the short stem. She bit off the last bite and raised her eyes to his as she chewed it slowly. "Thank you."

"You're welcome." His voice was as husky as hers.

The dancing flames in the hurricane lamps cast intriguing patterns of light and shadow over their faces. They stared long at each other until the man in line behind them loudly cleared his throat.

When they returned to the table, the wine steward was patiently waiting for Derek's approval before pouring the wine.

"To a wonderful week for both of us," Derek said, lifting his glass to hers after the steward discreetly withdrew. They clinked glasses, and she sipped the wine. "You like?"

She closed her eyes and savored the sunny flavor as it slid down her throat, warming as it went. "Very much."

They ate slowly. It appeared that Derek intended to spend the evening in her company. She should have been angry over his presumption that she would welcome him or that she had made no other plans. But anger required so much energy, and it hardly seemed worth the effort. She was too mystified, too caught up in the magic of the evening to be angry at anything.

The wine was potent. The alcohol went immediately to her head, making it feel light enough to float while her body was drugged with a delicious lassitude. She watched Derek's mouth as he ate, almost wishing he would pick up the conversation about kissing. His tongue flicked at the corners of his lips. *French*-kissing. Her stomach did a somersault.

"Have you ever been married?" he asked.

She toyed with the stem of her wineglass. "I was, until about a year ago."

"Divorce?"

"Yes."

"Rough?"

"Yes." End of subject. She made that eminently clear.

"Any family?"

"You mean children?" He nodded. "No children," she said wistfully. "No family either except for my sister, Kristin. She's sixteen. Still in school. It's just the two of us."

They seemed to tacitly agree that the less they knew about each other the better. They kept the conversation general, leaving out specifics. She told him only that she worked as a secretary. He didn't ask and she didn't volunteer whom she worked for or where she lived.

"What do you do?"

"I'm a farmer."

Carefully, never taking her eyes off his, she set her wineglass down. "A f-farmer?"

He smiled at her incredulity. "Does that surprise you?"

"Surprise me? Yes. No, shock is a better word."

He leaned forward slightly. "Why?"

"Admittedly, I haven't known any farmers, but you certainly don't fit the picture my mind conjures up."

"What would you guess me to be?"

"Hmm." She pretended to study him. "A professional polo player. A gambler. Maybe an entertainer."

"You see how wrong a person can be," he said, spreading his arms wide.

"Perhaps a gigolo." He looked genuinely wounded. "Are you teasing me? Are you really a farmer?"

"Yes." He laughed.

"What do you raise?"

"Crops," he said obliquely. "I breed a few horses. You know, a farm."

She got the message; the subject was closed. Well, fair was fair. She wasn't going to pry into his life. He had had the courtesy not to pry into hers.

They watched each other as they sipped the last of the wine.

"Well, I've struck out on tennis and snorkeling. Will you go to bed with me?"

"No!" she exclaimed on something between a laugh and a cry.

"Dance?"

She glanced at the other couples swaying under the stars to the haunting music. Smiling back at him, she said simply, "Yes."

He escorted her toward the dance floor, which extended out over the glassy waters of the bay. Facing her, he opened his arms, and she glided into their embrace. He enfolded her. With a hand opened wide over the small of her back, he pressed her closer.

She must have died out there on the beach this morning. She had suffered a stroke, a heart attack, something that had killed her instantly and painlessly. She had died on the beach this morning.

Because surely this was heaven.

Three

It felt good to be held in a man's arms. Caren hadn't realized how much she had missed just being held. She was an affectionate creature who had always enjoyed cuddling. Since the divorce, she hadn't allowed herself to think about such things, because the pain of loss was too much to bear.

She understood how babies could actually die from lack of being touched. Stroking was essential to the human animal. Her whole being had been starved for it.

She was also an intensely feminine woman and had missed having a masculine presence in her life. Derek's closeness made her feel that deficiency sharply. He was so much taller, and harder, and stronger than she. He was warm. She wanted to curl up against him, to draw comfort from his nearness and warmth.

His absolute masculinity emphasized the contrast between them. He smelled different and felt different. His clothes had a different texture from hers. She wanted to touch all of him, to remember with her senses of smell and touch what maleness was.

"I like your dress." His fingers strummed up and down her spine. The breathy words sifted through her hair, which she had left loose and casual. She was glad now she had. It added to the sensation of dreamy flight.

"Why?"

"Why do I like the dress? Because it allows me to touch your skin." His hand cupped her shoulder; then his fingers stroked her neck.

"I'm glad you like it." Surrendering to temptation, she curled her hand around the back of his neck and pulled several strands of his hair through her fingers.

He kissed her temple. Not really a kiss. He placed his lips beside her forehead and there they remained while he softly breathed in and out.

"I'd love to sleep with you, Caren."

Her gliding footsteps faltered. "You would?"

His lips skated down her cheek and settled in the vicinity of her ear. "Isn't it obvious? You attract me. I think you're very beautiful and incredibly sexy."

Was he a gigolo someone had hired to say these things to her? They were the things she desperately needed to hear. They spread over her wounded ego like a healing balm. Whether anything came of it or not, whether he was genuine or merely handing her a line guaranteed to work, she would always be grateful to the stranger Derek Allen for saying what she needed to hear.

"You do this all the time, don't you?"

He tilted her chin up to gaze into her troubled face. "What?"

"Meet a woman, charm her, take her to bed."

The tiger eyes fell away from hers. He studied the dainty gold ring in her ear for a long moment. When his eyes came back to hers, there was an unmistakable sadness in them. "Yes," he confessed softly.

She nodded slowly. It was what she had known. At least he was honest enough to admit it. His experience terrified her. She didn't belong with him.

"I don't," she said quietly. "At least I never have. I'm not sure I can be a casual lover. I don't want you to be disappointed and feel like you've wasted your time if—"

"Shh." Gently he pressed her head onto his chest. "I'm content just to hold you. You're very nice to dance with. We fit together well. For now, let's concentrate on dancing."

For a half hour or more they danced, talking seldom, but communicating on another level. She anticipated his moves and followed his lead as though they had been dancing together for years. He was tender in the way he held her, tender but possessive. And intimate. There was no mystery to his physique, for he held her close, their bodies continually rubbing against each other.

They returned to their table when the floor show began. Derek ordered her a tall, fruity drink. Its potency thrummed through her head in beat to the reggae drums. The regional costumes were vivid, the dancers were sinuous, the fire-eater daring, the music loud.

Derek and she got into the spirit of the show, clapping their hands to the music and laughing at the emcee's jokes.

When the show was over they strolled arm in arm through the complex on their way back to the bungalows. As they approached Caren's, her heart began to pound with anxiety. Would he demand a payoff?

She began to chatter nervously. "I really had a wonderful time. The dancing was nice, wasn't it? I don't know when I danced last. Thank you for joining me for dinner. I felt rather conspicu—"

He laid his three middle fingers against her lips to stop the inane flow of words. Her eyes melted into his as he closed in, pressing her between him and the door. He cupped her cheek with his other hand, sliding his fingers into her hair.

His eyes held hers. She felt her knees weakening and wondered how long they could support her. He was so close his heartbeats echoed in her chest. Her thighs felt warm and boneless; her breasts were aching and full. Had his fingers not been resting lightly on them, her lips would have been trembling.

With the tip of his middle finger, he followed the outline of her lips, first along the rim of the lower one from corner to corner, then over the top one, tracing the slight bow in its center.

"You have a very provocative mouth," he whispered in the stillness. "I think it could give me great pleasure."

She swallowed.

"Since I saw you on the beach, I've wanted to taste

you, taste this exquisite mouth.'' He slid his hand onto her neck, dipped his head down and to one side, and laid his lips against hers. Her eyes drifted closed and her hands found their way to his waist.

At first he merely brushed his lips back and forth over hers. His mouth was cool and firm and soft. She caught a hint of beard and stubble on one pass; otherwise, everything was softness and tenderness.

Then his tongue, warm and moist, flirted with the corners of her mouth and touched the bow on the upper lip that had interested him before. Involuntarily, her lips parted slightly. She was surprised to hear her own breath coming swiftly and unevenly through them. Her breasts were rapidly rising and falling in sexual agitation. Her hands were moving restlessly at his waist.

She wanted him.

He gave himself to her.

His tongue went deeply into her mouth with one sure, long thrust, as though he wanted no argument about it. He claimed her. There was no other word for the imperious way his lips settled hard and firm against hers while his tongue penetrated the innermost hollows of her mouth.

He was an excellent kisser. He didn't just kiss her mouth, he made love to it. He discovered and savored and filled her again and again with his nimble tongue.

Only once did he back away slightly to let her regain her breath. Even then he covered her face with light, quick kisses. Eyelids, nose, cheekbones, earlobes, all knew the sweet tribute of his lips. Then he recaptured her mouth, taking liberties as though they were his due.

His caresses were just as bold. He didn't work up to it, tentatively approach, grope. He simply moved his hand down to her breast and covered it. She whimpered against his ardent mouth as he filled his hand with her. He squeezed softly, reshaping, remolding, massaging.

A ribbon of desire began to coil through her as slowly but as surely as his hand moved over her breast and his tongue explored her mouth. His thumb feathered over the peaked center, and she reacted as though lightning had struck her. A gasp burst from her throat.

He enfolded her in his arms and hugged her tightly but tenderly, rocking her gently. His face was buried in the curve of her neck. His breath was hot and quick...and anguished. When at last he raised his head, his expression was tender. "You're very sweet." He kissed her softly on the mouth. It was a chaste kiss. "Good night."

The shadows swallowed up his retreating figure.

Caren let herself inside and walked trancelike to the bedroom. Without even turning on a light, she removed her clothes and got into bed. She lay perfectly still, as though to move would be to shatter something fragile and wake her from this marvelous dream.

The enchantment of the evening flowed through her like wine. She fell asleep almost instantly.

* * *

His telephone was ringing when he let himself into his dark bungalow. "Yes?" he said breathlessly, expectantly. Had she called to invite him to her bed?

His whole body sagged with disappointment when the caller identified himself. "How are you?" Derek asked, dropping down onto the bed.

"I am well. Your father was extremely tired, or he would have called you himself."

It was pointless to ask how they had tracked him down. He had made no secret of his trip, but he hadn't broadcast it, either. His father had a network of informants.

"How is he?" Derek asked of his father.

"He's...disappointed that you're not here to see him. He regretted that you left only a day before his arrival."

His father's aide had chosen the word "disappointed" carefully; it was euphemistic. His father was furious, Derek guessed. He wouldn't have taken kindly to Derek's bolting from town during his visit. But then, his father knew him well enough to know why he had left. Eventually he would be forgiven.

"I'm terribly sorry," Derek said with equal care. "I don't anticipate being away long. Perhaps he'll still be there when I return."

"Perhaps. At this point we have no way of knowing. I would suggest as a friend both to you and your father that you try to see him. He has much he wants to discuss with you."

"I want to see him too. I just didn't want to see him in Washington. He'll be busy while he's there."

"Yes. His schedule for the next few days is arduous. Your father has tremendous responsibilities. He takes them seriously and often goes beyond the call of duty."

Derek couldn't miss the reproachful hint that he himself might be less than responsible, but he chose to ignore it. "Tell him to rest as much as he can. Is my mother with him?"

"Yes."

Derek smiled. She would see to it that his father didn't neglect his health. "Give them both my love. And," he added as an afterthought, "I would rather my whereabouts not be made public just now."

"You're certain you can't return to Washington?"

It wasn't a suggestion. It was a subtle command. He glanced through the dense almond trees toward the bungalow next to his. Was she worth making his father angry?

He recalled her surprised, but pleased, expression when he had joined her for dinner. He remembered how rich her laughter sounded, how good she felt in his arms, how delicious her mouth tasted.

"No, I can't come back for a few days."

"Then I'll give your father that message. Good night, sir."

"Good night."

Derek returned the telephone receiver to its cradle and sat staring into the darkness. For as long as he could remember, he'd had to make choices, choices most people wouldn't have the vaguest notion of. They never got easier to make.

He began to peel off his clothes. When he was naked, he went to the terrace door and slid it open, letting in the breeze off the bay. Its caress was soft. Closing his eyes, he relished its cooling powers. He liked the balmy feel of it swirling over his skin, liked the way it whispered through the hair on his chest and thighs.

Opening his eyes to the beauty of the tropical night, he gazed at the sky. The stars weren't faded by city lights. They were brilliant, close, large. The moon looked like a disk of sugar candy one could reach up and sample. Its reflection shimmied in the waters of the bay. Swaying coconut palms cast shadows as long and narrow as pencils on the pale moonlit sand. The night lacked only one thing to make it perfect—

The woman.

Her eyes were almost as dark a velvet as the night sky. Parts of her body would be that velvety too. He wanted to touch each one. Her mouth was sweet. Once he had kissed it, he'd wanted never to stop. But common sense had ruled that he should. She couldn't be rushed, though her response to him was encouraging.

He remembered the way her body had softly slammed into his when he touched the tip of her breast. The notch of her thighs had cushioned his hard arousal and had almost robbed him of sanity. Then, as now, his hands formed fists as he strove to suppress his desire and maintain control. He clung to it precariously. For to lose control and take her would mean possibly to lose her. He didn't want to risk that.

If he had forced something to happen tonight, she would have regretted it tomorrow. She would have blamed him for heartlessly seducing her. Ordinarily, that wouldn't bother him. On any other tomorrow there would have been another woman waiting.

But this wasn't ordinary. He didn't want it to be over in one night. He thought this woman, this Caren Blakemore, with the shy demeanor and sweet body and beautiful face, was worth going to some trouble for. The victory would be made sweeter for the anticipation.

He returned to the bedroom and lay down on the cool sheets. He watched the play of shadows and moonlight as they chased each other across the ceiling. And, coming to terms with the discomfort of his body, he thought about the woman. As sleep claimed him, he could still feel the shape of her breast in his hand.

The morning light served to dispel the magic of the night before. As Caren sipped her coffee, she reviewed her behavior with dismay. How could she have lost control that way? Had he drugged her? Was the deceptively innocent drink he had ordered for her actually an alcoholic time bomb? Had the moonlight and music gone to her head?

For whatever reason, she had let a stranger, whom she had met only a mere twelve hours earlier, kiss her. Kiss her like *that*. Fondle her. It was appalling.

Sipping her coffee, she raised her feet to the rim of her chair and rested her head on her knees. Hypocrite, she accused herself. Only a few weeks ago Kristin had come to her in tears.

"He seemed like such a neat guy, you know? We really had a terrific time at the dance. I mean he's not into drugs or punk rock or anything. A really decent guy." Kristin had sniffed.

"But as soon as he parked in front of the dorm, he became an octopus. His kisses were nice. I liked that part. But, Sis, he wanted to...uh...well, you know. He said he only wanted to show me how much he liked me."

"They all say that," Caren had reassured her with a sad smile.

"They do?"

"Since Adam."

"And he asked me if I liked him, and I said yes, and then he said that if I did I'd let him...do it."

"They all say that too."

Kristin's face collapsed in a new rush of tears. "I liked him a lot. I still do. But even if he asks me out again, which I doubt, he'll want to do *that,* and I just don't want to yet. Some of the other girls think I'm dumb. They're already on the pill and do it all the time. But I don't care what they say, I'm not ready for it yet. I think it should be special."

Outwardly Caren tried to appear calm. On the inside, she was shrinking. Sixteen! On the pill.

"Then you shouldn't worry about it, darling," she

had said as she stroked back Kristin's hair. "When it's right, you'll know it."

"How?"

"You just will. I promise. There's more to it than wrestling in the back seat of a car. There should be real caring between the two people. If you give someone a part of yourself, he should feel responsible toward you, and vice-versa. Until both are ready to make that kind of commitment, the idea of sex is rather empty, don't you think?"

"Yes." Kristin leaned forward and rested her head on Caren's shoulder.

"Sex should involve more than your body. You should listen to your heart and spirit. You can't always trust your senses."

Now Caren's hand trembled as she poured another cup of coffee. She hadn't been listening to her heart and spirit last night. Her senses had been clamoring, and that was all she could hear. When Derek Allen kissed her, words like "responsibility" and "commitment" flew from her mind like startled birds from the trees.

Well, that was last night and this was today. She was seeing things clearly now. If she should happen to meet him on the beach, she'd be polite but aloof.

The very thought of venturing onto the beach filled her with dread. For that she resented him. She wouldn't let him ruin her vacation. Nor would she lurk up here in her bungalow like a frightened animal in a cave.

Loaded down with her beach paraphernalia, she

headed toward the surf. The beach in front of their bungalows was deserted. She wasn't sure if she was relieved or disappointed. She spread her towel on the hard-packed sand and liberally applied suntan lotion. Then, adjusting herself comfortably, she lay down.

She must have dozed, because his voice was the next thing her mind registered. Rousing herself, she turned her head. He was lying on a towel only a few feet away from her. He must move with the stealth of a great cat, she thought.

His smile stretched wide and complacent. "Good morning."

"Good morning."

"You're up early."

"I usually get up early."

"So do I, but I couldn't go to sleep for the longest time last night."

Like bait, his sentence dangled there in front of her. Obviously, he wanted her to ask him what had kept him awake. She was sure his answer would open up an avenue of conversation she intended to avoid. "I'm sorry," she murmured, and, turning her head, she closed her eyes again.

"I take it you want to be alone."

She sighed. She should have known it wasn't going to be easy. "I'd prefer it, yes."

"All right." She could hear him settling himself on his towel. "You be alone over there and I'll be alone over here."

She tried to rein in her smile, but it wouldn't be

held back. Like a fool she grinned up into the sun, which burned against her eyelids.

They lay in silence for a few minutes. She wished she knew if he were watching her, but she didn't risk looking at him to find out. If he was, what would she do? And if he wasn't, she'd be terribly disappointed and would wonder why not.

"You can take your top off if you wish," he said at last.

"I don't wish."

"I promise not to look."

"And I promise to fly to China under my own power."

He laughed good-naturedly. "I like you, Caren. You're honest."

"You're outrageous."

"Sure you won't sunbathe topless?"

"Positive."

"You'll get tan marks."

"I wouldn't if I had some privacy."

"Touché." He shifted. Curiosity got the better of her and she glanced at him. He was lying on his side facing her, his cheek propped in his palm. "You know what you need? One of those swimsuits you can tan through."

In spite of her determination to remain aloof, he had piqued her interest. "What in the world are you talking about?"

"They're new on the market this year. You can't see through them, but the fabric is woven in such a way as to let tanning rays through."

She eyed him suspiciously. "Are you making this up?"

"No!" he exclaimed, laughing. "I read about them in *People* magazine. Didn't you see the article?"

"I don't read *People* magazine."

"How do you keep informed?"

"*Time* magazine."

"It's not nearly as interesting."

"But much more informative."

"You weren't informed about the tan-through swimsuits."

"Touché," she said, and they both laughed.

Then Caren realized that, rather than taking her aloofness as a rebuff, he might be reading it as a come-on. She rolled to her back again and averted her head.

Derek idly sifted sand through the tube he made of his hand and gazed at her graceful form. He was glad she didn't read *People* magazine. Otherwise, she might have recognized him. At this point he would rather remain anonymous, simply Derek Allen.

She really had a gorgeous body. Her legs were long and slender, with narrow, tapering feet. Her stomach was flat and slightly concave as she lay on her back. Rising above it was her rib cage, crowned with the soft globes of her breasts. Their pert nipples were discernible against the tight bikini top.

Her profile was etched against the seascape, and Derek could find no flaw in it. The wind had done beguiling damage to the loose knot her hair had been wound into. Honey-colored wisps floated whimsically around her face.

His manhood stirred with desire.

"It really doesn't matter if you take your top off or not," he said softly. "I know what your breasts look like. I can lie here all day and fantasize about them."

Insults didn't seem to affect him. She would try another tactic—ignore him. She said nothing. Several minutes of silence passed.

"I've touched them, too."

Her eyes sprang wide, and she swiveled her head toward him. He was staring at her boldly. Sitting up, she used the diversion of fishing for the suntanning gel in her beach bag to hide her discomfiture. She unscrewed the cap with shaking hands and dropped it into the sand. She silently cursed her nervousness, and him for making her nervous. When she squeezed the gel into her hand, twice as much as she needed gushed out.

"Damn!"

"Here, let me do that before you make a mess of it."

Before she could protest, he was kneeling beside her and taking the plastic container from her hands. He replaced the cap and scraped the gel from her palm into his.

He rubbed his hands together slowly, methodically. His eyes captured hers, and she was powerless to look away. Even when he laid his hands on her shoulders and started spreading gel over them, she didn't flinch away from the hypnotic stare of his eyes.

"Don't you remember last night, Caren?"

"Yes," she responded like a somnambulist.

"Do you recall my kissing you?"

"Yes."

"Caressing you?"

She watched those strong brown hands move down her arms. The strength in his fingers was belied by the tenderness of his touch. She remembered the feel of them on her breasts. Closing her eyes, she swayed toward him slightly. "Yes."

"Then why are we pretending it didn't happen?"

He moved his hands to the expanse of stomach between the two pieces of the bikini and massaged in the gel. There was a catch in her voice when she answered. "Because it shouldn't have happened."

He leaned toward her, and like any slave she responded to even his unspoken orders. She reclined on the towel. He followed her down. His breath ghosted over her mouth as he asked, "Shouldn't it?"

"No," she groaned in desperation. If only his hands weren't so soothing, his breath so sweet, his eyes so compelling.

"Why?"

"This isn't me, that's why. I don't pick up men and talk to them about...about the things we've talked about. I'm playing a part."

He chuckled softly as he nibbled at her ear. "How untrue. You're the most honest woman I've ever met. That's part of your appeal. Every emotion, every thought is right there on your sleeve for the world to see. You don't know how to be any other way except genuine."

"I lead a very dull, ordinary life. I'm not equipped to deal with you."

With the leisure and appreciation of a voyeur, his eyes traveled down her body, then back up again. "You're equipped beautifully."

"You don't understand," she argued feebly as his mouth drifted over her collarbone. "This is wrong for me."

"Why? Did you get hurt last night?"

"No, but—"

"Nor was I hurt. Was it unpleasant?" Now his mouth was tracking the top of her bikini. Nibbling. Awaking parts of her that had been asleep for a long time.

"No, not unpleasant."

His mouth hovered over the peak of one breast. Not touching, not touching. But at that moment, Caren wanted it to be touching her. She wanted to feel his mouth on her breasts, which were flushed with desire. She could envision his tongue caressing, giving relief to flesh that strained upward toward him.

"It was one of the most pleasant evenings I've had in a long time." Raising his head, he pinned her to the sand with the intensity of his stare. "I mean that, Caren. Believe me."

Then his lips were moving warmly over hers again, and her arguments scattered. He probed the recess of her mouth with his tongue, and her arms crept up over his back. Her whole body came alive under the sweet dictatorship of his kiss. She arched against him and, like any cosseted pet who has been stroked and petted indulgently, she purred deep in her throat.

She offered no resistance when he eased open the top of her bikini and removed it. She only tightened her arms around him and welcomed the furred warmth of his chest against her naked breasts. He sighed his pleasure and lightly licked the tip of her nose before grafting his mouth to hers again.

He kissed her deeply. For a long time. His forearms rested on the sand on either side of her. With his thumbs only, he stroked the plumped-out sides of her breasts. She ached for more—more of his touch, more of his mouth, more of him. When he began to move away, she pried her heavy lashes open and gazed up at him hazily. "What are you doing?"

"I'm leaving you for a while."

"Oh." She couldn't disguise the disappointment in her voice.

He smiled. "I believe life should be one pleasurable experience after another. I robbed you of one yesterday." Playfully he ran his index finger over her lower lip. "You were enjoying your privacy immensely before I came along and ruined it." He kissed her shoulder. "As long as I'm here, you won't indulge yourself in sunbathing topless. So I'm leaving you free to do that." Standing, he reached for his towel and tossed it over his shoulder. "You have until two o'clock. At which time I'll be at your front door. Be ready."

"For what?"

"For me."

Four

〜◦⤸⤸◦〜

What was she, a wind-up toy? Did he think he could say "Hop" and she'd hop? Resentfully, she glared at her image in the mirror. You shouldn't even be here when he arrives, she told herself, much less be ready and eager.

Ready and eager for what?

He hadn't specified. She didn't know whether to dress up or to dress casually. Or did he expect her to be wearing nothing but an obliging smile when he arrived? If so, he had another thing coming.

She had wanted to go shopping today, so that was what she would dress for. A pair of madras shorts and a polo shirt were what he would find her wearing. But after she had dressed, she viewed herself ruefully. She looked like a sorority girl. Certainly not a femme fatale, which was no doubt what he was accustomed to.

When she heard his knock at the door, her heart leaped to her throat. In an effort to hide her panic, she slipped on a pair of sunglasses before she pulled the door open.

"Hi." He was leaning against the doorjamb, looking not the least bit worried that she might not have followed his instructions to the letter.

But she felt a great sense of relief. He was wearing shorts, a short-sleeved shirt, and topsiders. He didn't look like he was about to invite a woman into bed with him. In fact, had he been ten years younger, he could have been calling on her to ask her to wear his pin. She laughed at her private joke.

"Did I say something funny?"

"No, I just—" She broke off her sentence when she happened to glance over his shoulder toward the lane that led to the bungalow. "Are those for us?"

"Sure." Until now his arms had been behind his back. He brought them forward now. "Which color do you want?"

She stared at the bright, glossy helmets in stupefaction, then pointed toward the motorcycles as she stammered, "I...I can't ride one of those things."

"Have you ever tried?"

"No."

"Then how do you know you can't?" he taunted, and then cuffed her gently on the chin. "Got your key?" She nodded dumbly, still staring at the motorcycles parked in the lane. He shut the door behind her, and just as effectively shut off her retreat. He forced one of the helmets into her hand and nudged her forward. "Don't look so tragic. It's fun."

"I'll kill myself. Or someone else."

"No you won't. It's easy. Really. This is little more than a bicycle. You can ride a bicycle, can't you?"

She stared at him balefully, her chin going up. Locking her eyes with his, she plunked the helmet on her head. "Show me how."

He grinned, but tried to keep the smug satisfaction off his face. "There are three gears. You work them with your left foot. See? Here. First, second, third. Got that? The brakes are here on the handles. And don't forget to drive on the left side of the street."

Within five minutes she was cruising alongside him on a narrow, winding highway that was bordered on both sides by fields of sugarcane.

"This is great," she shouted over the growl of the motors. "I love it!"

"Just don't get overconfident."

"Why? Afraid I'll outrun you?"

"You'll never outrun me."

Her eyes left the road for an instant to look at him. In that heartbeat, she could tell he meant it, and in more ways than one.

He directed her to one of the shopping areas in the Montego Bay area. They parked and secured the bikes. "What would you like to do first?" he asked.

"I wanted to do some shopping today."

"Souvenirs?"

"No. Something for me."

"Clothing?"

"Yes."

He glanced at her speculatively, but said nothing.

Taking her elbow under his, he said, "We should be able to find a suitable shop around here somewhere."

They located an apparel shop tucked between a furniture store and an open-air fruit stand. Self-consciously, she browsed through the merchandise, ever mindful of Derek leaning against one of the mirrored walls watching her. As though sensing her unease, he pushed himself away from the wall and said, "I think I'll wait outside. It's stuffy in here."

Her smile was grateful. "I won't be long." He kissed her swiftly before exiting.

The shopkeeper beamed on them, probably thinking they were a "couple," and stepped forward to inquire politely, "May I help you?"

She knew the minute she saw it that the dress was what she wanted. It was of maize-yellow gauzy cotton. Straps about an inch wide tied the loose top onto her shoulders. It draped low on her chest and to the middle of her back. The skirt was full. The points of the uneven handkerchief hem came to the middle of her calf. She had a pair of flat, strappy sandals and a collection of bangle bracelets that would go perfectly with it.

When she stepped out onto the sidewalk, she stuffed the package into her oversize straw bag. Derek watched with interest. "It couldn't be much," he commented.

"It's a dress."

"A dress no bigger than that?" he asked with a leer. "Sounds interesting."

"It packs easily," she said primly.

They strolled through the shopping village, stopping when something caught their interest, and warding off the sidewalk vendors with as much politeness as possible. Like other couples on vacation, they walked hand in hand, sometimes swinging their arms back and forth.

Waiting for their drinks to arrive at an outdoor café, it occurred to Caren that she hadn't thought about Wade and her divorce since the day before. That was rare. The demise of her marriage had monopolized her thoughts for the last year. Derek Allen had made her forget it.

He had also made her feel like a woman again. It was amazing what a few words and a few caresses could do to restore a trampled ego.

She had been flirting with him all afternoon. Their conversation was spiced with double entendres and suggestive remarks. No matter what they appeared to be discussing, they were actually talking about sex. It was there in everything they said, every gesture, every look.

Derek reached across the table and snapped his fingers in front of her eyes. "Earth to Caren, Earth to Caren."

Spontaneously, she grabbed his hand and waggled it as she said, "I'm sorry. I was daydreaming. Did I miss something important?"

"Only some steamy stares I directed toward you. What kind of daydreams does a lady like you have? Average? Slightly naughty? Downright erotic? Was I in any of them?"

She wasn't about to lay out the story of her marriage and pore over the cause of its death as if this were an autopsy. Instead of dwelling on past sadness, she smiled seductively and fluttered her lashes at him. "You are conceited."

He squeezed her hand. "Was I in them?"

"In a few of them."

"The average, naughty, or erotic ones?"

"I never admitted to having any naughty or erotic ones."

"Do you?"

"Do *you?*"

"I'm having one right now." His eyes told her what his words left unsaid, and all her insides melted.

She was saved by the waiter who brought their drinks. "This is too pretty to drink," Caren exclaimed in a desperate attempt to cool the smoldering mood between them. She sipped the drink, which was garnished with a spear of fresh pineapple and an orange slice. It tasted as pretty as it looked. "Hmm. What is this? Remember, I have to maneuver that motorcycle back to…By the way, how did you drive both of those things to my bungalow?"

His eyebrows bobbed comically. "I have superhuman powers."

She could believe it. He had banished her unhappiness and depression. He had made her feel feminine and desirable again. She hadn't felt this frivolous and carefree since the divorce. Or even before. Had she ever felt this good?

"Go ahead and drink up. I told the bartender to go light on the rum."

When they had finished their drinks, they wandered back toward the parked bikes. Derek's arm was looped around her shoulders. Their hips bumped together companionably as they walked. They were loose and relaxed, and Caren could blame only a portion of her intoxication on the rum drink.

His mood changed so swiftly that at first she didn't realize what was happening. His whole body went tense beside hers. The curse that sizzled through his lips was vicious and terse and obscene. Then he muttered something in a language she didn't even recognize.

He spun around quickly, jerking her with him, and changed their direction as rapidly as he had changed his mood. She stared up into a hard, raging face she barely recognized as his. She glanced over her shoulder, looking for a reason for his metamorphosis.

All she saw was a heavyset man waddling along the sidewalk licking an ice-cream cone. A fancy camera hung from his neck, but he didn't look like a tourist. The white shirt, dark trousers, and loosened necktie looked out of place in a resort where most everyone else had on shorts and sandals.

"Come on," Derek ground through his teeth as he pulled her along. She couldn't keep up with the furious pace he was setting, which was almost a jog. They took a circuitous route, wending through the twisting streets, hustling through vendors' stalls, narrowly avoiding head-on collisions with other pedestrians.

"Derek, what—"

"Please hurry, Caren. We've got to get out of here."

When they reached the motorbikes, he virtually crammed her helmet on her head. "Here, put this on. Quick."

He straddled his bike and pumped it to life. Compelled to obey him for reasons beyond her understanding, she struggled to hold her purse on her shoulder and start the motorcycle. At last she succeeded. When he saw she was ready, he roared out ahead of her.

They raced through the streets at a breakneck pace that terrified her. In normal circumstances the narrow lanes would have been harrowing enough. But to navigate them on the left side, on a vehicle she wasn't used to, was suicidal.

At one corner, Derek braked his cycle so quickly he sprayed gravel and fishtailed. Cursing, he pointed her toward an alley. "This way." The fat man they'd seen earlier was huffing toward them.

She followed Derek without question, keeping the red light on the back of his bike in her sights and not daring to look at the row of houses whirring past.

At last they reached the outskirts of town, but Derek's pace didn't lessen. He drove like a demon, even though no one was pursuing them. Caren, trembling now in fear, as much of him as of the precarious ride, was startled when a rooster flew out of a yard and into her path. It squawked and flapped its wings only feet in front of her cycle before soaring out of the way in the nick of time.

She lost control of the bike. Swerving, she hopped a curb and barely braked in time to save herself from crashing into the wall of an abandoned service station.

She cut the ignition of the bike and climbed off, stumbling toward a shaded part of the wall. Leaning against it, she gulped for breath. She heard the other bike coughing to a halt, but didn't turn around until she felt Derek's hands on her shoulders.

"Caren, are you all right?"

She rounded on him. "I want to know what the *hell* that was all about, and I want to know now." She all but stomped her foot for emphasis. Her eyes were flashing with fury. She yanked off the helmet and threw it to the ground. With the helmet off, her hair came tumbling down around her shoulders. "Who were we running from and why? Who was the fat man?" She aimed a straight, stiff index finger at the end of his nose. "And don't tell me he wasn't anybody, because I saw him twice."

"You have a right to be angry."

"You're damn right I do."

"And you're exciting as hell when you're angry."

He raised a hand to her flushed cheek and stroked it. She swatted it away angrily. "I want an explanation of why you almost got us both killed."

"Are you hurt?"

His gentle concern after such a tumult sapped the

last of her patience. "Give me an explanation!" she shouted. "Are you married? Is that it? Is the man with the camera a private detective trailing you for a jealous wife?"

"No, he's no detective."

"Are you married?"

"I don't have a wife. Never have."

She searched his face, relieved that he wasn't married, but still anxiety-ridden over his abrupt change of personality when he saw the man with the camera. "Drugs? Are you a criminal running from the police? Are you wanted for some horrible crime?"

He grinned sympathetically and shook his head. "Nothing that colorful, I assure you."

"Because if you were married or an outlaw of some kind— Well, I couldn't get into anything like that."

"What *could* you get into?" he asked raspily only an instant before he pressed a hot, yearning kiss onto her mouth. She struggled against him, angry at him for ignoring her questions and angry with herself for letting him get away with it.

But his mouth was too masterful. Her struggles became less frantic and her protests were reduced to whimpers of pleasure. In seconds her arms were locked behind his head and she was arching her body against his. He sandwiched her between the wall and himself in a way that was both possessive and protective.

"Caren, Caren," he murmured against her cheek.

"I want you." He pressed his hips into the soft hollow between hers. He was hard. She could feel him.

One hand encircled her neck while the other made a loose fist. With the backs of his fingers, he fanned her breast until he felt the crest harden. Groaning, he kissed her deeply again, drawing her will and her better judgment out of her body and infusing her with himself.

"Will you come to me tonight?" Her eyes drifted up to that burning golden gaze. "For dinner," he added.

Not only for dinner. For bed. And she knew it. And he knew she knew it.

"Please." He kissed her softly, barely touching his lips to hers. It was more a transference of air than a kiss. "Please."

She nodded mutely. He drew her to him, tucking her head under his chin. He sheltered her in his embrace until they were able to drive.

When they stood facing each other at the door of her bungalow, his eyes sliced down her body. She got the impression he was stripping away every article of clothing with them. "I'll expect you at my bungalow around sunset," he said.

"All right."

They had left the cycles at the main complex of the resort. Derek turned and, without another word, walked toward his bungalow.

Sweat rolled down her body in rivers.

When Derek left her, she had been too keyed up

to nap, but her nerves would be tied in knots by sunset if she didn't relax. Exercise, she had thought, was a panacea for frustration.

After pulling on a leotard and a pair of shorts, she had walked to the well-equipped health club in the compound. Her muscles had been stretched and strained until they were tingling. Her heart had pounded after punishing calisthenics. Dismay over the events of the afternoon had eventually been worked out. Now she leaned against the redwood wall of the sauna, trying to sweat out the last of her ambiguity over Derek Allen.

Why did the evening to come bother her? What was she afraid of? This was what she had come here for, wasn't it, to shed her depression, to celebrate her survival of the divorce, to experience a rebirth into the world of the living?

Sure, Derek's behavior that afternoon had been peculiar, but no one was perfect. He came close. He was gorgeous. He was infinitely male. For whatever miraculous reason, he found her attractive. She had felt his desire for her in his kiss, felt it in...

That, too. Yes, he was definitely male. And she wanted him.

So why was she hesitating? Why the precaution?

Because she knew nothing about him.

But didn't she know all she needed to know? It wasn't as if anything permanent would come of this. The details of his life would remain a mystery to her just as hers would to him. They would enjoy each other while they were together, bid each other an affectionate and poignant farewell, and never see each other again. That was all there was to it.

Wasn't it?

Why did she feel it wouldn't be that simple?

Because life rarely was.

"I assure you I don't know—"

"When I checked in," Derek said tightly, "I requested that my name be given to no one, that should someone call asking for me, the resort was to give out no information whatsoever. Twice now the confidence I placed in your establishment has been violated." Derek showed no mercy on the resort's general manager.

"I regret any unfortunate encounters you may have had, Mr. Allen, but I assure you that everyone on staff was made aware of your request. Perhaps those who invaded your privacy were informed of your whereabouts by someone outside the resort," he offered hopefully.

"Perhaps," Derek said tersely. Where Speck Daniels was concerned, anything was possible. "I reiterate that I want my stay here to be private."

"I understand. Anything we can do—"

"You can show me your goodwill by having dinner sent to the bungalow tonight. I want it here before sundown, and I don't want to be disturbed before midmorning tomorrow, when I want a brunch served."

"Or course, sir. Dinner for one—"

"For two."

There followed a discreet silence before the general manager cleared his throat and said, "Of course. We'll plan—"

"No. I've planned the menu." He ran down the list he'd made. "Got it?"

"Yes, sir. Will there be anything else?"

"Oh, yes. Much more. I hope you're taking notes. I want everything to be according to my specifications and I want everything perfect."

"Hi."

The door to the sauna opened, and a young woman about Caren's age joined her. Caren didn't particularly welcome the company. She was engrossed in her disturbing thoughts. But she smiled and said a bright "Hello."

"Jeez, as if it isn't hot enough on the beach," the woman said, mopping her face with a towel. "What am I doing in here? Never mind. I know what I'm doing. I'm sweating off calories. I've been eating like a vandal since I got here. This is a perpetual dieter's nightmare. Or dream. I can't decide which."

"You don't look like you need to diet," Caren observed.

"Thanks, but you know it's a national obsession to stay trim." She sighed. "I just wish every other woman would go to pot, then I could relax and get there myself." Caren laughed with her. The woman looked at her closely. "Were you with an absolutely gorgeous hunk at dinner last night?"

Had Caren's face not already been flushed from the

heat of the sauna, it would have warmed with pleasure. "Yes." Then, realizing she was soon to become the gorgeous hunk's lover, she hunched her shoulders and shivered. "He is gorgeous, isn't he?"

The woman rolled her eyes heavenward. "Delicious. That hair! And those eyes. Course, I adore my Sam."

"Is he here with you?"

"Yeah. We've been having a blast."

"Where are you from?" Caren hadn't had a conversation with another woman about men in over a year. She discovered she was enjoying this "girl talk."

"Cincinnati. Isn't this place yummy? Sam has been as randy as an alleycat since we got here." She giggled. "I love it."

Caren smiled. "How long have you been married?"

The young woman burst out laughing. "We're not married."

"Oh," Caren said in a small voice. "I'm sorry. I thought—"

"I'm not married, but *Sam* is. I'd die if his wife found out we were down here together. What a bitch. She makes his life hell."

Her voice droned on, but Caren didn't hear any more of it. To hear the young woman talk, the wife was the troublesome party, the fly in the ointment, the villain.

But Caren's sympathies were with her. Had Wade's girlfriend talked about her this way? Had he?

Had all his business trips out of town actually been larks with his girlfriend?

Leaving the other woman talking, Caren excused herself and rushed toward her bungalow. Now she recalled why the resort's brochures had been so accessible in her desk drawer. One day she'd found them in Wade's coat pocket and had thought he was planning a vacation for her. When she had teased him about it, he confessed that he had wanted it to be a surprise.

They never took that vacation. Only a week after she'd found the brochures, he walked out of her life. She'd forgotten all about them until the night Larry had issued his ultimatum. Now she realized that Wade had collected them not with her in mind, but his girlfriend.

Was she so different from everyone else in the world? Did no one hold anything sacred anymore? Was marriage a joke and she the only one who hadn't yet caught the punch line?

People played games, acted out roles. Relationships were temporary and demanded nothing of a person except a healthy appetite for sex. Was it tacitly understood that no one brought their *spouse* to a resort like this, but brought their lover? Or did singles come here for the sole purpose of...

Her footsteps faltered on the path.

Wasn't that what she was doing here? Hadn't she come specifically looking for an affair? Disgust tasted brassy in her mouth. This scene wasn't for her. She didn't belong. She couldn't play these games. What had made her think she could?

In these bedroom games she was unprepared and inadequate. For the last two days she had been foolishly convincing herself a man could find her desirable. But if she couldn't hold a man like Wade Blakemore, who was only moderately good-looking, intelligent, and sexy, how could she expect to entice a man like Derek Allen?

Meeting the woman in the sauna was like looking Wade's girlfriend in the face. She had thought herself cured of the hurt, yet here it was again, eating its way inside her, grinding her newfound self-confidence into dust.

As soon as she reached the bungalow, she hung the new dress out of sight in the closet and shut the door firmly. She wasn't going to meet Derek tonight. She wouldn't make a fool of herself. Tomorrow she would pack and leave, then return to Washington, where she should have stayed in the first place.

She showered, dressed in her old sundress, then lay down on the bed. The telephone rang a few minutes later. She let it ring. It continued to ring at five-minute intervals. She tuned it out, as she did every thought too painful to contemplate. Lying on her back, she stared up at the ceiling unmoved and unmoving.

She didn't stir until she heard the latch on the terrace door rattling. She propped herself up on her elbows only seconds before the looming shadow behind the sheer drapes materialized into Derek Allen.

"Go away," she cried.

"What's the matter? Why are you lying here in the dark?"

"Nothing's the matter. I just want to be alone."

"Why didn't you answer the phone?"

"Why didn't you give up and stop calling?"

He advanced into the room, angry now. He had imagined her ill or injured. To find her merely sullen both relieved and infuriated him. "I wanted to know what was keeping you."

"I'm not coming."

"The hell you're not." He placed one knee on the bed and leaned toward her. "I invited you, you accepted. It's incredibly rude to let someone stand by expecting you and then not show up or even call with an explanation."

"I'm sorry," she conceded, edging away from him. "I should have called, but I didn't want to argue with you. I thought you'd take the hint and get discouraged."

He laughed harshly. "I told you once today that you'll never outrun me." He reached for her, but she avoided his hands.

"Leave me alone, Derek. I don't want to have dinner with you. I don't want to have anything with you. With any man. Now, if you don't get out of here, I'll have to call the manager."

He laughed again. "I assure you he'll be most unsympathetic. If I held a hoop in front of him, he'd jump through it."

"And that's what you expect me to do, I suppose?" she snapped.

His lips slowly fashioned a sensuous smile. "Fight me if you want, Caren love. That will make it even more exciting."

He scooped her into his arms and off the bed. Then, sweeping through the sheer drapes as though they were vapor, he carried her out into the night.

Five

~~~~~~

She went rigid with indignation. It served no purpose. He ignored the fulminating look she gave him as his long strides ate up the distance between her bungalow and his. In fact, he looked rather pleased with himself.

Well, if he wanted her to beg for release or plead with him to leave her alone, he would be disappointed. As soon as they arrived at his bungalow and he set her down, she would calmly announce her intention to leave and do so.

She wouldn't give him the satisfaction of knowing she was angry, even a little afraid. No man she had ever met before would have had the nerve to high-handedly carry a woman to his lair, not in this day and age of equality between the sexes.

But there had always been something primitive in Derek Allen's bearing. The established rules seemed not to apply to him. If they did, he flagrantly disobeyed them.

"Here we are," he said blandly as he passed

through his own terrace door. He wasn't even winded from carrying her.

In spite of her determination to remain indifferent to his caveman tactics, she gasped in astonishment when they cleared the terrace door.

The sitting room of the bungalow had been transformed. The furniture had been moved out of the way to the corners of the room. A mattress had been placed in the center of the floor. It was covered with white satin sheets. Tossed over the foot of it was a thick, fleecy sheepskin, also pure white. At the other end were piled dozens of pillows. Of varying shapes and sizes, covered in myriad colors and fabrics, they invited one to recline indolently.

Draped over the entire bed was an old-fashioned mosquito net. At the ceiling it was gathered to a point over the center of the mattress; on the floor it was arranged to surround the bed like a transparent tent.

The room was subtly lit by scores of candles placed in every available spot. The air was redolent with the perfumes of pikake, plumeria, honeysuckle, and jasmine. Stationed next to the "tent" was a portable service cart. Silver serving dishes emitted their own heavenly smells. A bottle of white wine was chilling in a silver wine cooler overflowing with ice cubes as perfect and crystal as diamonds. Fresh flowers were in abundance. Some had been artfully arranged in vases, others were strewn about carelessly. Soft mood music was emanating from invisible speakers.

Speechless, mouth slightly agape, Caren didn't even realize that Derek had unceremoniously dumped her in the middle of the bed until her bottom struck it. Then for several seconds she sat there, stunned, gazing around at this exotic, erotic playground in awe.

It wasn't until she looked up at the man that her reason returned and she shook herself out of the daze. Derek was standing with his feet wide apart, his hands on his hips, looking down on her as though she were a subordinate who needed to be reminded who the master was. Each burning candle cast a tall, fearsome shadow of him on the walls. Literally, he surrounded her.

The gold stripes in his rich brown hair attracted the candlelight. Flickers of light were also reflected in his eyes. His dark skin blended into the deep shadows of the room. His white Swiss army shirt with its rolled-up sleeves was unbuttoned almost to his waist. The broad muscled chest with it sensuous carpet of sun-gilded hair was disturbingly visible. His dark trousers... Don't look, don't look, she told herself.

She looked. That was a mistake. The trousers fitted far too well.

He was desirous. He was dangerous. Caren's heart began to pound.

"I'm waiting." His lips had thinned to a hard, unyielding line.

Her knees were bent, her arms straight and stiff behind her as they supported her upper body. He was looming so close over her that she had to tilt her head back in order to meet his intimidating gaze. Her hair hung free down her back.

"Waiting for what? For me to swoon?" she said defiantly.

"For you to tell me what changed your mind about coming here tonight. Why you were up there hiding in the dark." He gestured with his head toward her bungalow.

"I wasn't hiding."

"I think you were. Otherwise, you would have answered my call and politely refused my invitation. What gives, Caren? Why the drastic change from this afternoon?"

She wet her lips nervously and damned herself even as she did. He noticed. His eyes missed nothing. Tossing her head in what she hoped was a gesture of nonchalance, she said, "I was upset after that death-defying motorcycle ride. I wasn't thinking clearly when I agreed to come here tonight. I would have agreed to anything."

His lips tilted up at one corner. He let her squirm for an interminable amount of time before he said, "Don't ever try to lie to me again. You're terrible at it. Now, I'm asking again, why?"

"I didn't want to," she flared.

He dropped to his knees in front of her and grabbed her shoulders as though he wanted to shake her. "That's a damn lie. We've wanted each other from the beginning. Don't tell me you don't want me. I won't buy it." His hands slid closer to her neck and gentled in their grip. "Why the reversal, Caren love?"

The fight went out of her then. That tender address,

his caressing fingers, the liquid warmth in his eyes were her undoing. She couldn't pretend to be a firebrand any more than she could pretend to be a siren. "I was afraid," she said, dropping her eyes to her lap.

"Of me?" he asked on a disbelieving note.

She shook her head. "Of me. Of doing something stupid, of embarrassing myself. I told you, I'm no good at this sort of thing."

A moment of silence passed before he asked softly, "Shouldn't I be the judge of that?" He touched her hair, smoothed his hand from the crown of her head to her neck.

Her head came up abruptly. "I don't want your pity."

He moved like lightning. His hand yanked her head forward and his mouth was hungrily grinding against hers before she could catch her breath. He kissed her savagely, and when he was done he released her just as suddenly.

"Did that feel like pity? Now, tell me where you got this ridiculous theory that you're somehow inferior."

"Not inferior exactly."

"Exactly what, then?"

"Outclassed. I'm not suited to this type of thing."

"Who told you you weren't?"

"My ex-husband," she replied angrily.

"Your own husband insulted you that way?"

"Not in so many words."

Derek blinked. "I don't understand."

"I don't expect you to."

"So explain it to me."

"No."

"Why?"

"It's a sad, boring tale."

"We've got all night."

"Don't you have anything better—"

"Dammit, I said to tell me!" He roared like a tiger, which had just been denied his dinner.

"All right," she shouted back. "If it will get me out of here and away from you any faster, I'll tell you."

She pushed him away from her and crossed her legs Indian-fashion. Her fingers clasped and unclasped as she began to speak.

"I was married for seven years. I thought we were happy. Oh sure, some of the magic wore off after a while. That's to be expected, isn't it? Things became routine."

"What things? Sex? Sex became routine?"

Why didn't she tell him it was none of his damn business? Her expression was hostile when she glared up at him, but the earnestness in his face dissolved her militance.

Maybe she needed to talk this out. She hadn't bared her soul to anyone since the night Wade walked out. She hadn't wanted to burden Kristin with her problems. Besides, Kristin was too young to relate to them. Most of Caren's friends had gone through bitter divorces themselves. There was little sympathy to be gleaned from them. Her few happily married friends couldn't understand the feeling of utter rejection she'd felt.

So instead of coming back to Derek with both barrels loaded, she answered calmly. "That was part of it. We were active, just not imaginative. But there was more to it than that. He became distracted, distant. We didn't talk much, and when I tried to draw him out, he would shrug it off and say that he was having problems at work."

"Go on."

"There isn't much more. It's classic, I'm afraid. One evening he came home and over dinner he told me he wanted a divorce."

"He gave you no valid reason?"

She laughed without humor. "A very good one. *The* reason. Another woman. My husband left me for another woman. There you have it. Finis. The end."

"And for that reason you feel that you're sexually inadequate?"

"Wouldn't you?"

"No."

"Well I did, *do*. I'm not talking strictly about sex. It encompasses much more than that."

"Do you still love this fool?"

Her eyes swung back up to his. "No." She was going to share something with this stranger that she hadn't shared with anyone else. She would have thought divulging such a confidence was impossible until she heard the words tumbling out. "I don't think I loved him then, either."

"Why were you married to him, then?"

"I loved the idea of stability that marriage offered. The security. My father died when Kristin was a baby. My mother reared us by herself. I saw her loneliness, the struggle she had living as a single woman. I think I married Wade because he was the first to ask me. Maybe I was afraid his was the only offer I'd ever get. We were mutually attracted. He had a good job with a future. I fell in love with the American dream."

"But not the man."

"In retrospect, no. I don't think I really loved him. Not the way I should have."

Caren felt a great burden falling away from her, one she had carried for over a year. Wade hadn't been solely responsible for their failed marriage. It felt good to finally acknowledge her part in it. Now, having faced it, she could let go.

Slowly, and a trifle self-consciously, she looked at Derek. "You called him a fool. Why?"

He touched her cheek. "Just like a woman. You're fishing for compliments."

Ducking her head, she admitted softly, "Maybe I am."

"Don't transfer Wade's guilt to yourself." The serious tone in his voice brought her eyes back to his. "You were willing to work at the marriage. He wasn't. He insulted you by leaving you for another woman. You've been terribly hurt."

He laid his palm along her cheek. "Tonight I will take away all your hurt. I will show you how lovely and desirable you are. Tomorrow this foolish man will be only a bad memory. My loving will banish his hateful presence from your heart.''

He fastened his mouth to hers with a sweet suction. Beyond that, it was a chaste kiss. It had none of the savagery of the one previous, but a remarkable tenderness.

When at last he freed her lips, she sighed deeply. It was a good beginning. She felt the shackles falling away.

''Would you like some wine?'' he asked as he flicked a strand of her hair over her shoulder.

''Please.''

He pushed the mosquito netting aside so he could reach the wine cooler. Wrapping the bottle in a white linen towel, he carried it to the bed and deftly uncorked it. After he filled the two waiting goblets with the sparkling golden wine, he handed one glass to Caren.

''Your mouth is sweeter than any wine.''

It wasn't a typical toast, but he clinked his glass with hers and they drank. He leaned forward and kissed her. His lips and tongue were cool from the wine. She thirsted for them when he withdrew. Her eyes were lambent in the soft lighting as she gazed at him.

''I like the setting you've created,'' she said after a lengthy stare. ''You have a vivid imagination.''

He chuckled at that. ''Perhaps I should have been a movie director.''

''Or an actor.''

"That would never have done," he said, shaking his head.

Newfound confidence was bubbling inside her with each sip of wine. "Why?" she asked teasingly.

"I don't like being photographed," he said with an abruptness that brought the conversation to a standstill.

She was digesting that oblique statement when he asked if she was hungry. "I guess I am," she said, pausing to consider. "I went to the health club in the complex this afternoon and—"

He stopped her sentence with an ardent kiss. After first leisurely investigating her mouth, his tongue bathed her lower lip. "And what?"

"I forget," she murmured as their mouths melded together once again.

"I hope you like the dinner I ordered." He turned his back on her only long enough to crouch in front of the serving cart and lift the heavy silver covers from the chafing dishes.

"It smells heavenly."

He filled one large plate with food. "Stretch your legs out in front of you," he directed her. She complied, and he set the plate on her lap. He extended his legs in the opposite direction and sat hip to hip beside her, facing her. Placing the hand nearest her on the far side of her legs, he bridged her thighs with his torso.

"Jerk chicken, a spicy marinated chicken cooked slowly over coals. Very popular on the island. Stamp and Go, another national dish."

"That's what it's called?"

He nodded. "It's codfish minced with peppers and spices, rolled into balls, batter-dipped, and deep-fried." There was also a selection of papaya and pineapple, and fresh vegetables. She was fascinated, both by the array of indigenous food and his smooth recital.

By the time he finished enumerating the dishes on the plate, her mouth was watering. "I don't have any silverware."

His eyes locked with hers. "You don't need any. That's why I selected only finger-food. I'm going to feed you."

A strange sensation trilled through her vitals. She'd never had such an erotic proposal. And it wasn't so much what he said as the seductive way he said it.

He lifted a piece of chicken breast from the plate and held it up to her. Too dazed to do anything else, she opened her mouth and took the morsel between her teeth. Her eyes never leaving his, she chewed slowly. It was scrumptious. "Good?" Derek asked.

"Hmm. Yes."

"May I have one?"

She stared at him for the duration of a heartbeat, then picked up a slice of chicken and raised it to his lips. He nibbled a bite of it, then chewed, watching her all the time. When he swallowed that bite, he took the rest in his mouth.

They sampled each dish on the plate in that manner. Slowly. Silently. Only their eyes speaking to each other. Caren felt she must be in some bizarre dream—from which she hoped she never awoke. She felt like the heroine of an exotic fairy tale too fantastic to be true. Derek was the hero—handsome, sexy, bold, tender, mesmerizing—also too fantastic to be true.

He raised himself slightly and secured most of her hair in a gentle fist. Lifting it off her neck, he leaned forward and pressed his mouth to the hollow above her collarbone. Her head fell back. His breath was warm on her skin. She felt the elusive damp caress of his tongue. His lips rubbed up and down her neck. He murmured something, but she couldn't distinguish the words. They weren't important. She knew what he was saying.

When he returned to his original position they sipped from their wine stems. He poured more from the bottle. He fed her a bite of juicy pineapple, then blotted her lips with a linen napkin. His eyes roamed her face.

"You're very beautiful, Caren. I want to see more of you."

He lifted his hand to the top button of her sundress and undid it. She was embarrassed by the old sundress. She had slipped it on after her shower because it was comfortable and loose.

"I planned on wearing my new dress tonight," she said apologetically.

"Another time."

His eyes held hers captive while he undid all the buttons as far as her waist. Not until he pushed the panels of her bodice aside did he lower his eyes.

He studied her for a long moment, his tiger eyes glowing hotly. "Beautiful," he whispered. With an attitude that was almost reverent, he stroked the underside of one breast with his index finger. "So soft." He folded his hand around the fullness of her breast, lifted it, circled the aureola with his thumb. Her eyes slid closed as he finessed its crest. "No," he whispered tautly, "watch me."

She opened her eyes. His long, lean fingers were dark against her skin. They made her look very beautiful. What they did to her was beautiful. He smiled up at her as his fingertips appreciated the results of his efforts. "You please me."

It took them an hour to finish their meal, bite by sensuous bite. In between they shared kisses and caresses that left Caren weak with a new hunger.

Once he hooked his hand around the back of her neck and drew her down to him for a tempestuous kiss. She was left breathless and tingling.

Another time he carried her hand to his chest and pressed it over his heart, stroking the back of it as his eyes poured their fiery gleam over her.

For dessert they ate fried bananas dipped in sugar and cinnamon. He fed her a bite and laughed when some of the sugary mixture clung to her lips. He gathered it up on the tip of his finger and extended it to her mouth. "Clean it off."

His softly urgent tone of voice was compelling. Without hesitation, Caren licked the sugar from the tip of his finger. He pressed it between her lips. She sucked it inside and stroked it with her tongue.

His breath hissed sharply through clenched teeth. His eyes shone like topazes. "I knew your mouth would give me pleasure," he said thickly.

With one sweeping motion of his arm, the dishes were moved aside and he lowered himself over her as she reclined against the pillows. Her arms opened wide to receive him and she drew his weight possessively against her.

She wanted to absorb him, to have him press and press until she was a part of him, living inside that tanned, sleek skin, that vital body. Her fingers twisted through his hair. She wanted to examine every strand, to solve the mystery of its striped color.

But later. Now, she wanted only the taste of him, the feel of his tongue moving languorously inside her mouth. He gave her what she wanted, but it wasn't enough. Her legs shifted restlessly against his.

He raised his head and gazed down into her fevered face. "Don't hurry it. We have all night." He lifted himself off her, and she was mortified to realize how wanton she must look. Her dress was unbuttoned to her waist, folded aside, revealing her trembling, flushed breasts. The hem had ridden up to her thighs. The lacy edge of her panties was showing. Her hair was a riot of disarrayed strands.

She sat up, clutching her bodice together and shoving down her skirt. She made a self-conscious gesture to restore order to her hair, though she knew that was futile.

"You're delightful," Derek said, his eyes sparkling with humor. "A hellcat one minute, a shy maiden the next. God, what a joy it would be to learn all the facets of you.''

He turned away and began to methodically cover the chafing dishes. When all the food was cleared away, he rolled the cart to the far side of the room.

"Do you like the music?" he asked.

"It's fine."

"You must tell me if there's anything you don't like." He was talking about more than the music, and she knew it. She nodded. He came back toward the bed, slipped off his shoes, and ducked under the net. He offered her his hand. She took it, and he raised her to her feet.

With unhurried leisure, he kissed her, drawing her inexorably closer to him, though his hands only rested lightly on her shoulders. Then she felt her dress slipping away. He slid it down her torso, past her hips and down her legs until it dropped to the mattress. She was left only in her panties.

She should have been shy. She wasn't. His adoring gaze wouldn't permit her to be. Covering a breast with each hand, he caressed her. He played with her like a treasured toy, his delight evident on the lean, shadowed planes of his face and in the light that shone in his eyes.

When her breasts were primed for his mouth, he dipped his head and took her between his lips. Caren staggered against him, clasping his head with her hands. "Derek," she cried softly.

"Yes, Caren love, yes."

She got lost in the magic of his mouth. His caresses

were poetic in their tenderness and pagan in their daring. His tongue was governed only by the desire to bring them both pleasure. His hands lay lightly on either side of her waist, seesawing back and forth in that curved indentation. On one pass they slipped lower until they reached her panties. He carried the garment down her legs until it pooled around her feet. She stepped out of it.

He raised himself to his full height and let his eyes feast on her. Hungrily they toured, his gaze almost tangible as it stroked down her body. It beckoned all her erogenous parts to pay attention. They obeyed. Her arousal was profound and couldn't be disguised.

He smiled as he examined her breasts. Then his eyes coasted down, and his jaw tensed with mounting passion. He was intrigued by the soft shadow between her thighs. He brushed it with the tips of his fingers.

Caren held her breath.

He dropped to his knees, spread his hands wide over her derriere and drew her to him. He kissed that silky nest with gentle fervency. Rockets went off in Caren's head. Never had she experienced such a sweet, unselfish caress.

A sob tore from her throat. Instantly Derek was on his feet again, holding her, cupping the back of her head with his hand and pressing her comfortably against his chest. "Shh, shh. Does that kind of intimacy repel you?"

"No, no," she moaned. "It's just... Oh, Derek, hold me!"

He did for a long while, swaying with her. When

her trembling had subsided, he eased her away. "I have on too many clothes, don't you think?" he asked. "Would you undress me?"

Her eyes went wide with panic, then gazed down at the expanse of his chest. "Yes," she said solemnly. "If you want me to."

"I want you to want to."

Hesitantly her fingers went to the few buttons on his shirt that were still fastened. She tugged the shirt-tail from his waistband and finished unbuttoning it. Placing her hands on his shoulders, she peeled the shirt off. He pulled his arms free of the sleeves and tossed the shirt to the mattress.

She reached for the fastener of his slacks. Her hands fell away. She reached for it again. Again she lost her courage.

"I'm sorry," she whispered.

"It's all right. I will." He unfastened his trousers and pushed them down his legs. Woodenly she stared at the middle of his chest as he rid himself of his briefs as well.

Without another word, he knelt and gathered up their discarded clothing. Stepping from under the netting, he carried the clothes to a chair and carefully folded each garment. Caren watched him at his task, at first amazed that he was doing it, then amazed that he could look so manly doing such a domestic chore.

He epitomized male beauty. He was beautifully proportioned. The muscles of his chest, back, arms, and legs were well defined, but graceful. His strength lay in his leanness. His skin was the same toasty color all over, dusted with gold-tipped body hair that clustered darker and thicker around his sex.

"You're beautiful."

She wasn't even aware she had spoken her thoughts aloud until he swung his head toward her and speared her with his eyes. The wild, untamed air about him was more pronounced now that he was naked, and her heart tripped with excitement, as though she were about to leap off a high cliff or plunge down the hill of a roller coaster.

He advanced toward the satin island in the center of the room, but paused on his way to pick up a tray from a table. On the small brass salver was a collection of vials, each containing a golden liquid.

"Lie down." She lowered herself to the mountain of pillows. "On your stomach," he said. She turned over.

He stepped onto the mattress and dropped to his knees beside her. Carefully he set the tray down. "You must relax," he whispered, running his hand from her shoulder to the backs of her knees. His warm palm felt wonderful against the small of her back, her buttocks, the backs of her thighs. She rested her cheek on the back of her hand and closed her eyes.

"Am I going to get a massage?" she asked with a yawn.

He smacked her bottom playfully. "Not if it's going to put you to sleep."

Not a chance, she thought with alarm when he straddled her thighs. He braced himself up on his knees, but she could feel the hard strength of his thighs against the outside of hers. He brushed her hair over her head, leaving her nape vulnerable to his gliding fingertips and warm breath.

Taking up one of the vials, he poured its contents into his palm. Her nose was filled with an exotic flowering fragrance that she couldn't quite name. Not as delicate as carnation. Not as heavy as gardenia.

"Hmm, that's wonderful," she said drowsily.

"What? The scented oil or my hands?"

"Both."

He kneaded her shoulders, freeing them of any remaining tension. The muscles seemed to melt beneath the coaxing of his strong fingers. He eased her hands from beneath her cheek and spread her arms out on either side of her. He squeezed the biceps with just the right amount of pressure until Caren thought she hadn't the energy or will to lift a feather. Each of her fingers was wrung through his, the oil making them slide easily.

Each vertebra was treated to a rotating massage of his thumb. He dug into the small of her back with the heels of his hands, rolling, then easing the pressure. When his hands slid over her buttocks, she shuddered with pleasure. His talented fingers edged down her legs a glorious inch at a time. He clasped the backs of her thighs, squeezed, massaged, then gave up all pretense of massage and caressed.

She moaned as his hands took liberties. Questing. Finding. Stroking. Until her womanhood was full and throbbing, aching for fulfillment. Her hips rolled from side to side in an agony of longing. He lay atop her and nipped the back of her neck with his teeth as his hands slid beneath her to caress her breasts.

"You are so dear," he whispered, "so precious. You feel so good beneath me."

His shape was imprinted on her back. He was deliciously heavy, hot and straining with desire, anchoring her to the satin bed.

He eased off her and turned her over to face him. His kiss was searing, his tongue rampant in her mouth. He parted her legs and draped them over his kneeling thighs.

She turned her face into the pillow. "No, no," he rasped. "I want to watch your face," he said, raising himself above her.

He was velvety, hard, pulsing with passion and life. He guided himself to the flowering center of her womanhood. Touched her. She moaned his name and laid her hands on his chest, her fingers curling into the supple flesh. Her lower lip was caught between her teeth. "I want you, Derek."

"Caren, Caren love." He pressed himself between the petals of her femininity. "Draw me inside you. Deeply, deeply." With a milking motion, her body invited him into her until he filled her completely and his body was locked tightly to hers.

His face twisted into a grimace of sublime pleasure as he thrust again and again into the silken sheath. He whispered words that were strangers to her ears, but she echoed them in her heart.

When her body began to quicken around his, he

covered her breasts with his chest, buried his face in the curve of her neck, and let go the reins of his passion.

Sated, exhausted, breathless, they lay together as one, their hearts celebrating *la petite mort*.

Six

She opened her eyes slowly, yawned, stretched, then gazed around her. Had last night been only a dream? Sunlight filtered hazily through the netting, contributing to her dreamlike state. Everything around her looked diffuse, fuzzy.

There were the candles, burned down now into hardened pools of colorful wax. The flowers in the vases were still fresh, whereas the blooms that had been scattered about were curling and limp, but no less fragrant. The cart with the silver platters was still parked against the far wall. The ice in the wine cooler had melted.

She lay naked and indolent on the satin sheets. The fur of the lambskin rug tickled her toes. She was alone.

Derek's scent still clung to the satin pillow beside hers. The imprint of his body was evident on the sheet close to where she lay.

But even if these telltale traces of him hadn't been there, she would still know that last night had been no dream. It had been real. The man had engraved himself on her body, on her soul. After only one night, she knew him more intimately than she had known a man she had been married to and lived with for seven years.

Smiling the complacent smile of a sexually satisfied woman, she stepped out of the net tent and crossed to the terrace door. She spotted him immediately in the surf. As sleek and agile as an eel, he cut cleanly through the water. Strong powerful arms which she knew to be capable of great tenderness pulled him through the water until he had swum farther out than she felt comfortable with.

Then his brown back bowed and arched and he disappeared beneath the surface in a shallow dive. When his head emerged a full minute later, he shook it free of water and began to kick himself back to shore with the legs that had been entwined with hers throughout the night.

He came out of the water with the surety of a nautical god. Following a path her lips had charted several times the night before, sea water trickled down the smooth muscles of his arms. Crystal droplets rolled down the hair-matted chest, rivered to the center of his torso, eddied around his navel, and followed that silky line of tawny hair toward his masculinity.

He was naked.

Caren laughed softly with deep affection. Had she ever known anyone so comfortable with nakedness, male or female? Wade hadn't been inordinately shy, but she remembered his being naked only in bed or in the shower. He would have never traveled from point A to point B wearing absolutely nothing. Derek knew no such restriction. He was totally at ease with his unclothed body.

The sun bathed him now in a golden glow and reflected off the water sheeting his body. He moved with the sinuous graceful tread of a great cat, with no wasted motion, no abrupt movements. His muscles stretched and rippled and bunched with the suppleness of elastic.

Last night this man, this stranger, had taught her a new language of love. She had awakened this morning with a whole vocabulary of emotions she hadn't even known existed before spending a night in Derek Allen's bed. He hadn't only coaxed her dormant senses to life, he had instructed them on all they were capable of feeling and entitled to experience.

The things he had said were evocative. The things he had done were erotic. The things she had done were beyond reason.

Caren raised her hands to fevered cheeks. Had that responsive woman truly been she? Had she behaved as she vividly remembered?

Yet she felt not one twinge of shame. Because though they had taken human sexuality to its limits of pleasure, nothing they had done had been depraved.

Only beautiful. Only sweet. Only giving.

She certainly didn't feel used, but honored. Discovered, not debased. Dignified rather than debauched.

When the discreet knock sounded on the door, she glanced toward the beach. Derek was standing on the hard-packed sand, drying his back with a towel he had carried down with him. Caren hastily scrambled toward the clothing folded on the back of the chair, fumbled for her sundress, pulled it on, and haphazardly fastened the buttons on the bodice.

"Yes?" she called through the door.

"Brunch, madam."

She opened the door to two bellmen, who rolled in another service cart. They bid her a good morning as she stood there self-consciously shifting from one foot to the other. If medals were given out to hotel room-service waiters exhibiting the most discretion, these two deserved them.

After that one hello, they ignored her as they went about their business. They set up the table, lit a flame beneath the coffee warmer, poured icy fruit juice into frosted glasses, and removed the dinner cart from the night before. Not once did they glance at the bizarre bed in the middle of the floor, though it must have sparked their curiosity.

Just as they were withdrawing, Derek came through the terrace door. Caren whirled around and slumped with relief when she saw that he had knotted a towel around his waist. Coming to her without delay, he clasped her hand and squeezed it before inspecting the brunch table, nodding his approval to the bellmen and bidding them goodbye as he closed the door behind them.

"Good morning." Once the door was closed behind the waiters, he turned to her. His eyes were hungry.

"Good morning."

"Have you been awake long?"

"Only a few minutes."

"I hate it that you woke up alone."

"I didn't mind. I was watching you swim when they arrived with the brunch. It looks delicious."

He whipped off the towel and negligently let it fall to the floor. "*You* look delicious." His whisper reached her only seconds before he closed the distance between them.

Wrapping both hands around the back of her neck and lacing his fingers together there, he drew her up for his first kiss of the morning. There were no unnecessary preliminaries, no apologies for his desire. His tongue sank into her mouth as his head tilted to one side. The kiss was long, drugging. That now familiar lassitude stole over Caren as it continued.

His hands slid down her front to free the buttons of her dress. After slipping it from her, he lifted her high and hard against him.

"The water was invigorating," he said with a mischievous grin.

"So I can feel," she breathed against his mouth as he led her to the bed. She lay back on the pillows, the mounds of her breasts becoming perfect targets for his seeking lips. "What about brunch?" she moaned as his tongue curled around one sleepy-pink tip.

"After this."

"And then what?"

"More of the same."

They sighed in unison as he possessed her.

That set the pattern for the days that followed. They made no long-range plans. They took things as the came. They ate, slept, played, swam, lay on the beach, and made love as it suited their whims.

This was a living fantasy Caren had stepped into. She knew it, knew that at the end of the week she would revert back to herself just as Cinderella had at the stroke of midnight. She would return to her life and never see Derek again.

But she indulged herself. It was *her* fantasy, *she* was the heroine, and she was going to participate in and enjoy it while it lasted. Hadn't that been the reason behind this trip? Wasn't this what she had wanted? What she had desperately needed?

But wasn't it also far more than she had bargained for?

Derek was the most sensual person she had ever met. He made of eating, drinking, swimming, sleeping, and making love sensual experiences that she had never imagined they could be.

He challenged her to try foods she had never eaten. She discovered them to be delicious. She acquired a taste for potent liqueurs that warmed her insides and unleashed her senses. She came to crave the feel of the sun and sand and sea on her naked skin. Her hair was left free to catch the tropical breeze. She delighted in the wide, glossy leaves of the almond trees and marveled at the vivid color of the bougainvillea vines. The sky had never looked so blue to her.

And when it came to lovemaking, she realized she had been almost virginal compared to all Derek taught her. She had never imagined making love could so consume one's body and heart and soul.

In his embraces, a victim of his hypnotizing kisses and tender caresses, she lost all restraint and inhibition. They made love on the terrace of his bungalow, their bodies oiled for sunbathing, until sweat glistened on them. In the shower, on the bed, on the boat they rented for an afternoon of sailing. She had told him that her sex life with Wade had become routine and unimaginative. Derek made it his business to rectify that. Nothing they did was routine or unimaginative.

His lovemaking was passionate and intense. Whether it was feverish and fierce and fast, or languid and leisurely and loving, she had his total concentration. He gave everything of himself to the act. So did she. It was both thrilling and frightening.

"You're staring," he chided softly one night over dinner. They had decided to leave the bungalow, where more often than not they took their meals, and go to the complex to enjoy the music and dancing along with the buffet.

She was wearing the dress she had purchased in town. Her hair had been piled into a loose knot on top of her head and secured with a brilliant yellow hibiscus blossom. She felt utterly feminine and soft, a perfect contrast to Derek's masculinity. His eyes skimmed her sexily while he sipped his wine.

"Am I staring? I'm sorry."

"I'm not complaining. I just wish I knew what was going on behind your beautiful brown eyes when you stare at me like that. You do it often."

"Do I?"

"Yes." He leaned across the table and whisked an airy kiss over her mouth. "What do you see when you look at me with such intensity?"

"I don't know," she answered honestly. "It's like you're..." Shaking her head, she laughed. "Never mind, it's crazy."

He took her hand and pressed it. "Go on, tell me."

She watched his thumb as it stroked naughty messages into her palm. "You're a mystery. Sometimes you're ordinary."

"Is that a compliment or a put-down?" he asked with a teasing glint in his eye.

She smiled distractedly, her mind busy converting her thoughts into words and making them understandable. "What I mean is, sometimes you're wholly American. You use vernacular and idioms, gestures that everyone else uses. You could be any guy on the street."

"I am," he said, serious now. Almost defensive.

"Yes. But then..." She bit her lower lip. "But the other times, especially when we're making love, you change."

"I'll say I do," he drawled. "In public I can generally control my body, but when I'm alone with you and you're naked, it becomes—"

"I don't mean that you change physically," she rushed to interrupt, glancing around them nervously.

He chuckled and stroked the backs of her fingers. "What do you mean?"

"That you become someone else. It's like there are two of you living in one skin. One is very American and one very...I don't know...foreign. Your speech patterns change. The words you use are more elaborate. Sometimes you speak to me in a language I don't even recognize."

He sat back in his chair and twirled his wine stem. The motion did more than just put space between them. It signaled his aversion to the topic and his reluctance to discuss it further. "I studied several languages when I was in school. I have a knack for picking them up easily."

That was a plausible explanation, but Caren thought there was more to it than that. And the closed, tense expression on his face didn't do anything to relieve her suspicions. Obviously, he didn't want to explain, and it wasn't any of her business. She regretted ever mentioning it.

"I told you it was silly." She smiled at him in a conciliatory way. "Simply put, you're just more lover than I've ever had before."

His good mood returned immediately. Moving close to her again, he searched her eyes. "How many lovers have you had, Caren?"

She faltered, and for a moment her eyes slid away

from his green-gold gaze. "Two," she confessed softly. "My husband and you. How many have you had?"

It was amazing how badly it hurt to think of how and where he had learned the erotic arts he practiced so adroitly. How many lovers did it take to teach a man how to fulfill a woman's most secret desires?

He raised her hand to his lips and kissed the knuckles. "Many, Caren." When he raised his eyes to hers they were fiery and penetrating. "But never like this. Never like you."

Derek was surprised to discover that he meant it. Those words had been uttered hundreds of times to different women, but they had been just empty words excerpted from his collection of phrases guaranteed to please a woman.

Caren Blakemore had been different from the beginning. Her shyness had appealed to him first. The passion he had unleashed in her had been a pleasant surprise, but he had made love to passionate women before.

What was it about Caren that was unique? Something. And that indefinable something scared hell out of him. Each time they made love, he left more than his seed with her. He left a small bit of his soul, something he'd never given another woman.

At first he hadn't even been conscious of it. It was as he lay beside her early one morning and watched her while she slept that it came to him quietly how much her sweetness touched him.

He was always glad to see her when they had been

apart even for a few minutes. He enjoyed more than sex with her. He liked her sense of humor, her intelligent conversation, and that damned...*something* that kept him jealous of every thought that wasn't disclosed to him.

And he had realized as he lay there listening to her soft breathing and watching the slight rise and fall of her chest that she wasn't going to be easy to leave, this delicate woman with eyes as soft as dark velvet and hair the color of warm honey.

That kind of thinking was treacherous. It had disturbed him that particular morning and it disturbed him now. The creamy flawlessness of her complexion was highlighted by the candlelight in the center of the table. Her eyes were so deep he felt he could sink into them, get inside her, and never find his way out.

He had awakened her that morning to gentle lovemaking. He hadn't been able to stop himself then and he couldn't now.

"Dance with me, Caren, so I can hold you."

Caren walked into his arms when he stood and extended them to her. She clung to him. For a moment there she had gotten too close. He had retreated into his privacy. No personal questions, she reminded herself. The less you know about him the better. The week will soon be over.

But the thought of its being over left her feeling bereft.

That night there was a fury to their lovemaking that hadn't been there before. It was as though both of them wanted to make up for lost time. When at last they fell asleep, Derek was holding her close.

She didn't sleep well. It was very early when she woke up. The sky was a pale lavender. Only the gentlest waves made their way to the shore. The bay was calm. What few boats were anchored offshore looked like stationary fixtures against the cloudless horizon.

As he had been on most mornings, Derek was up before her. She saw him, not swimming as usual, but sitting alone on the beach, staring out over the water.

Suddenly she wanted to be with him, to feel the reassuring warmth of his body. It was a compulsion generated by the stark fear that he might disappear if she didn't touch him immediately. She pulled on the only garment she had with her, the gauzy dress she had worn the night before, and hastened down to the beach.

He heard her approach only seconds before she launched herself toward him. He opened his arms and she flew into them. He fell back onto the sand, rolling her beneath him and pinning her there.

His anxiety matched hers. His kiss was ravenous. His hands threaded through her hair and he wound thick strands of it around his fingers. His mouth moved over hers greedily as his tongue delved deep.

When at last he raised his head, they gasped for breath. "What are you doing down here so early?"

"Every morning I stand up there and watch you swim in the sea. This morning I wanted a close-up view." She was now brave enough, confident enough, to comb her fingers through his chest hair, to lift her head and nuzzle his neck.

"You might get more than you bargained for," he growled as he noted her skimpy attire. In her rush, she hadn't taken time to put on any underwear beneath the dress.

"Promise?" Her tone of voice was as smoky as her eyes.

Making a low sound in his throat, Derek stood and yanked her to her feet. He ran toward the water with her in tow. She shrieked as the cool water swirled round her ankles, then her calves, and finally her thighs as Derek pulled her farther and farther out.

Turning, he grinned boyishly. "What's the matter?"

"It's cold."

"Is it?"

He spread his hand over the top of her head and dunked her. She came up coughing seawater. "Why, you—"

She lunged for him, but he executed a neat horizontal dive and plunged beneath the surface. He circled her like a shark homing in on a feast. She screamed playfully when he surged out of the water with a mighty roar, his teeth bared.

She plodded through the water toward shore. The wet dress clung to her and impeded her footsteps. Derek dived again and clasped her ankle, bringing her down with a huge splash. When she surfaced, he pulled her against him and cut off her furious sputterings with a bone-melting kiss.

His mouth was hot against skin now cooled by the water. He kissed her as though he would never release her, as though he wanted to draw all of her into himself.

She arched against him, pressing herself along his strong leanness. Her arms closed around his neck. The water lapped at their thighs. The sun's rays, just peeking over the horizon, spilled over them like molten gold.

Derek broke off the kiss abruptly and stared into her eyes fiercely. He trapped her head between his hands, tunneling his fingers through her wet hair. His breathing was harsh. He was a man struggling to keep a tenuous hold on his emotions and passions. They won.

Bracketing her rib cage between his hands, he lifted her high above him. She rested her hands on his shoulders for support. He gazed up into her face, then let his eyes steal over her hungrily. Her body was clearly defined beneath the wet cloth plastered to it. The dress was all but transparent, and sexier than nakedness.

Her breasts were full, crowned with dusky peaks. He easily detected the dimple of her navel. He swore softly when he glanced at the shadowy cleft between her thighs.

"You're beautiful, Caren, and I want you so much. Do you have any idea what it's like for me when I'm deep inside you?"

He pressed his face into her stomach and rolled it

from side to side. His mouth was open. His breath was hot on her skin through the wet fabric.

The muscles of his arms bulged as he lowered her just enough to reach her breasts with his mouth. He fastened on one tight crest and sucked sweetly. His tongue nudged her, lashed her, beat a tattoo of heat and desire against her.

Her head fell back, and she lifted her transported face to the morning sky. Mindlessly, she chanted his name like a prayer in some pagan ritual. Gradually he lowered her, taking love bites of her flesh as he did. The wet skirt stuck to him, leaving her bare as she descended. Her thighs were slick and wet against the smooth shaft of his sex.

He groaned her name and sealed her lips with his. He buried his tongue in her mouth as he lifted her up against his lap. Her legs folded around his hips naturally. With one swift, sure thrust he made them one.

The world could have tilted off its axis and she wouldn't have known it. In fact, that was what she thought had happened when Derek lowered them into the shallow water. Her hair floated out behind her like a liquid halo. Her limbs seemed weightless. She knew only the rhythmic thrusts of Derek's body into hers. It was a coupling so elemental that when he reached as high as he could and filled her with his fire, they cried out their ecstasy on harmonizing notes.

Gradually they sifted down, like spiraling leaves off the tallest branches of the trees. Then they lay limp and unmoving in the mild surf.

The sun rose. The wind picked up and slapped

against broad palm fronds. The boats at anchor for the night began to set sail in the bay. Sea birds took flight. The landscape was waking from a peaceful sleep.

And still they lay, exhausted, the survivors of a tempest.

She stirred, and her eyes opened.

She was in the bed in her own bungalow. They had gone there for a few hours of sleep when they returned from the beach. Derek was bending over her. He kissed her cheek softly.

"Sorry I woke you up. I left you a note. I'm going snorkeling for a while. You get some more sleep."

"You'll be careful?"

"I promise not to let any sharks get me," he said, smiling and kissing her on the nose. Then his lips came down on hers lovingly. "You made this a wonderful day, Caren love."

"For me too."

He kissed her again. "Sweet dreams."

He slipped through the door and shut it quietly behind him. The silence in the dim room surrounded her. All she could hear was the rapid pounding of her heart.

She loved him.

As well as she knew for a fact that the sun would rise again tomorrow, she knew that she loved him.

He had left the room and taken her heart with him. The loneliness was unbearable. When they left each other for good, he would take her heart then, too. The loneliness would be more unbearable.

Rolling to her side, she gripped the pillow and squeezed her eyes closed against the tears forming in them. How could this have happened?

She should have known it wouldn't be a casual affair that she could throw away like a candy wrapper. Hadn't she told Kristin as much? Sex was more to her than just a physical act. It involved the heart.

Yet she hadn't heeded the danger signals. She had fallen heedlessly in love with a man she would never see again after this week. And the longer she was with him—

She sat upright in bed with a sudden thought. She must leave. Now. So there would never be any soul-destroying, heart-wrenching goodbyes. She couldn't tolerate them. She couldn't stand to watch him go on his merry way, leaving her with her heart breaking and bleeding. She couldn't abide a cheerful send-off.

"It's been great, Caren love. Have a good life."

No, she couldn't abide that at all.

Bounding out of bed, she began riffling through closets and drawers, madly gathering her possessions and tossing them into suitcases. She must hurry. If he came back, looked at her, touched her...

When she was done, she scanned the bungalow, looking for something she might have missed. Her eyes fell on the note tucked beneath her handbag.

Caren, I've gone snorkeling. That is, if I can find the energy. You made me weak with wanting you. Derek.

The handwriting was economical and crisp. He did that as he did everything else, with no wasted motions, no superfluous movements.

The message blurred before her eyes. She should crumple the note and throw it away, but she couldn't force herself to. Weeks from now, months, years, it might be evidence that this dream week had actually taken place. She put the note in her handbag.

Locking the bungalow behind her, she hurried through the compound to the central reception desk. "I want to check out," she told the smiling clerk.

His smile collapsed. "But your reservation is good until the end of the week. If anything isn't to your liking—"

"No, it's nothing like that. It's been lovely, but I have to go home." She wanted to scream at him to hurry and prepare her bill. At any moment she expected to hear Derek come up behind her and demand to know what she was doing. She wouldn't put it past him to lift her in his arms again and carry her out of the busy lobby.

Even more likely, she would change her mind about leaving and flee back to the bungalow, back to him, to savor every golden minute of the time she had with him.

But she couldn't. A clean break was better. She would never survive another rejection from a man she loved. Derek had given her back her self-esteem. Leaving now would preserve it.

Smothered by a miasma of depression, she boarded the airport shuttle and miraculously got a seat on the next airplane. The trip to D.C. was uneventful, though she had to make a connecting flight in New York.

Her car, having been parked for several days at National Airport, was reluctant to start. As she took the route to Georgetown, the problems in her life began to resurface. She had successfully shelved them for a week. Now they had to be faced.

Money was foremost in her mind. She shouldn't have wasted what savings she had on a lavish vacation. What had she been thinking? Kristin's schooling was so expensive. And there were clothes, and fees, and books. The list was endless.

She needed that promotion. Larry could pull strings. But he was upset with her. She probably wasn't in the running for the job anymore.

Worry weighed as heavily on her as her suitcases as she lugged them up the stairs to her apartment. The interior was stuffy and close. Dismal. Bleak. Funereal. She raised the windows.

She glanced at the suitcases standing just inside the door. They were an unwelcome sight. She should unpack them tonight. The chore wouldn't take her mind off Derek, but at least it might exhaust her so she could sleep.

But she lacked the will and the energy to do it. She left the luggage where it stood, peeled off her wrinkled pants suit, took a mild sleeping pill that had been prescribed soon after her divorce, and climbed into bed.

The pill and her own weariness combined to put her to sleep quickly.

She was awakened by a rude and insistent knocking on her door. Reflexively she reached for Derek. The emptiness of the bed served to bring back all the misery. She choked back a sob, as though she'd been crying in her sleep.

Groggily checking the clock on the bedside table, she noted it was just after eight o'clock in the morning. Who in the world was at her door at this hour?

She stumbled to the closet, pulled on a robe, and went to her front door, asking cautiously, "Who is it?"

The reply was gruff and official. "FBI."

Seven

"F_B..."

Was this a joke? She put her eye to the peephole. The two men standing on her threshold looked like they had neither told nor laughed at a joke in their lives. Dutifully they were holding up their badges. "FBI?" With trembling fingers she slid the dead bolt free, unlatched the chain lock, and pulled open the door.

"Ms. Caren Blakemore?"

"Yes."

"I'm Inspector Graham. This is Inspector Vecchio. Will you please get dressed and come with us?"

"Come with you? Now? What for?" she asked, aghast. "Are you sure you have the right person?"

Inspector Graham flipped open a small notebook. "Ms. Caren Blakemore, 223 Franklin Place, Georgetown. Age twenty-eight. Formerly married to Wade Blakemore, who works at the Bureau of Engraving and Printing. You are a clerical employee at the State Department under the supervision of Mr. Larry Watson. You have a sister, Kristin, age sixteen, currently enrolled in Westwood Academy.''

She sagged into the nearest chair. Bewildered and frightened, she shook her head as she tried to assemble her thoughts. ''I don't understand. What's going on?''

''That will be explained shortly. Will you get dressed, please?'' Vecchio was tougher, more brusque than Graham. She disliked him instantly.

''Am I under arrest?''

A look passed between the two men. ''Temporarily in our custody,'' Graham said. ''We'll wait for you.''

Like a ghost she moved into her bedroom and closed the door behind her. She dressed mechanically. When she couldn't find the blouse she wanted, she remembered that her suitcases were still packed and standing inside the front door of the apartment.

She did the best she could with what cosmetics were in her bathroom and brushed her hair. She didn't have time to do more than that. Graham called to her through the bedroom door.

''Coming.'' Her knees were shaking, but she bravely opened the door and faced the agents. ''I'm ready. Should I bring anything with me? How long will I be?''

''I'm sorry. I don't know.''

''Let's go,'' Vecchio said curtly.

The two agents flanked her on the staircase. They had said she wasn't under arrest, but that was what it felt like. She and Graham got into the back seat of an innocuous-looking automobile, while Vecchio slid behind the wheel.

She didn't ask where they were taking her. It didn't matter. The very fact that she was in the custody of the FBI made the particulars unimportant.

What had she done?

The question played again and again in her mind like a stuck record. It had to have something to do with work. Had she misplaced another document? Had her mistake warranted an investigation this time?

Surely not. She was privy to certain classified documents, but not at that high a level. What could it be? And what would this mean? To her? Her job? Kristin?

She began to tremble.

Vecchio let her and Graham out at the curb in front of the State Department. Graham, with a hand on her elbow, led her inside. She was escorted into an office unknown to her, and she almost collapsed in relief when Larry Watson sprang to his feet the moment she cleared the door. She got the impression he had been sitting waiting in a state of anxiety for some time.

"Larry! Thank heaven." She rushed toward him in relief and gratitude.

He all but flinched away from her. "Caren."

Her feet came to a dead standstill the instant he spoke her name in that terse, angry way. She clasped her damp hands together at her waist. "Larry, what's going on? What is all this about?"

Her initial relief at seeing him deserted her and was

replaced by a cold, chilling dread. Something terrible had happened; she had unwittingly committed a transgression, and the consequences would no doubt be severe.

"Sit down," Larry ordered in a tone he had never used with her before.

More out of a need to keep herself from crumpling than to obey his command, she dropped into the nearest chair. "Tell me what's going on." Though she strove to control it, her voice rose hysterically.

Diplomatically, Inspector Graham excused himself. "I'll be outside." He left them alone.

When the door closed behind him, Larry glared at her, cramming his hands into his pockets as if to keep from wrapping them around her neck and strangling her. Caren had never seen him so angry. He was fairly bristling.

"You have embarrassed this office, and I have to take that personally, Caren. How could you have done it?" he ground out through his teeth. "I never would have thought you capable of something like this." He swung away as though the sight of her was too hateful for him to stand.

"Done what?" she cried. "What have I done that's so terrible? I haven't been here for a week. No one's told me anything. How have I embarrassed this office, much less you? I can't explain or defend myself until I know what I'm accused of."

He cursed softly, his shoulders hunching in anger. "Did you have a nice vacation?" he asked abruptly.

The question was so out of context it disoriented

her. She rubbed her forehead as though to calm her tumbling thoughts. "Yes, it was very nice." Suddenly she saw Derek, but she pushed the image of him aside. This crisis demanded her full concentration.

"I'll bet it was *nice*," Larry sneered, facing her again. "Did you gloat the whole time you were down there?"

She looked up at the man she had worked for for several years. He had become a stranger. Disgust was written on every feature of his face. Whatever she had done, it couldn't be that horrendous. She hardly wielded the kind of power to induce such fury in her boss. This time Larry really had blown her error all out of proportion. Her patience snapped, and she surged to her feet.

"Gloat over what? Tell me, dammit."

Her anger only inflamed his. "I want to know one thing. Did you do it to get back at me for chewing you out that day before you left? Was that your motivation? Or was it something altogether different? Or did you merely want to humiliate the President or the Secretary of State or the entire United States government? Tell me, Caren. *Why did you do it?*"

He was shouting by the time he finished. Her momentary bravado dissolving before his rage, she cringed backward. Her mouth hung slack as she stared up at him.

Before either had time to say more, the door opened. Caren whirled, expecting nothing short of a hooded executioner. Instead she recognized an under secretary to the Secretary of State. Her heart began to pound and her palms all but dripped perspiration as he fixed her with an accusing stare.

"Ms. Blakemore." He nodded her into a chair. She backed up toward it and fell onto its cushioned seat the moment the backs of her knees struck it.

"I'm Ivan Carrington, advisor to—"

"Yes," she interrupted shakily. "I know who you are, Mr. Carrington."

"You're in a sticky situation, Ms. Blakemore," he said without preamble.

She wet her lips and looked up at Inspector Graham, who had followed Carrington through the door. "I've gathered that, Mr. Carrington. But no one, not the FBI agents, not a man I considered my friend—" she cast a reproachful glance at Larry "—not anyone, has told me what that situation is."

He sat in a chair facing her, laid a leather briefcase on the small table between them, and folded his arms across his chest. He treated her to a lengthy stare. Was he measuring her guilt or innocence? That was how it appeared.

"You were in Jamaica this week."

It wasn't a question; it was a statement. Caren wondered how he knew that or of what concern her vacation was to him. "Yes."

"In the company of Derek Allen."

Blood rushed to her head until the pressure behind her eyes was almost unbearable. Even her vision blurred, and she prayed she wouldn't do something so undignified as faint. Meanwhile, her heart kept up that pounding current of blood flowing to her head. "Yes," she croaked. "He and I spent some time together. What has he got—"

"How long have you known Mr. Allen?"

"I...I didn't," she stuttered. "I met him in Jamaica."

The three men exchanged glances all around. Then Carrington said, "Didn't you think your meeting was a rather strange coincidence, Ms. Blakemore?"

She was thoroughly perplexed. "Coincidence? I don't understand."

"How well do you know Mr. Allen?" Carrington's tone was clipped, that of an inquisitor.

She blushed deeply and avoided the hawkish eyes. "I...we...not very well."

Slowly, Carrington reached for the briefcase. Methodically, precisely, he worked the combination lock and pressed the fasteners open. They clicked loudly. Caren jumped as though the noise were a gunshot. Carrington took a manila envelope from the briefcase and slid its contents onto the table.

The world wavered around her sickly. She would have blacked out had she not been spellbound by the collection of glossy eight-by-ten prints, all black and white, all of her and Derek. All lurid. All stark in clarity. In the surf, her wet dress clinging to the thighs locked around Derek's waist. On the beach, their naked bodies twined together. Each picture erotic and explicit. Damning.

"I think you know Mr. Allen slightly more than

you would have had us believe," Carrington said dryly.

Caren's chin dropped to her chest as hot tears of shame and mortification squeezed from beneath her eyelids. "Please," she begged softly.

Only after she heard the rustle of the pictures being gathered back into the envelope and the briefcase being snapped closed did she open her eyes. She brushed her tears away with the back of her fist.

Carrington leaned toward her. "Now let's try again. What do you know about Mr. Allen?"

"Nothing. Only his name."

"Which name?"

"I don't understand," she said earnestly.

"Have you ever heard him referred to by any other name?"

"No."

"The Tiger Prince?"

"No."

"Never?"

"No."

"Oh, come on, Caren, stop lying," Larry shouted from behind her.

She swiveled her head toward him. "I'm not lying! I don't know what any of this is about."

"I'll handle this, Watson, if you don't mind." Carrington's voice was as cold and lethal as a steel blade.

"Certainly, sir," Larry demurred and stepped back. "You've never heard Allen called the Tiger Prince?" Carrington asked her. "It's a nickname."

"I didn't know he had a nickname," she said dully.

The pictures wouldn't fade from her mind. They kept flashing behind her eyelids like a sleazy peep show, sickening in their detail. What had been so sweet, tender, and loving in actuality had turned to smut in the camera's lens.

"Do you know a photographer named Raymond Daniels? Speck Daniels he calls himself."

"No."

"He's planning to send these pictures in for the front page of the next edition of *Street Scene,* Ms. Blakemore."

Her head shot up, and she looked at him through glazed eyes. "*Why?* I still don't understand why. What possible interest—"

The door opened, and Vecchio stuck his head in. "They're ready for you, sir," he said to Carrington.

Carrington rose quickly and extended his hand. "Ms. Blakemore."

Numbly, she got to her feet and let herself be led from the room. She noted that Carrington had brought his briefcase with its incriminating contents with him. They passed through the echoing corridors and entered one of the top-level conference rooms.

Caren gazed around her in awe. A football game could have been played on the table in the room. It was massive. At one end sat Secretary of State Draper and a group of his aides and advisors. Carrington joined them.

Caren's knees began to tremble. She thought they

might have buckled beneath her if Graham hadn't taken her arm and led her to the middle of the table, where he helped her into a high-backed chair.

She glanced down the length of the table to the group of people at the other end.

Surely this was a dream. Or a nightmare.

She recognized sheik Amin Al-Tasan from his pictures. As a pro-Western Arab who often acted as spokesman for the OPEC nations, he was constantly in the news. His wealth was legendary, as was his power in the Arab world and his influence in the West. Caren remembered reading that he was coming to Washington.

He sat in the end chair, facing Secretary of State Draper at the opposite end. His burnoose and kaffiyeh were white. His swarthy face was as handsome in person as it was in his pictures. He had a sensually full mouth and a long nose, slightly hooked on the bridge. Black brows arched like widespread wings over deep-set eyes.

And those eyes were fixed on Caren Blakemore with a hostile stare.

One of the sheik's entourage leaned forward and whispered something in his ear. He waved the aide off with a beringed hand, his stare never faltering from the woman sitting in the middle of the table.

Caren stared at the sheik, transfixed by his very presence and his apparent hatred of her. It was incomprehensible that a man of his worldwide notoriety would be sharing the same room with her. But that the air in that room would be crackling with such tension was doubly incredible. What could they possibly have in common that would generate such animosity?

Despite his obvious antipathy, she would have gone on gazing at the compelling picture the sheik and his entourage made had there not been a distraction on the other side of the room.

Caren turned her head in that direction in time to see another man entering the mammoth chamber. He was dressed in a trim, European-tailored three-piece suit of navy blue. His shirt was startlingly white against his tanned face, as was the white kaffiyeh which was attached to his head with a silk-braided cord. The whispered conversations going on around the conference table ceased abruptly as he came in.

It was Derek Allen.

Caren wondered how may shocks one normally healthy heart could sustain before it refused to function anymore.

All eyes were trained on Derek as he walked the length of the room. His eyes had homed in on the sheik, and there they stayed as he walked with regal dignity toward him.

He stopped, salaamed, then leaned down and embraced the older man, kissing him on both wind-ravaged cheeks. ''Father,'' he whispered respectfully.

The word echoed through the still room. It reached Caren Blakemore's ears, and a wave of dizziness seized her. Her eyelids fluttered closed, and she swayed in her chair. She gripped the edge of the table to keep herself upright.

Now it all came together. Like metal shavings, the bits of information came scurrying toward the unifying magnet—Derek Allen was son to sheik Al-Tasan. The magnitude of the trouble she was in swept over her in inundating waves.

After greeting his father, Derek was led toward the Secretary of State, who stood for him. An aide introduced them. "Mr. Secretary, Prince Ali Al-Tasan."

They shook hands. Derek was then seated directly across the table from Caren. She couldn't meet his eyes. She kept hers on her white, bloodless hands, which were twisting in her lap.

Prince Ali Al-Tasan. Son of one of the most influential sheiks in the world. He had been her lover.

She couldn't resist raising her eyes and looking at him to make certain he was real. She hadn't known what to expect, but it certainly wasn't the total implacability of his features. The green-gold eyes were trained on her, but they gave away nothing, none of what he thought of the situation or the proceedings going on around them.

He might have been a complete stranger for the unemotional way he looked at her. Would she be the one held accountable for this mess? Did he intend for her alone to take the blame?

She turned her attention to the verbal volley going on between the two delegations. Secretary of State Draper said little without consulting his bank of advisors. The sheik had a spokesman whose feelings were screened by a pair of opaque sunglasses. Some of the legal jargon escaped Caren. She weeded out the diplomatic sugar-coating and finally discerned the bare facts.

The State Department thought it possible that she had passed classified information to Derek, who in turn had turned it over to his father. Sheik Al-Tasan was in Washington to negotiate oil prices on behalf of OPEC. The picture they painted was black.

Carrington addressed her. "Ms. Blakemore, did you discuss anything having to do with oil prices while you were in the…uh…company of Mr. Al-Tasan?"

"I know nothing about oil prices. Nor did I know his name was Al-Tasan." She glanced at Derek accusingly. His expression remained impassive.

"Isn't it strange that the day you asked for a vacation—"

"I didn't ask for a vacation. Mr. Watson, my supervisor, insisted that I take one."

"But you had cross words that day, did you not?"

"Yes, but—"

"And you weren't feeling too gracious toward this department because you were being passed over for a promotion."

"That had nothing to do—"

"Why did you choose to go to that particular resort in Jamaica at that particular time?"

"On a whim!" she cried. "It was purely arbitrary."

The disbelieving faces that stared back at her told her unequivocally they thought she was lying.

"You had never met Mr. Al-Tasan before?"

"I met Derek Allen on the beach at the resort the day after I arrived."

"You did not recognize him as Ali Al-Tasan, known around the world as the jet-setting Tiger Prince?"

"No, I did not."

"Do you expect us to believe that, Ms. Blakemore?" Carrington asked incredulously.

"It's the truth!"

"You spent almost all your time with Mr. Al-Tasan, became intimate with him, and you expect us to believe that he was a total stranger to you?"

She wet her lips, ducked her head, and answered a soft "Yes." She glanced at the sheik. He was staring at her as though he would order her to be stoned at any moment.

Other women had casual affairs and went blithely on their way with no recriminations or repercussions. Even married women got away with adulterous afternoon "parties." She, Caren Blakemore, quiet, unassuming, scared-of-her-own-shadow Caren Blakemore had an affair, her first, and it turned into an international incident. She thought of the pictures of her and Derek and covered her face with clammy hands.

"Ms. Blakemore, didn't know me by any name except Derek Allen." Derek's voice sliced through the muttered conversations. The delegations at both ends of the table fell silent.

"It is as she says," he went on in a level voice. "I met her quite by accident on the beach."

"You introduced yourself only as Derek Allen?" Carrington fired the question at him.

Caren lowered her hands from her face in time to see the bureaucrat go quiet beneath Derek's stare. Apparently, Derek wasn't accustomed to being spoken to in so imperious a manner. But then, he was a prince, wasn't he?

"That's right."

"You didn't know her before?"

"No."

"Did you know where she was employed?"

"If I didn't know her, how could I possibly know where she worked?" Derek asked reasonably.

"She didn't know of your connections with OPEC?"

"I have no connections with OPEC. That is my father's business."

"But you have a vested interest in the oil prices," Carrington suggested.

"None except for what I pay for gasoline at my local service station. I am an American farmer. I love my country. Why would I betray it any more than Ms. Blakemore would?"

"Did you talk about political philosophy?"

Derek stared at the man, an intimidating, lethal, confidence-shattering stare. Then he asked a question of his own. "You've no doubt seen Mr. Daniel's pictures of us?"

"Yes."

"Would *you* have been talking about political philosophy?"

The room erupted into laughter. Derek smiled in celebration of the point he had scored. But when he glanced at Caren, his smile rapidly disappeared. Her face went from scarlet to chalk-white even as he watched. She looked as if she were on the verge of fainting. He stood abruptly, and the laughter ceased.

"I wish to see Ms. Blakemore alone."

"That's out of the question," Carrington said adamantly. "This is—"

"I think this whole mess can be expeditiously cleared up if I'm permitted to see Ms. Blakemore alone."

"We can't allow two parties involved in possibly treasonous activities to—"

"Do you doubt my son's integrity?"

It was the first time the sheik had spoken. His voice was as dry and raspy as a desert wind, and it swept through the room like a sandstorm.

When Carrington opened his mouth to speak, Secretary of State Draper raised his hand to silence him. It wouldn't do to offend Amin Al-Tasan. He was a valuable link between the United States and the Arab nations.

"Of course, Mr. Al-Tasan," Secretary Draper said to Derek. Over his shoulder he spoke to an aide. "Make a room available. For fifteen minutes?" he addressed the sheik inquiringly.

Al-Tasan nodded his approval.

Derek and Caren were led from the chamber into a small ante-office. The door was closed behind them and they were left alone. She had preceded him into the room, so her back was to him. He didn't speak. At last she turned and faced him, one question uppermost in her mind.

"Did you know who I was, where I worked, when you 'accidentally' met me on the beach?"

"No."

"Did you?" she shouted.

"No," he replied in the same unperturbed tone.

Tears sprang into her eyes. To think that his motive for making love to her had been political was too humiliating to tolerate. Had he romanced her only to get information out of her? Had she been a pawn in an international game?

"Why didn't you tell me who you were?"

"I did. My name is Derek Allen."

"Also Prince Ali Al-Tasan."

"An accident of my birth. My legal American name is Derek Allen."

"And you're a farmer," she said peevishly.

"Yes. I have a farm in Virginia."

"And thousands of oil wells in Saudi Arabia!"

He shifted uncomfortably. "They belong to my father."

"Is your nickname the Tiger Prince?"

"Yes. That's usually the way I'm written up in the tabloids."

"I don't read that kind of garbage, so tell me, why are you called that?"

He made an impatient gesture with his hands. "A journalist dubbed me that years ago, and it's stuck. It

has something to do with my hair and coloring and—
Never mind.''

"The time for secrets and reticence has passed,
Derek. Or should I salaam and call you Prince Ali?''

He responded angrily. ''I'm known as the Tiger
Prince because of my rebellious disassociation with
the Arab world and because of my playboy lifestyle.''
Silence as heavy and dense as a woolen blanket fell
over the room.

''I see,'' Caren said at last as she lowered herself
into a chair. ''And I was your latest conquest.'' She
plucked at her hem before she looked up and asked,
''You recognized the man in town that day, didn't
you?''

''His name is Speck Daniels. He is slime. He free-
lances and sells to the trashiest magazines and tabloids. He's always hounding me. The night before I
left for Jamaica I had an altercation with him, more
virulent than the others we've had.''

''He tracked you to Jamaica?''

''Apparently. Somehow he found out where I was
staying.''

''The pictures?'' she asked hoarsely.

''I guess he anchored a boat offshore and photographed us with a telephoto lens. I had no idea he'd
go to those lengths to get even. I underestimated him.

''He sent the pictures to the State Department last
night in an effort to embarrass me during my father's
visit to Washington. It was a coincidence that the
officials here recognized you as one of their own.
Daniels didn't know he had such a prize. I'm certain

he does now, and he'll see to it that the photographs are published. Those that get by the censors.''

They shared an uneasy silence, unable to meet each other's eyes.

Caren massaged her temple, thinking of Kristin. What would the scandal do to her? She would be disgraced, laughed at, talked about, snubbed.

Her own future was ruined as far as working in the State Department or any other government agency was concerned. Her credibility would never survive a scandal like this, whether she was guilty or not. If she made it through this at all, she and Kristin would have to leave the Washington area. And go where?

She looked up at the man standing in front of her chair. His face was the same, but the kaffiyeh was foreign. His eyes were the same, but distant. The hands that were held loosely at his sides were achingly familiar with their long slender fingers sprinkled with blond hairs. She had felt those hands on her body, yet they seemed untouchable now. She had been more intimate with this man than with any other human being in her life. Yet he was a stranger to her.

''Who are you?''

He took a chair facing hers. ''My mother, Cheryl Allen, was a student in London when she met my father. He was studying English and Western civilization, already sensing that East and West would one day have to peaceably coexist. They fell in love, married.

''My father had been married before and had a son, my brother Hamid, who is his heir. Hamid's mother died in childbirth. By the time my grandfather, the old sheik, found out about my father's marriage to a Christian woman, my mother was already pregnant with me. The old sheik was furious and demanded that my father return home. But he stayed with Mother until I was born and saw that she was safely returned to the United States.''

He stood and began pacing. ''My father accepted his duty. He returned home, verbally divorced my mother, married an Arab woman, and started another family. When the old sheik died, Father assumed the reins of control. He has been a good ruler. He has helped to bring Western technology, medicine, and science into his country.''

Caren tried to absorb all this, but it was like a story, too bizarre to be true. Did things like this really happen? Were there people like Amin and Ali Al-Tasan in the world? Not the world she knew. Or was he still part of a fantasy?

''And your mother?'' she probed.

''She returned to the United States and raised me as an American and a Christian.''

''But your father seemed to...''

''Love me?'' He smiled. ''He does. And I love him. Deeply. I respect him. That's why I hate that this has happened. He hasn't exactly approved of my escapades in the past, though he's been forced to turn a blind eye and a deaf ear. I've embarrassed him on numerous occasions. He sees this as another of my wild, irresponsible flings.''

''Wasn't it?''

The look he shot her stopped her breath. "No, Caren. Even had I known our being together was an untenable situation, I would have pursued you. Never doubt that. I saw you. I wanted you. I had to have you."

She swallowed hard and turned away. "Well, you had me. There are pictures to document your success." Much to her chagrin, she began to cry. She covered her face with her hands. "It really doesn't matter what we talked about or whether I transferred government secrets to you or not. We're as good as guilty because the evidence is so incriminating. Can you imagine how I felt when Carrington spilled those pictures out on the table?"

Derek cursed and raked a hand through his hair. "God, I'm sorry." He knew her shyness, knew those moments must have been hell for her. "Daniels will pay dearly for taking those pictures."

Her shoulders shook as she sobbed. "Damn you. Why didn't you tell me who you were? What am I going to do?"

"I have a solution."

She struggled for control and turned to face him at last. Sniffing back her tears, she asked, "What? I'm listening."

"We could marry."

Eight

❧❧❧

She stared into Derek's lean face. As it had been earlier, it was impassive. He was expressionless. His inflection hadn't altered. He could have just told her the time of day instead of suggesting that they get married.

The absurdity of it suddenly struck her, and she began to laugh. Tentative ripples of mirth grew until within seconds she was almost hysterical. It was either laugh or bang her head against the wall. Laughter was the least destructive means of releasing her emotions.

Derek let her laughter subside before he said calmly, "I take it you find the suggestion amusing."

"I find the suggestion ridiculous. You *are* joking, aren't you?"

"I'm quite serious. And I assure you they are." He tilted his head toward the conference chamber.

Caren sobered instantly. Every glimmer of humor fled. The transformation was so complete that it seemed her face had always been as void of gaiety as it was now. Propping her elbow on the arm of her chair, she let her forehead fall into the cup of her palm. "Yes, I know they are."

"Then don't you think the idea at least bears discussing?"

She looked at him angrily. "You're going to waste our fifteen minutes engaging in some sort of game with me?"

Angry in his own right, Derek's lips tightened. "I told you I was serious. If we go back in there and announce that you are now my fiancée, soon to be my wife, the situation alters dramatically. You will find people treat the daughter-in-law of Sheik Al-Tasan with a certain respect. This time, Ms. Blakemore, consider marriage a means of protection."

"For you?" she asked scornfully.

"For you," he said calmly. "I don't need protection. My father will see to that."

She simmered beneath his haughty gaze. It was the first time he had ever turned that royal condescension on her and she didn't like it. Not a bit. Others might cower before it, but she'd be damned before she would.

Spitefully she wondered what his reaction would be if she accepted his proposal. Probably a fatal heart attack. This grand gesture was surely all for show. Very well. She'd play devil's advocate and see just how far he would go before he balked.

"So I'm to believe that you're offering me marriage out of the goodness of your heart?"

A hint of a smile flickered in his tiger eyes. It was

so fleeting and so subtle that she was sure she must have imagined it. "Well after all, I feel somewhat responsible for the situation we find ourselves in. I was the seducer, you were the seduced."

His voice was as sensuous as velvet on naked skin and reminded her all too well how easily that seduction had been accomplished. He really owed her nothing. She had gone into the affair with both eyes open. She had been a willing participant once her initial wariness had been broken down.

What a fool he must think she was! He had seen the pictures too. He had been reminded of her unqualified passion in the arms of a stranger. If he had forgotten her fevered responses to him, the pictures were certain to have jostled his memory. Her pride took a stinging blow at the thought.

She left the chair and went to a window that offered a splendid panorama of the nation's capital. She was a patriot. She loved her country. Sight of the Washington Monument and Lincoln Memorial never failed to bring a lump to her throat. Now she was being accused of betraying the country she loved. And all because of this man who frivolously offered marriage as a means of solving her problem.

He probably considered this just another lark, one that his millionaire father would bail him out of. But she would suffer for those days of passion in Jamaica for the rest of her life. Even so, she wasn't going to grab at his mocking offer as though it was a lifeline.

"I'll never marry again," she said.

"Because your first husband was a louse?"

She spun around to face him. "Because I'll never be under a man's thumb again, nor be deluded by pronouncements of love."

"You're under no such delusion this time. We haven't mentioned love, have we?"

"Of course not," she muttered, turning back to the window. "I only meant that I'll never be at the beck and call of another man."

"I was born in the second half of the twentieth century. I don't hold to any archaic principles about marriage or the woman's place in it. I would hardly expect you to jump to obey my commands."

"Wouldn't you? I think that's what you expect from everyone, Prince Al-Tasan."

He sighed tiredly. "I'm quickly losing patience with you, Caren."

Lord, she wished he wouldn't use her first name. Now she knew why it had a different flavor when it came off his tongue and through his lips. His second language was no doubt Arabic. His slight accent lent a musical, lyrical quality to her name.

"We are into the last five minutes of our reprieve," he said. "We can swear from now until Doomsday that we didn't know anything about each other but our names, that we spoke of nearly everything except politics, that we departed—at least you departed, which is an issue I intend to get to the bottom of later—without ever having learned where the other lived and worked.

"Ultimately, it doesn't matter whether they believe us or not. Our integrity will still be compromised by the press." He paused. "Please look at me while I'm speaking to you."

Reluctantly she turned to face him. Reluctant because she *was* obeying a command. Reluctant because she didn't want him to see her raw fear of his logic. Reluctant because she could feel the first stirrings of surrender tapping at the barricades in her mind. Reluctant because his male beauty and his compelling eyes had, from the beginning, been more than she could resist.

"I've offered the only means I can think of for us to get out of this mess. Do you accept it?"

She gnawed on her bottom lip. He fully expected her to say yes. She could see that confidence in the cool calculation of his eyes. He expected her to throw herself into the harbor of his arms and beg him to save her with his money and influence.

That she resented. She also resented the fact that the bizarre proposal had begun to make perfect sense.

While she ruminated, he pressed his point. "You've no doubt lost your job as a result of this."

"No doubt."

"How will you support yourself until you find another?"

"That's none of your business."

"I'm making it my business."

"I don't need your charity!"

He came lunging toward her and gripped her shoulders hard, shaking her slightly. "Now is not the time for you to come down with a case of stupid, stubborn pride, Caren. I'm offering you my help, not my charity.''

"I'll make do," she said tightly, knowing all the while that he was right.

"On what? What about Kristin?"

Her head snapped back so that she could meet his eyes. That he remembered her sister's name shocked her. "What about her?"

"Can you keep her in private school on an unemployment check? And besides that, what effects would a scandal like this have on her?" He paused to draw a deep breath. "When it comes to handling sticky situations, I'm a pro, but the two of you are babes in the woods. Neither one of you is prepared for the stink something like this can cause, believe me."

"Please, Derek," she said miserably, twisting free of his hold. She didn't actually work herself free; he released her. Only because he chose to. If he really wanted to, he could hold her forever. She knew it. It was a frightful, suffocating thought, and she struggled against it.

"What woman in her right mind would want to become the wife of a man internationally known for his philandering as the Tiger Prince?"

"Would you rather be known as my wife or as one of my mistresses?"

"*One* of them? How many are there?"

"Read the latest edition of *Street Scene*. I'm sure it'll provide an accurate accounting."

"Then won't I just blend into the background, become one in the ranks?"

"Hardly."

"Why?" She envisioned leggy models and chesty starlets and sulky princesses and rich socialites. "Am I so different?"

"Yes," he snapped. "You're fresh as a daisy. That in itself is unusual. And you also work in the State Department of the United States. My father is negotiating with the United States on behalf of the OPEC nations. Hasn't this soaked in yet, Caren? You're in a helluva lot of trouble."

"Thanks to you!" she cried. "Now you want to marry me. Have you lost your mind, or have I lost mine? Linking myself to you is no solution to this mess. I'd only be letting myself in for more trouble. At least a mistress is a temporary position."

"So is being my wife."

She recoiled, stunned and speechless. He'd taken the wind right out of her sails. "Oh, I see."

"As soon as this blows over and some other poor sucker becomes the victim of bloodsucking journalists, we'll get a discreet divorce."

How naive she had been. From her mother's lap she had been taught that the institution of marriage was holy and sacred and inviolate and everlasting. Wade had disillusioned her first about its longevity. Still, even after the divorce, she had stupidly clung to the belief that marriage was sacred.

Derek was making it sound as though they would be subletting an apartment for the summer. It was temporary. Nothing to move into permanently, nothing to get too attached to, nothing to get too comfortable with, nothing to stamp as personally yours.

"Then why bother?" Into that question went an honest curiosity to know his reason for the proposal.

"Because if you're my wife, my father will spare no expense, he'll move heaven and earth, to get us out of this mess and keep us off the front pages of the tabloids. If you're just another one of my women, he won't lift a finger to help you. You'll be on your own."

For that she had no argument. She *was* on her own. She had no one to turn to in this crisis, save for Kristin, who would be as terrified and unskilled in facing it as she.

"Your father would protect me if I became your wife?"

"You would be his daughter. He places tremendous importance on family loyalty."

It was almost laughable. Amin Al-Tasan had sacrificed the woman he loved and her child, returned to his own land and married another woman, sired her children, yet Caren was supposed to believe that family loyalty was important to him.

She wanted to believe it, because it was the only choice she had. She needed the sheik's help. And why not take it? If Derek Allen had been a shoe salesman from Cleveland on vacation in Jamaica she wouldn't be in this predicament. As it was, he was of a royal Arab family. Why not use the power available to him?

She raised her head and searched the swirling agate depths of his eyes for a flicker of the passion she had read in them before. It wasn't there. Even standing as close as they were, he was remote, a stranger.

"Well?" he asked impatiently.

Before she could answer, someone knocked on the door. Without taking his eyes off hers, Derek called, "We're coming." Then, softly, "Caren?" The steady jewel eyes, the firm slant of his mouth, the determination in his chin willed her to answer.

"All right."

The two words were barely out of her mouth before she regretted them. She had taken the coward's way out again. She had done the bidding of a man. Her future was in his hands. But what choice had she had?

Derek accepted her answer without reaction, at least none that was apparent. He went to the door, opened it, nodded at Graham, who was waiting for them, and extended his hand to Caren.

She laid her palm in his and together they went back into the chamber. As they entered the room, the hushed conversation ceased. Derek seated her first, then, rather than going around the table and resuming the chair he had previously occupied, he sat next to her.

Still holding her hand where everyone could see it, he addressed Secretary of State Draper. "Ms. Blake-more and I met by accident in Jamaica." He grinned so engagingly that even she believed him when he said, "It was love at first sight."

The officials' stupefaction couldn't be concealed as

they listened to the Tiger Prince admit that he'd fallen head over heels in love. It would take quite a woman to bag this prize. Several eyed Caren in such a speculative way, it made her skin crawl.

"Because I didn't want anything to jeopardize this fragile new relationship," Derek went on, "I kept my heritage a secret from Caren. I regret that now. She was informed of it by strangers before I had a chance to return to the States and explain it to her myself." His tone was mildly reproachful. "But all that is behind us. She's consented to become my wife. We plan to marry immediately."

This piece of news caused a paralysis in the room. Several moments ticked by before anyone moved, then, as if on cue, everyone began babbling at once.

The sheik accepted the announcement with no more reaction than a slight widening of his eyes. Members of his entourage guffawed and passed jokes among them that Caren was glad she couldn't translate.

The reaction from the opposite end of the table was rather more restrained. Aides and lawyers bent at their waists to whisper into Draper's ear, each voicing protests and alternatives.

Carrington was outraged. "Mr. Al-Tasan, we find this jest outrageous, and if you think—"

"It's not a jest," Derek said coldly. "I intend to marry Ms. Blakemore as soon as a license can be procured, and there's not a damn thing you can do about it."

"And we're supposed to conveniently forget that

Ms. Blakemore could have compromised this department by her liaison with you?"

"She didn't," Derek said crisply. Caren could tell by every taut line in his body that his temper was rising. She glanced at the sheik. His glare was no longer focused on her, but on the diplomat who was ill-advisedly doubting his son's honesty.

Carrington persisted. "Can you prove that Ms. Blakemore did not give you classified information pertinent to the negotiations now underway?"

Derek leaned back in his chair, suddenly relaxed. "Can you prove she did?"

If Carrington wasn't perceptive enough to see that he was painting himself into a corner, the Secretary of State was. He raised his hand in a restraining gesture, and Carrington had no choice but to swallow his next argument.

Slowly the sheik rose from his chair. "It is as my son says." The whispery voice had all the thunderous impact of a prophet's oration. "As Ms. Blakemore is about to become a member of my immediate family, she is under my protection." His hawk eyes drilled into Carrington. "I do not countenance any of my family being interrogated."

Secretary of State Draper was eating crow, if the distasteful expression on his face was any indication. But he got to his feet and met the sheik halfway to the door.

"I'm glad we could settle this so expeditiously, Mr. Al-Tasan." He bowed slightly. The sheik acknowledged the homage with nothing more than a slow blinking of his eyes and slight inclination of his head. He marched out, his white burnoose flapping behind him, his entourage in his wake.

Their exit cleared the way for Derek and Caren. Derek helped her to her feet and kept his hand beneath her elbow in support. Avoiding as many eyes as she could, she went through the door.

Larry Watson was already in the corridor. Lifting her arm out of Derek's clasp, she faced him. "I met him by accident in Jamaica, Larry. It was an incredible coincidence. I swear to you that I didn't know who he was until he walked into this room today."

Larry glanced down at his shoes shamefacedly. "Damn, Caren. I'm sorry for everything I said. I couldn't believe it of you, but—"

She laid a comforting hand on his arm but quickly withdrew it when she felt Derek stiffen beside her. "The evidence was pretty incriminating, I'll grant you," she said forgivingly.

"You know they'll ask for your resignation. Maybe I can intervene."

She shook her head. "Don't bother. I consider myself finished here. I don't want you to get involved any more than you already have been."

He looked pained. "I'll clean out your desk and send the contents to you."

"Thank you."

He glanced at Derek, then looked at her worriedly. "Are you sure you know what you're doing?"

She smiled at him with far more confidence than she felt. "Under the circumstances, I'm doing what

I have to do. Don't worry. I'll be fine.'' She felt the possessive clasp of Derek's hand on her arm again. ''Goodbye, Larry.''

'''Bye, Caren. Stay in touch. If you ever need anything—''

Derek led her away before she heard the last of Larry's offer. He rudely prevented anyone else from entering the elevator with them. He punched the first-floor button, then turned to her.

''Who was that?''

''Larry Watson. My boss. *Former* boss.''

''Only your boss?''

His angry, demanding tone brought her head up. ''What do you mean?''

''You know what I mean.''

The symptoms in any other man—rapid breathing, flashing eyes, tense muscles, a working jaw—would have spelled jealousy. In Derek it could only mean that he was stingy with his possessions. ''Yes,'' she said shrewishly. ''Only my boss.''

''Good.'' His reply was blamed. Caren fumed.

The rest of the trip passed in silence. When they emerged from the elevator, one of the sheik's entourage salaamed to Derek, then embraced him and began to speak to him in rapid Arabic. She could have been invisible for all the attention the servant gave to her. Would it always be like this? Would she always be an appendage of the Tiger Prince?

No. Only until the divorce. It was rather odd that she was already thinking of divorce before she was even married.

"My father wants to see us in his hotel suite," Derek told her as the man withdrew and rejoined the sheik, who had granted the media reps a spontaneous press conference.

"Now?" she asked, hating the quaver in her voice.

"When my father beckons, it's always 'now.'"

A row of black limousines was waiting at the curb outside the building. Robe-clad chauffeurs stood at attention beside them. Derek walked to the first one in line and stood beside its back door for several seconds. Caren thought Derek must have selected the wrong car, because the chauffeur made no move to open the door for him.

Then he did the strangest thing. He carried two fingers to his lips, kissed them, then pressed the kiss onto the window of the back seat.

He took Caren's arm and directed her to the last limousine in the row. The chauffeur rushed to open the door for them. When they were settled into the lush velour upholstery, she asked, "What was that for?"

"What?"

"That kiss."

He looked down into her face. "For my mother."

Her lower lip fell away from the upper as she stared at him. "Your mother? She's in that car? But I thought... He's married to... Your mother is with the sheik?"

"She's always with him. When she can be."

"I don't understand. He's married to another woman, but your mother stays with him? Why?"

He fixed a gold-green stare on her. "Because he wishes it."

She would have pursued the topic of his mother had not the sheik chosen that moment to exit the building amidst a swarm of reporters trying to get one last word from him. They traveled in a motorcade through downtown Washington D.C. to the hotel where the sheik was in residence.

Caren and Derek were told to wait in an anteroom of the suite. Caren sat tensely in a ladder-back chair while Derek, perfectly at ease, ambled around the room.

If he were relieved to have just escaped embroilment in an international incident, he gave no indication of it. He took a drink of water from an iced carafe, gazed out the window whistling a tune through his teeth, studied the artwork on the wall.

His insouciance was disgusting to Caren, who was a package of raw nerves. When he offered her a drink of water, she shook her head, but didn't speak. Her tongue seemed to have been glued to the roof of her mouth. She couldn't remember being so nervous and on edge since waiting in the dentist's office to have root canal work done.

She jumped when Derek turned to her abruptly. "Why did you leave me?"

After all that had happened since then, she could barely remember the anguish she had gone through when deciding to leave him. "Do we have to talk about that now?" she asked wearily.

"Yes."

"I don't want to."

"I do," he said firmly. He came to stand directly in front of her, forcing her to drop her head back if she wanted to look into his face rather than his lap. That in itself was unnerving. "Why did you sneak away like that?"

"I felt it was best."

"For whom?"

"For both of us."

"Why?"

"The week was drawing to a close."

"So?"

"I thought we would never see each other again. I didn't want any sentimental goodbyes. Wouldn't you have rather had it that way too?"

"You didn't leave me much choice, did you?"

"You didn't leave me much choice this morning."

"Ah—" he raised his index finger "—but you made the right choice."

"I'm beginning to doubt that. We're already arguing."

He reached out and brushed an errant strand of hair from her cheek. "It's common for newlyweds to argue on their wedding day, I believe. Something to do with the…tension."

His caress had reminded her how unkempt she must look, but at his suggestive drawl her eyes flew up to his. Now those eyes were familiar. Now they were smoldering with the sultry heat of a tropical night. "I don't feel much like a bride." She tried to sound waspish, but the words came out plaintively.

His eyes took a scorching path from her mouth to her throat and across her breasts. Both his hands were cupping her face now, tilting her head up and back until her chin was almost touching his belt buckle. He dragged his thumb along her lower lip, then raised his stormy eyes back to hers.

"I promise you will before the day is over." It was a vow that made her shiver in dread. Or were those tingles chasing up and down her spine anticipation? "Why did you leave me, Caren?"

"I told you," she said in desperation. His charm was working on her, and she mustn't let it.

"You're lying. There was more to it than not wanting to say goodbye." He stroked her cheekbones. "Didn't you think I'd come after you?"

"No. I thought I'd never see you again."

"You forgot that I told you you'd never outrun me. You haven't have you?" His hands slid away from her cheeks in a soft caress.

No sooner had he released her than the door to the suite opened and a servant summoned them inside. Caren's heart was thudding, and she wasn't sure her jellied knees could hold her up after her stirring exchange with Derek.

The servant bowed deeply as they passed through the door. She halted on the threshold, astonished. To her amazement, the room was perfectly ordinary.

She had expected piles of pillows, bolts of fabric draped from the ceiling, hookahs emitting the smoke of an acrid Turkish tobacco at best and a controlled substance at worst. Where were the harem dancers with jewels winking in their navels? None of that would have surprised her as much as the ordinariness of the room.

The furniture was French Provincial and a trifle too fussy for her taste, but it was beautifully arranged and accessorized. A buffet of food had been laid out on a sideboard, though it didn't seem to have been touched. A wet bar stood ready with every conceivable kind of wine and liquor. The glasses sparkled in the sunlight that streamed in through the windows, the drapes having been pushed aside.

Most ordinary of all were the man and woman sitting close together on the sofa. At least the man was sitting on the sofa. The woman was perched on its padded arm. One of her arms was looped around the man's shoulders in an attitude of casual familiarity. His nearest arm was secured about her dainty waist.

Caren barely recognized the sheik without the flowing burnoose and kaffiyeh. But his eyes, those deep-set, penetrating eyes couldn't belong to anyone other than Amin Al-Tasan.

His face was weather-beaten and sun-ravaged, but breathtaking in its rugged appeal. He wore his hair as Derek wore his, longish and loose, but Al-Tasan's was much darker. Their hairlines were identical. In shirtsleeves the powerful chest and arms that Derek had inherited were visible. His trousers were European-tailored. Handcrafted Italian loafers were on his feet. But the most arresting thing about him was the energy he radiated. Like his son, he captivated and held the attention.

Cheryl Allen was the first to speak. She disengaged

herself from Al-Tasan and came to Derek with her arms widespread. "Hello, dear."

Derek took his mother in his arms with a warm hug. He kissed her soft brown hair. She was a trim woman who barely reached her son's shoulder. Her skin was smooth and obviously well tended. She was extremely attractive, attractive enough to hold the attention and affection of the handsome Al-Tasan.

"Mother, you look fabulous. Is that a new dress?"

"We flew up to New York yesterday evening to do some shopping. Amin picked this out. Do you like it?"

"Very much," Derek replied, though Cheryl Allen was no longer listening to him. Her friendly green eyes were curiously assessing Caren. "Mother, this is Caren Blakemore. Soon to be your daughter-in-law."

Cheryl's smile was hospitable and kind. "So I've heard." She took Caren's ice-cold hand and pressed it affectionately. "I've wanted a daughter-in-law for a long time."

Caren was surprised by her sweetness and generosity, and gave her a weak, tremulous smile. "It's a pleasure to meet you, Ms. uh..." She foundered. What did one call a sheik's former wife?

"Call me Cheryl," she said hastily, seeing Caren's distress. "Let's sit down, shall we? Would you like something to drink?" She turned toward the man who had sat as still as stone through the entire conversation. "Amin, darling, what would you like?"

"I would like for you to stop flittering around, trying to make this unorthodox occasion seem orthodox.

Come sit beside me. Derek is perfectly capable of
getting himself and his fiancée a drink.''

He patted the arm of the sofa, and Cheryl returned
to it. ''As a Moslem, I don't drink alcohol, Ms.
Blakemore, but please feel free to indulge,'' Al-Tasan
said.

Caren's back went up. Was he testing her? ''Thank
you, but I don't care for anything right now.''

Derek was barely suppressing a smile, and his eyes
were dancing with mischief as he led her to a chair.
''Father, Caren isn't a heavy drinker, if that's what
you're trying to find out. In Jamaica I tried plying
her with liquor several times. I wasn't particularly
successful.''

He went to the bar and poured himself a glass of
mineral water, adding ice cubes with decisive, splash-
ing plunks and squeezing the lime with gusto.

His body language bespoke supreme indifference.
Caren glanced worriedly at the sheik. He was looking
not at Derek but at her. He was smiling. ''She's very
pretty, Ali.''

''Thank you. I think so too.''

Caren was startled when Derek sank down close
beside her and draped an arm across her shoulders.
He kissed her temple with husbandly affection.

''She has caused me a great deal of trouble today,''
Al-Tasan said.

Caren had had all she was going to take of being
talked around. She wasn't deaf, or mute, or imbecilic.
''No more than you've caused me, Mr. Al-Tasan.''

The sheik's eyebrows rose quickly, then lowered
into a significant scowl. The hand that had been idly

stroking Cheryl's back stilled. "She has a sharp tongue, too," he said. Suddenly that exquisite desert face broke into a wide grin that displayed incredibly white teeth. He bellowed with laughter. "She reminds me of you when we first me, *cherie*." He pinched Cheryl's arm affectionately. "Very saucy. I like that. I detest mewling women. Don't you, Ali?"

The next half-hour was considerably less tense than the first five minutes had been. Caren was mildly piqued when Al-Tasan grilled her about her background, but Derek's warning eyes kept her tongue civil. It was she who was being forced into this marriage, not the other way around. Yet she was the one under scrutiny.

At last Al-Tasan gave them both a long, lingering perusal. "You have my permission to marry."

Caren didn't remember asking his permission. Nonetheless, she remained silent as Derek inclined his head respectfully and said, "Thank you, Father."

Al-Tasan stood and came toward them. Derek pulled Caren to her feet. The sheik framed her face between his hands. She could see her pale image reflected in his ebony eyes. Surprising her, he kissed her on both cheeks before setting her away from him. "Daughter."

Turning to Derek, he said, "I would like a private word with you, Ali." Derek followed his father into the adjoining room.

Servants materialized to wait on Caren and Cheryl, who insisted Caren join her in drinking a cup of tea and eating a cucumber sandwich.

"I'm delighted over this marriage, no matter what

circumstances brought it about. For years Amin and I have worried about Derek, wanting him to settle down and start a family.'' The Wedgwood cup and saucer rattled in Caren's hand at the mention of a family. Cheryl either didn't notice or chose not to comment. ''He's been rather wild. My fault, I suppose. But he had such a difficult time growing up, with things as they were,'' she finished lamely, glancing up at Caren with a sad smile.

Caren's heart went out to the woman in pity. Before she could think of anything consoling to say, the door to the next room opened and the two men filled it. Al-Tasan gripped his son in a hug and kissed his cheeks heartily. Derek responded likewise.

He came to Caren and took her arm. Al-Tasan smiled on them both. ''We will arrange to see you soon.'' He extended his hand toward Cheryl. ''*Cherie*, come here.'' The raspy whisper conveyed untold intimacy.

Cheryl Allen, the gracious woman who looked totally composed and able to handle any situation, set her teacup aside, smiled at her son and Caren, then went immediately to take Al-Tasan's outstretched hand. He drew her inside the bedroom and closed the door. She had been summoned, and Derek and Caren had been dismissed, all with the same degree of finality.

Nine

——∞∞——

"**D**on't expect me to be like that."

They were in the limousine again, gliding through the streets of Washington in an island of luxury. They had even been isolated from the driver by a sliding panel of glass after Derek had given him her address. How he had learned where she lived she didn't know, but she was inured to surprises by now. Her eyes were sightless as she gazed out her window.

"Like what?" he inquired. She could feel his body shifting, turning in the seat to face her. She kept her head averted.

"Like your mother. The way she fawns over your father, heeds his slightest wish, fetches and carries for him." Now, she looked at him fully, lest he mistake her earnestness. "I will not be that kind of wife to you."

Anger would have been the expected response. Possibly even fury. A slow, lazy grin that hiked up one corner of his lips was the last reaction she would have anticipated. Yet that was what she got. That and a warm palm that curled around the side of her neck, that applied just enough pressure to draw her face beneath his.

"What kind of wife will you be, Caren love?"

Then his mouth covered hers. He tasted and savored with all the pleasure of a gourmet at a feast. His lips were pliant yet demanding as they moved over hers, persuading them to open for his tongue. It invaded swiftly, possessed completely, stroked tantalizingly.

He unfastened the top two buttons of the simple blouse she had dressed in that morning and slid his hand onto her collarbone. The long, lean fingers curved over her shoulder. It was an intimate caress in that it was negligent, as though he took it for granted she wouldn't object.

Indeed she was powerless to do so. Because this embrace was the first real thing that had happened to her today. He had removed the kaffiyeh, and he looked like the Derek she knew. This was familiar. This she recognized. This she could accept.

Knowing a response would compromise her recent declaration of independence, she nevertheless surrendered as her body wanted her to. She kissed him back. And when he raised her brassiere strap off her shoulder and ran his fingers back and forth beneath it, a low sigh vibrated in her throat.

At last he lifted his lips from hers. "I've wanted to do that all day. At moments I didn't think I could stop myself." His lips roamed along her jaw, to her ear, down her neck, leaving a chain of damp kisses and the fragrant vapor of his breath. "I was mad as hell at you for running away from me."

"Why? Did it hurt your ego?" Was she the first woman to scorn his attentions?

"No. I just wasn't finished with you yet," he whispered in her ear a heartbeat before his tongue sponged the earlobe. "I hadn't had near enough of this."

His mouth made love to hers again, expressively, evocatively, until her insides were rolling with a shameful craving. She twisted in the embrace to bring her breasts in contact with his chest. Her arm curved around his neck and she succumbed to the carnality of the kiss.

She didn't even know the limousine had come to a halt until Derek released her. She sat up, furious with him for his complacency and with herself for handing that smugness to him on a silver platter. The chauffeur opened the door for them. Hastily she reached for the buttons on her blouse. Derek caught her wrist.

"Leave them. You're no longer a government employee, and I won't have you lacing yourself up as tight as a Victorian spinster. I like you looking feminine."

She bit back a retort because she didn't want to create a ruckus in front of the driver, and because several neighbors and passersby were eyeing the limousine with open curiosity. Besides, Derek had a firm grip on her upper arm and was already ushering her up the stairs.

She almost stumbled over the suitcases still standing just inside the apartment door. "I didn't unpack last night."

"Yes, making good an escape from a villain like me is exhausting, I would imagine," he said dryly.

Since the chauffeur was standing sentinel outside and out of hearing, she spun around, her fists digging into her hips. "I would appreciate it if you'd refrain from making any more snide comments about that."

"And you'd better dismiss any notions of running away from me again."

"You have no claims on me."

"In half an hour I will."

"Half an hour?" she asked, the fight suddenly draining out of her.

"My father is arranging for us to meet a judge. He'll have all the essential documents."

It was really going to happen. She was going to marry Derek Allen, otherwise know as Ali Al-Tasan, and she knew neither of them.

"You'd better get your things together," he said in a considerably softer voice. "I think it will be best if we get out of Washington and go to the farm. We'll stay there until things quiet down. Take only what you need right away. I'll buy you the rest later."

She wanted to take issue with the proprietary way he was arranging her future, but she was too tired. "I'll be right out." Waving a hand vaguely in the direction of the sofa, she said, "Make yourself at home."

She wandered aimlessly through the bedroom and bathroom, looking for something worth packing and taking with her. There was nothing. Was she too dazed now to attach significance or sentiment to anything, or had her life actually been that dull?

One thing did register—she didn't want to be married in the skirt and blouse that were the first articles of clothing she had reached for that morning. Going back into the living room, she picked up her smaller suitcase. "Do I have time to shower?" she asked Derek. He was flipping through a magazine with no more anxiety than a man waiting for a bus. It was highly irritating.

"Of course. Would you like me to wash your back?"

"No."

"Anything you say, love."

Under the circumstances, the endearment grated. Her spine was ramrod straight as she stalked back to the bedroom. The door was closed none too gently behind her. She showered, shampooed, and applied makeup, taking an inordinate amount of time, perversely hoping to ruffle him.

But when she joined him he was as calm as he'd been before.

She had dressed in an off-white silk sheath belted with a braid of vibrant silk cords and an oversize hammered-brass buckle. She had smoothed her hair back into a chignon on her nape. Her only jewelry was a pair of pearl earrings. The ensemble was chic, smart, elegantly simple. She tried to match her expression to its sophistication.

Derek tossed the magazine aside and slowly got to his feet, his eyes prowling appreciatively.

"I'm ready," she said hastily before he could comment on her appearance. "I'll just take these things that are already packed."

He nodded and opened the door, issuing a spate of orders to the chauffeur. Once the suitcases had been carried out, he asked, "Is there anything you should do to secure the apartment?"

"For now, I'll just lock it. I had had milk and newspaper deliveries suspended until further notice when I went to Jamaica."

There was no need to notify her landlord, because she didn't know when she would be back. How long would this "marriage" last? A week? Two? A month?

Derek had said he was angry she had left him, not because he loved her, not because he was fond of her, but because he hadn't had enough of her. And the kiss that followed his statement indicated exactly what he'd been referring to. She would need a place to come to when Derek's sexual appetite for her had been satisfied.

What he expected out of the marriage was apparent, an expense-free mistress. Prince Al-Tasan was in for a rude awakening.

She waited until they were once again ensconced in the back seat of the limousine to make her announcement. And actually it was Derek who opened the conversation.

"You look gorgeous, Caren. Prettier than I've ever seen you. I'm extremely proud of my bride."

"Thank you." She fiddled with the tassel on her belt. "I felt self-conscious about being dressed as I was when you were wearing a suit. I didn't know when I pulled on those clothes this morning that I might be married in them."

"I'm in a real dilemma."

"A dilemma?"

"I want to kiss you, but I don't want to muss you. Which selfishness should I give in to?" He tilted his head and studied her. "You're too pretty to mess up. I'll compromise." He took her hand, lifted it to his mouth, and planted an explicit kiss on the palm.

It was a kiss she felt in the heart of her femininity, which blossomed, warmed, liquefied at the touch of his lips and that wicked, wicked tongue. "I have the loveliest, sweetest, sexiest bride in history," he murmured into the hollow of her hand, which until now she hadn't realized was an erogenous zone.

Prying her hand away, she put several inches of space between them on the seat. Clearing her throat, trying to still the knocking of her heart, she said, "I have to talk to you about something, Derek."

"What kind of underwear are you wearing?"

"What kind of question is that?"

"The kind a groom is entitled to ask his bride."

"I might not be a bride after you hear what I have to say."

"Oh?" It was spoken casually, as though he were

only mildly interested. But the veeing of his sun-gilded brows gave him away.

The peachy lip gloss she had put on was doing a poor job of keeping her lips moist. She dampened them with a flick of her tongue. "I'll go through with this marriage ceremony because it's necessary. But that's all it'll be."

"I'm not sure I grasp your meaning."

She took a deep breath. "I mean that it will only be a ceremony. Nothing else."

"Nothing else?"

Why was he being so dense? Was he deliberately baiting her, forcing her to spell it out? "Nothing else that marriage implies."

The silence dragged on while the driver effortlessly maneuvered the limousine through Washington traffic.

Derek ended the silence at last. "That is to say that you don't intend to grant me conjugal rights?"

"That's exactly what I'm saying," she said, raising her chin a notch to show him she meant business.

"You won't share a bed with me?"

"No."

"Make love at all?"

"Not at all."

He rattled the pane of glass between them and the driver with his roar of laughter, showing another trait he shared with his father. She stared at him in huffy silence. What had she said that he found so damn amusing?

"Caren love." He reached for her hand, and when

she would have kept it from him he wrapped his hard fingers around it and drew it toward his chest. "Do you realize how ridiculous it sounds for you to make that condition?"

"Tell me why."

"Very well." His attitude was one of patient condescension, as if he were explaining the mysteries of life to a child. "In the first place, you are in no position to be making conditions of any sort. We're both in trouble, but you're the most vulnerable."

"By virtue of my sex, by virtue of the size of my bank account, by virtue of my work, which I liked and was very good at!" she stormed.

He nodded in concession. "I didn't say it was fair; I'm only stating the facts. Granted, you had more to lose. I offered you a solution to a serious problem. Don't you think it's rather unsportsmanlike and downright petty of you to be putting conditions on *my* offer?"

Furious and humiliated, she clamped her lips shut. "In the second place," he continued smoothly, "we want each other. There's never been any doubt about that."

"In Jamaica, yes. It was romantic. It was removed from the real world. The sea, the moon, the music, the flowers, the wine. I got caught up in the romance of it, that's all. Now my feet are back on the ground. They landed rather hard, I might add. After all that's happened as a result of my indiscretion, how could you think that I'd want to continue it?"

"I don't analyze reasons for human behavior,

Caren. I deal only with the facts.'' He leaned toward her, bringing his mouth a scant few inches from hers. ''You want me right now just as much as I want you. I know your body well. I see the signs. One reason I like that dress is that it fits you so well and conforms to your sweet shape. I detected the response of your breasts when I kissed your palm only moments ago. Didn't you think I'd notice? And when you shift uncomfortably and recross your legs, don't you think I can imagine the responses in other parts of your body?''

Scalding tears flooded her eyes. ''Stop it, please.'' She squeezed her lids closed and pressed her lips together so he wouldn't see their trembling.

''You want me, Caren. Still. More than ever. And if you'd shake off that prudish attitude you've developed since returning to the States and look at me closely, you'd know how badly I want you. I certainly can't hide my desire. Now why this absurd stipulation on our marriage?'' His voice had risen angrily until the last sentence was a demand to know.

''Because you've caused me enough grief as it is. I don't want to be your wife. I certainly don't want to be a temporary playmate until the newness wears off. I won't be one of a harem that spans the globe. I won't sleep with you.''

''Isn't that rather like shutting the barn door after the horse is out?''

''That's just the kind of ungentlemanly thing I'd expect you to say. I slept with you before because I wanted to. It was by choice. Now I choose not to. And I won't."

"But the circumstances have changed. After we're married I'll have the right to insist," he said, seemingly not in the least perturbed by her tirade.

"Would you?"

"I might."

She felt a tremor of fear, but hid it behind a show of anger. "How? By knocking me over the head with a club and dragging me to your bed? Like father, like son. You snap your fingers and I'm expected to jump. Women are chattels, is that it? Created by God and put on this earth for your entertainment. Well, guess again, Mr. Derek Allen. I won't live in that kind of slavery, not even for a little while. So you can tell Abdul up there to turn this car around and take me back home. I'll solve my problem some other way."

He could have backhanded her and she wouldn't have been surprised. But he merely smiled and said chidingly, "His name is Mohammed, and no, he's not going to take you back home. I stand by my offer. I'll marry you. And you can stew in your own juice, deny that you want me in your bed, pout and sulk all you want to, and I won't force my detestable loving on you."

Once again he had effectively turned the tables on her and made her feel foolish for blowing her top. "Oh, well, good." She eyed him suspiciously. He had conceded much too quickly. "What will you be doing while I'm sulking, pouting, et cetera?"

She didn't trust his smile. It was far too feline, far

too much like a great cat who had just spotted a weakened prey. The smell of victory was in his flared nostrils. The glow of triumph was in his eyes. The satisfaction of effortless, imminent success curved his wide, sensuous lips. "I'll be changing your mind."

The message, strong in content, was spoken with no more abrasiveness than a gentle kiss. It was like the whispery vows of passion his lips had made against her breasts and down the valley of her stomach, over her belly, and around her navel. It was spoken in the same misty voice that found her ear in the aftermath of lovemaking. He had said, "You always please me, Caren. I love the way your body gloves mine so tight and warm. It feels so good."

That softly threatening promise brought back all the memories of his lovemaking, and she wondered why she was denying herself. She sat, transfixed, staring into the hypnotic swirls of his eyes and only blinked herself out of the trance when the driver opened the door.

"We're here," Derek said, assisting her to the sidewalk.

"Will your parents be here?"

"No. Where father goes, there's always fanfare. He wanted to spare you further embarrassment."

Caren moved like an automaton into the building. None of this seemed real. She met the judge, shook his hand, and graciously accepted his best wishes on her union with Derek. She signed her name to the documents slid beneath the poised pen. She took her place beside Derek. She repeated the words of the marriage vows.

Then she knew. When the words echoed back through her head, she realized why she had made that condition, why she was terrified of this alliance.

She never wanted it to end.

She wanted to be Derek Allen's wife. The vows weren't merely words to her. As she spoke them, they took on special meaning. She had fallen in love with Derek before she had fallen into his bed. Giving of herself had been an outpouring of love. Marriage to him would be a commitment, physical and spiritual. To her it wasn't a farce.

But to him…

As he spoke the words that bound her life to his, she lifted her eyes. He was watching her, and a shock went through her. It was almost as though he were speaking to her sincerely. But she couldn't let herself believe that for one moment. Her eyes drifted away.

It would hurt, Lord how it would hurt, when she was cast aside, when this "play" marriage was dissolved. To spare herself further hurt, she must remain aloof and independent. She would live with him in polite coexistence, but there would be no intimacy. If she became a wife to him in every sense of the word, she feared that when the time came for them to separate, she would beg him to let her stay.

When they came to that part of the ceremony when they were to exchange rings, Derek shocked her by presenting her with a narrow gold band. It was engraved with an intricate design and looked antique.

"One of my mother's, given to her by my father," Derek explained softly when she raised inquiring eyes. "It's been in the family for generations. They wanted me to give it to the woman I married."

Dazedly, Caren watched Derek slip the beautiful ring onto her finger. It fitted perfectly. The solemnizing kiss that followed was tender but potent. Keeping to her resolve would be the hardest challenge of her life.

The judge pumped Derek's hand and offered them the hospitality of a drink in his office. Derek declined, and the judge, understanding the groom's impatience, sent them off with his blessings. Caren wouldn't have been surprised by his effusiveness had she known the amount of the check that now lined his pocket.

They were driven to a high-rise apartment building in a posh neighborhood. The limousine glided into the shadowed underground parking garage like a sleek serpent into its pit. Standing beside a parked Excalibur was a servant who immediately began transferring Caren's suitcases into the quaint trunk on the rear of the car.

"I thought you might be more comfortable taking this car to the farm rather than riding all the way in a limousine," Derek said. As if riding in an Excalibur were any less novel than riding in a chauffeur-driven limousine.

Derek bade his father's servants goodbye and took the ramp back out into the fading sunlight. This day was almost over, and still Caren couldn't believe any of it had actually happened.

"In case you're wondering, those photographs of us and all the negatives are now in my father's possession." She blushed to think about them, but he settled her mind immediately. "They will be destroyed if they haven't been already."

"How did he keep them from being published?"

"I gave him the name of the photographer, Speck Daniels. No doubt my father made him an offer he couldn't refuse. I doubt he'll be taking pictures like that anymore."

Caren swiveled her head around to see if he were joking. He wasn't. She shivered in the cool night air, and only partly because they were driving at breakneck speed with the convertible top down. What would have happened to her had she become sheik Amin Al-Tasan's enemy rather than his daughter-in-law?

"What about *Street Scene* magazine?" she asked huskily. "I thought they were planning a whole issue around us."

"Oh, they were. But Father threatened them with a lawsuit that would have eaten up not only the profits from that issue, but for the next ten years as well."

"When did you learn about this?"

"This afternoon when he called me into the bedroom."

"But he hadn't had time to do all that," she exclaimed in dismay.

Braking at a traffic light, Derek turned his head and smiled. "No, but those were his plans. And when he says he is going to do something, you can consider it done.''

She had paid little attention to where they were going. But when the surroundings became familiar, she glanced at him in awe. ''You seem surprised,'' he said as he pulled the car to a stop outside the private school.

''I am. How did you know?''

''I have my ways,'' he said enigmatically. Getting out of the car, he came around to open her door. Taking her arm as she alighted, he walked with her up the lichen-covered brick walkway. ''I think Kristin should be informed of our marriage before I whisk you off for the honeymoon, don't you?'' He placed a arm around her shoulders and hugged her close. ''Besides, I'm anxious to meet my sister-in-law.''

The usually austere headmistress was all aflutter when Caren introduced Derek as her husband, especially since she recognized him. Her blue curls bounced and a stumpy, efficient hand toyed with the collar of her prim blouse. Kristin was paged immediately.

While they waited, the headmistress asked leading questions that she hoped would produce material for her consuming curiosity. Without giving any real information, Derek charmed her with his easy banter and that heart-tripping, bone-melting, hormone-stirring smile.

Kristin came bounding down the stairs with no more poise than an energetic sixteen-year-old was supposed to have. The headmistress turned on the

heel of one functional shoe and frowned. The un-
voiced reproach was lost on Kristin, who stopped so
suddenly she seemed to wobble for a few seconds
when she saw her sister on the arm of the most gorgeous man she'd ever seen.

For a moment she wavered there on the stairs, gaping at Derek in amazement. Then she made a conscious effort to close her mouth and proceeded down
the stairs, with much more decorum this time.

Caren, sympathizing because she knew the impact
Derek could have on a female, went toward her sister.
She had been so preoccupied with what this marriage
would mean to her that she hadn't taken Kristin's
feelings into account, not until this moment. She
hugged her younger sister hard.

"Hello, Kristin."

Kristin returned the embrace, but her hug was per-
functory. Caren rather imagined that Kristin was still
staring over her shoulder at Derek. "Hi. You're back
from your trip?"

"Yes," Caren said, pushing her away so she could
see her face and gauge her reaction to what was coming. "I came back a few days early."

"Why?" So far Kristin's eyes had remained fixed
on the man who was gracing the foyer of the boarding
school in a way it had never been graced before.

"Well," Caren hedged. Now that the moment had
come, she didn't quite know how to break the news.
"Something came up...I met...this is Derek Allen,"
she said quickly. "Derek, my sister, Kristin."

Entranced, Kristin floated toward him. "Hello,

Kristin,'' he said smoothly. ''I've been anxious to meet you.''

''You have? Why?'' she sighed. Caren wanted to shake her as hard as she could. She didn't want Kristin to become too enchanted with him.

''Because I'm family now. Caren and I were married this afternoon.''

Kristin's mouth worked uselessly. Her eyes went from one adult to the other. Finally getting a grip on herself, she stammered, ''M-ma-married?''

Derek took Caren's hand and pulled her beneath his sheltering arm. ''I met your sister in Jamaica and fell in love with her.'' He let his eyes sear into Caren's before finishing. ''I chased her back to the States and pleaded with her to marry me. She consented, and I rushed her to the judge's chambers before she could change her mind. I hope you're not offended that you weren't invited to the ceremony.''

It was trite and absurd, but Kristin and the headmistress lapped up every fictional word of his extemporaneous tale. He painted a word picture straight out of a Doris Day movie, and by the time he completed it with a soft kiss on Caren's mute lips, his audience was tingling with romantic excitement and hovering on the verge of sentimental tears.

''Oh, God, Sis,'' Kristin gushed, catching Caren in a hug so enthusiastic it almost broke her neck. ''It's positively wonderful. Oh, God. And to think I'm the one who told you to go to Jamaica. I just had this feeling, you know, that something really wonderful was going to happen to you. Oh, *God!*''

Derek interrupted Kristin's exuberant congratulations by asking the headmistress's permission to take her out for a celebratory dinner. She granted it effervescently.

Kristin raced up the stairs to change. Derek spent the time besieging the headmistress with questions about the curriculum and Kristin's progress.

As though he cares, Caren thought petulantly.

But to see the earnest concern on his face, one would think he did. She grudgingly had to admit that this visit to Kristin was thoughtful and showed some sensitivity.

Kristin came down dressed in her Sunday best. When they stepped into the courtyard and she saw the car, the "Oh, Gods" started all over again. Derek laughingly told her she would have to sit in the rumble seat, but she let him help her into it with all the grace of a queen being assisted into a royal carriage. Derek inspired that kind of confidence in a woman.

He took them to a restaurant only a few minutes' drive from the school. It was a family-owned Italian restaurant with enough atmosphere to mellow the most cantankerous soul. The food was delicious, the wine heady, the service impeccable.

Derek's good looks and cosmopolitan manner thoroughly enthralled Kristin. Caren knew him well enough by now to know that it wasn't a conscious effort on his part. He charmed without thinking about it. He talked little about himself, but asked Kristin about her studies, her interests, her hobbies.

"Only one thing really bothers me." At his coaxing, she had happily expounded on her life at school. She was frowning now as she twirled the stem of her wineglass. He had poured the wine for her without even asking. Caren knew how many points that must have scored him. He was treating Kristin as an adult. Nothing would please a girl her age more.

"What's that?" Derek asked from his corner of the booth. Idly he was strumming Caren's shoulder with the tips of his fingers. All evening he had perpetuated the myth that their marriage was normal and inspired by love. He couldn't have been more courteous or attentive to her every need.

His eyes often strayed to her, and even a near-sighted man could read the heat in them. They declared loud and clear: *This is my wedding day. You are my bride. And I can't wait to take you to bed.* Caren's insides rearranged themselves with every loving word, every touch.

"Boys," Kristin answered Derek glumly. She looked at her sister. "You know the guy I told you about before you left on your trip?"

"Yes."

"He hasn't called me back. I knew he wouldn't."

"He's obviously an idiot," Derek said dismissively. He got to his feet, leaned across the table, and kissed the top of Kristin's head. "If you ever have any problems, you come to me. All right?"

"All right," Kristin answered happily.

"If you ladies will excuse me, I need to make a telephone call. I'll be right back." He blessed—or cursed—Caren with another of those smoky glances before he went toward the front of the restaurant.

Her skin still burned under that gaze long after he left. Hoping to hide her blush, she stared into the ruby facets of her wineglass.

As though she had been waiting all night for the opportunity, Kristin leaned across the table and unabashedly asked, ''Is he positively yummy in bed?''

Ten

"Kristin!"

"Well?"

"That's a terrible thing for you to ask."

"I want to know. And don't pretend that you haven't been to bed with him, because I can tell you have by the way he looks at you, like he's about to gobble you up. Was it dreamy?"

Caren tried to hold back her smile. How wonderful it would be if Derek loved her and she could share the joy of it with Kristin. "You've met him," she answered evasively. "What do you think?"

"Oh, *God!* I think he's gorgeous. The girls in the dorm will die when they they see him, positively *die*. He's more of a hunk than the Chippendale men. The body is excellent. I mean, the bod is…well, *excellent*. I love his hair and, oh, Caren, he's just so nice and…" She flapped her hands in agitation, unable to find the words to describe Derek. "He's my brother-in-law! Wow! I still can't believe it. And that car! Is he terribly rich?"

"I suppose so. He's half Arab, Kristin. His name is Ali Al-Tasan. His father is sheik Amin Al-Tasan. Have you heard of him?"

Kristin's eyes were bugging. "The oil well Al-Tasan? Friend of prime ministers and kings Al-Tasan? *That* Al-Tasan? Are you kidding me?"

Caren shook her head. As briefly as possible she told Kristin the story of Derek's life, or what she knew of it. "He has an apartment in D.C., but we're going to his farm in Virginia."

"He probably has houses all over the world."

"Probably. I don't know."

"Do you think we'll get to travel? Caren, my God! Do you realize what this can mean to us? Little ol' us?"

"We'll just take each day as it comes." There was no sense bursting Kristin's bubble now. When the marriage was dissolved, she'd explain it all to her then. Or perhaps not. She might just pretend that it hadn't worked out.

Derek returned to the table, asked if they wanted anything else, and, when they declined, escorted them back to the car. At the door of the school, Kristin gave him an exuberant hug.

"Thank you for making my sister happy again."

He laughed, ruffling her hair. "It's been my pleasure." He pressed a hundred-dollar bill into her hand. "Here's some spending money."

Caren swallowed a protest. Kristin had had to do without so much since the divorce. She had been made to suffer through no fault of her own. What was a hundred dollars to Derek? And if it would provide Kristin some new clothes, why not?

"Thanks! Isn't it terrific to have money again, Caren?"

"Kristin!"

"Well, isn't it? We've been paupers since that jerk walked out on you. Now we won't have to count every penny. You won't have to work. Oh, Caren, you can go back to sculpting!"

"You had better say good night and go inside before the headmistress comes out looking for you." Caren didn't like the track the conversation was taking. She didn't want Kristin to get accustomed to the luxuries that Derek could provide.

They said their goodbyes, exchanging hugs and kisses all around. Derek gave Kristin the telephone number of his home in Virginia and the mailing address.

"Can I call collect?" Clearly she felt at ease with him enough to tease.

He tweaked her nose. "I expect you to, brat. And often. If you ever need anything, notify us. Promise?"

"Promise."

Once they were on their way, Caren sank into the leather seat of the car and rested her head on its back. Her eyes closed almost automatically. "Thank you for being so generous with Kristin. She's had it rough, even though I managed to keep her in that school. I promised our mother I'd give Kristin the best education possible. Wade and I were the only family she had. When we broke up it was a psychological adjustment for Kristin too. I apologize for her candor. She always says exactly what's on her mind.''

"Such candor is commendable. I wish some of it would rub off on her older sister.''

She sat up and shot him a scathing look. "What do you want me to do? Tell you your bod is excellent?''

He laughed. "Is that what she said?''

"According to her, and she speaks for all the girls in the dorm, you're better than the Chippendale men.''

"Wow!''

"She said that too.''

"What?''

"Wow.''

"Oh.''

They were on the outskirts of the city by now. Derek guided the car to the shoulder of the highway.

He let the motor idle while he looked at Caren closely. "I'd say you're exhausted.''

"It seems like a long time since the FBI agents got me out of bed this morning.''

He frowned. "That must have been terribly frightening.''

"I wouldn't recommend it over an alarm clock.''

He touched her cheek briefly. "Let's put the top up. You can sleep all the way home.''

Home. The word connoted permanence. It had a safe, secure, stable, solid ring to it. But it wouldn't be home for her. Before she even moved in, she knew her residence would be temporary.

"There," he said, latching down the convertible top. "Lean back, take a nap, and when you wake up, we'll be there." Leaning across the console, he kissed her lips lightly, then reengaged the gears and steered back onto the highway.

Caren was too fatigued to argue. She found a comfortable position for her head, adjusted her legs, and let her eyelids drift closed. The throb of the motor lulled her with its steady vibration.

The taste of Derek lingered on her lips. The scent of his cologne filled her head. She was aware of his warm, strong presence beside her. His body...really was...excellent....

"Caren love."

She awoke to the delicious sensation of soft lips moving against her cheek, whispering her name. She stirred, but slightly, not wanting to wake up.

"Darling, we're home." The lips whispered against that spot just below her ear where all her nerve endings seemed to be concentrated. "Caren?"

"Hmm?"

"Are you awake enough to walk?"

"Hmm."

There followed a light chuckle. Then a strong arm went around her back, another hooked under her knees, and she was lifted up.

Derek.

She recognized the hardness of his powerful chest

beneath her breast. As always, their hearts seemed to beat in time. Her arms were too heavy to lift around his neck, but she burrowed her head beneath his chin. The skin on his throat was warm. She pressed her lips to it.

She got a vague impression of excited whispers, of steps, of light. Opening one sleepy eye, she saw a sweeping staircase that reminded her of *Gone With the Wind*. But keeping even one eye open was too much of an effort, so she closed it, laying one hand on Derek's chest and snuggling closer.

There was a reason why she shouldn't be entrusting herself to him. It kept niggling at the back of her mind, but the thought wouldn't quite ripen. She ignored it and basked in his strong warmth.

She rocked with the motion of his body as he carried her upstairs and down a hallway. The lights were dimmer in the room where he stopped. She didn't open her eyes, but sensed less light falling on her lids. Not until she was laid on a bed did her eyes flicker open; she saw above her a canopy.

"Are you sure there isn't something—"

"Thank you, no, Daisy. I'll see that she gets into bed. We've kept you up late enough. Good night."

"Good night."

Caren heard the voices, but they didn't rouse her completely. She was aware of a door closing softly, then silence.

Her body dipped as he sat down on the side of the bed. Laying a hand on her cheek, he rubbed his thumb over her cheekbone. "Poor baby," he whispered in the soft lamplight. "You're so tired."

He pressed a brief, light kiss on her forehead. When he raised his head he saw the smile curving her lips. He touched the corner of her mouth with his fingertip. Unfortunately Caren didn't see his tender expression. Her eyes were still closed.

With one hand supporting her neck, he raised her head and began pulling the pins from her chignon. When all the honey-blond strands were free and spilling over his hand, he combed through them with his fingers. He inched his supporting arm down until he could angle her forward and work the zipper of her dress. He eased it off her and let her recline.

Trying very hard to keep his eyes off the perfection of her breasts in their lacy brassiere, he pulled the dress down her body and legs. He slipped off her shoes and set them neatly together on the floor beneath the bed. He was in no hurry.

The half-slip wasn't expensive. Nylon. But it had a deep border of lace that was infinitely feminine. She looked very pretty lying there with her hair making a wispy crown around her head, her body relaxed, her breasts rising and falling gently with each breath, her thighs screened by the lacy slip. She was utterly feminine. Fragile. Helpless.

His masculinity responded, thick and hot. But he forced the desire to cool as he curled his fingers in the elastic waist of the petticoat and removed it.

Because of his vast experiences, Derek was rarely shocked. But he was genuinely surprised when he saw the garter belt and stockings. He had expected pantyhose. This secret, flamboyant side of her delighted him. His bride was multifaceted, and he couldn't wait to discover each dazzling aspect of her personality.

She certainly wasn't predictable. He'd had his fill of predictable women, women who had been around the block so many times with so many men before him, he was bored before he ever got to their beds.

But this woman...

He gazed at her, reveling in his freedom to do so without her knowing it. This woman was different. She constantly amazed, angered, and aroused him, but he hadn't been bored since he met her. He didn't anticipate being bored for a long time to come.

With deft fingers he unhooked the garters. Settling his palms on either side of her leg, he rolled the stocking down. Over the slender thigh, the well-shaped knee, the shapely calf, the trim ankle, the dainty foot.

One night in Jamaica he had tracked each inch of that leg with his lips. He knew how the softness of her inner thigh felt against his tongue. The back of her knee was an exciting spot that made her writhe with passion when kissed. He had taken love bites of the fleshy part of her calf, kissed the soles of her feet, nibbled her toes.

He cursed his vivid memory. It wasn't doing the growing bulge in his trousers any good.

With much less leisure and reflection, he removed her other stocking. Slipping his hand beneath her hips, he found the fastener of the garter belt and un-snapped it. It was a confection of lace and satin that made him smile as he tossed it aside. He had slept with women adorned in Dior creations designed to allure, but he didn't remember a time in his life when he had enjoyed a woman's lingerie more than now.

There wasn't much to her panties. A scrap of fab-ric, a panel of lace, several inches of thin elastic to hold them together. They rode just below her bikini line. Between their waistband and her tanned tummy was a ribbon of pale flesh he longed to trace with his tongue. Through the lace…oh, God, that sweet soft triangle of down.

He could also see tan lines through her bra. They were much fainter, since she had sunbathed without her bikini top often those last golden days they'd spent together.

Once again sliding his hand beneath her back, he grappled with her bra strap and breathed a sigh of relief when it came undone without waking her. He slipped it off.

His breath dammed up in his throat. He squeezed his eyes shut and took several long, deep breaths be-fore he opened them again to look at his wife. Her breasts were high and round, softened now by her sleeping position. The coral crests were pert even in this relaxed state. He knew their color, their taste, their texture, and ached for his mouth to be intimate with them again.

He couldn't. She would never learn to trust him if he took advantage of her now. But he had to touch her or die. The tips of his fingers glided down the smooth satin of her throat, then back up. Down again, then back up.

"Derek?"

His name was a breathy, sleepy mumble, but it went through him like a shot. His hand stilled, and he folded it loosely around her neck. "Yes, love?"

She arched her back, stretching languorously, lifting her breasts, moving her legs sinuously on the linens that Daisy, the maid, had been thoughtful enough to fold back before they arrived.

Derek's heart labored to pump his blood. His brain sent sluggish signals to his body, but it was incapable of obeying them. They told him to either remove himself from the temptation or to yield to it, but not to sit there like a fool, with his vision blurring and his palms sweating.

Sexual restraint was new to him. He'd never exercised it before. He thought any man who ever had should be canonized.

Caren's hand moved restlessly on the sheet as though seeking something. When it found his thigh, it rested there and she sighed his name again.

That small amount of encouragement was enough to send him hurling over the brink. He leaned over and cupped her head between his hands. "Caren, you look beautiful in my bed."

Then he kissed her. At first his mouth merely settled on hers. He applied a minimum of pressure. But when her response was a low purr of contentment rather than a scream of protest, he began to brush his lips back and forth against hers.

Eventually her mouth parted, then his. He breathed her sweet breath, tasted her essence before he allowed his tongue to investigate the slick inner lining of her lip. He explored her teeth with the tip of his tongue. Then it drove deep, deep into the hollow of her mouth.

She moaned softly. Her hand crept up his thigh to his waist. It slid up his chest to his neck. She pulled him closer as her body arched up to meet his.

Though the kiss was both heaven and hell for him, he was exultant. Whether she would admit it or not, she wanted him. Her subconscious was ruling now, and everything in her was reaching out for him. All those protests to their sleeping together were just so much stubbornness—stubbornness he swore he would wear down.

His hand found her breast full, the nipple already hard with yearning. His caress elicited another moan.

"Caren, Caren, why do you deny me? Deny yourself?"

He lifted his head, demanding an answer with his eyes. Hers were still closed. Even as he watched, her mouth opened wide and she yawned broadly. Her head dug deeper into the pillow, and she slipped into the blackness of sleep.

He laughed ruefully. "That's the first time one of my kisses has put a woman to sleep." He stood and drew the sheet over her. God, she is beautiful, he said to himself. A tumbled angel.

His body was outraged. He wanted to make love to her, but he had given his word he wouldn't force her. But just to sleep beside her, to hold her through the night...

Well, why not? She was his wife. This was his house. His bed. By God, he'd sleep wherever he damn well pleased.

Swiftly he stripped. Crossing naked to the window, he opened it and let the country breeze, just tinged with the first hint of autumn, cool his body.

It did little good. As soon as he got beneath the covers, Caren sought his warmth. She molded her spine to the S formed by his torso, lap, and bent knees. Her hips cuddled his body where it was currently most vulnerable.

His fever came back, raging.

Sunlight awakened her. Bright, brilliant, blinding rays. They slanted into the room from the open window. She rolled to her back and surveyed her surroundings with eyes suddenly wide awake.

She was lying in a canopied bed. The other furnishings in the room, like the bed, were two centuries old. The polished hardwood floor was covered with a rug, Aubusson if her eyes weren't deceiving her. Its muted tones matched the pastels that decorated the room.

She contracted every muscle in her body, then let them gradually relax. She felt very good, which was surprising after all that had happened yesterday.

Raising herself on her elbows, she noticed the pillow close to hers, so close that the hand-embroidered edges of the cases overlapped. There was also a dent in the linens, and rumpled covers at the foot of the bed, which was too far down for her feet to have reached.

Derek had slept with her.

She was naked except for her panties. Just as she noticed the articles of clothing strewn over the bed and on the floor nearby, the door opened and a heavy-set woman bustled in carrying a silver tray.

"Well, good morning! I'm glad you're awake. I've been dying to meet you, Mrs. Allen. I'm Daisy Holland, but you call me Daisy."

Caren yanked the sheet up over her breasts and stuttered a shaky good morning. Daisy set the tray on the bedside table and began gathering up the clothing littering the room as though it were nothing out of the ordinary.

"That man, I swear, he's neat as a pin with everything else, but he drops his clothes wherever he takes them off. And look at the way he scattered your pretty things around." She made a *tsk*ing sound as she scooped up Caren's garter belt and brassiere. The stockings were draped over her shoulder. Caren smiled sickly. Daisy didn't notice her embarrassment as she went about straightening the spacious room, keeping up a lively chatter.

"I couldn't believe when he called and said he was bringing his bride home. About time, too, if you ask me. I sat up last night waiting to meet you. But you, poor little thing, were so tuckered out when you got here. Derek carried you up the stairs without hardly letting me get a good look at you. I offered to get you undressed and ready for bed, but he wouldn't have it. Said he'd take care of you himself. Treated you just like a doll."

"Where is Derek now?"

"He went out riding, as he does every morning. He told me to tell you he would meet you for breakfast whenever you're ready. I brought you up some coffee to drink while you're dressing, but you stay in bed, dearie, as long as you feel like it."

"No, I need to get up." Luckily, Daisy disappeared into the adjoining room at that moment. Caren slipped out of bed and pulled on her robe, which had been thoughtfully laid on the nearby chair.

Daisy returned and gestured over her shoulder. "I sneaked in this morning and unpacked your things in the dressing room. If you can't find something, just holler. Here, let me pour a cup of coffee for you. Do you take cream and sugar?"

Caren felt confused. She had never been waited on in her life and had no idea how one went about handling servants, especially in such awkward circumstances.

When Caren descended the staircase a half-hour later, she and Daisy had come to terms. Caren had kindly explained that she was capable of doing most things for herself, but granted Daisy permission to fuss over her "just a little bit" because, as Daisy had stressed, she was now mistress of the house and it had needed a mistress for a long time.

"This beautiful old house needs a woman and children. I've told Derek that a hundred times. I see he's finally listened to me. Isn't your hair pretty, though? My, my, you look like an angel, which perfectly complements Derek's devilish looks. Oh, my. I hope you didn't take offense. But you know how dashing and devilish—"

"Yes, I know," Caren had reassured her with a smile.

As she went down the stairs she tried to orient herself to the layout of the house. Upstairs the room she had slept in was one of two that shared a bath and dressing area and comprised the master suite.

On the bottom stair, she paused uncertainly, looking to her left and right, trying to decide where the kitchen and breakfast might be.

"You look lost," Derek said, stepping into the wide vestibule whose ceiling was two stories tall. "I was about to come up and drag you out of bed, lazybones. It's a gorgeous day, and I want to show you around the farm. Sleep well?"

Without any hesitation, he came to her, caught her in his embrace, and kissed her until she was breathless. "Good morning," he whispered against her lips before he raised his head.

So much for the cool tolerance she was going to treat him to. Her knees turned to jelly and her voice was scratchy as she replied, "Good morning."

He was dressed in a loose white shirt, casually un-

buttoned to the middle of his chest, and khaki jodhpurs. She had never known anyone who actually wore
jodhpurs. She was certain no one wore them with the
panache Derek did.

Highly glossed brown leather boots encased his
high-arched feet and long calves up to his knees. The
riding pants had leather inserts on the insides of his
thighs. With his hair windblown and his cheeks
ruddy, he looked fabulous.

He was leading her through a parlor with a grand
piano in one corner and a marble fireplace in the
other. They entered a dining room where King
George III would have felt right at home. Caren knew
her mouth must be slack with dismay. She had toured
historic homes that weren't nearly so lavishly fur-
nished and decorated and well preserved.

"I usually don't eat a large breakfast," Derek said.
"I'm having fruit and croissants. If you'd like Daisy
to cook you an egg or waffles—"

"No, this looks wonderful," she said as he seated
her perpendicular to his chair at the head of the thirty-
foot table. There were fresh flowers arranged in a
Lalique bowl at its center.

And one red rose at her place setting.

He picked up the long-stemmed bloom, kissed it,
and passed it to her. "Welcome home, Caren."

Taking the rose and unconsciously raising it to her
lips as though to capture his kiss, she replied, "Thank
you."

The china and sterling were priceless. She would
never treat it so casually as Derek did as he served

her from the platters of fruit and fragrant baskets of homemade rolls and danish. He poured steaming coffee from a silver service. They ate in silence for several moments.

She was sipping from her coffee cup when he asked, "Do you ride, Caren?"

"Yes. At least I have. It's been a while."

"Good," he said, smiling broadly. "I've picked out a mount for you. I hope you like her. Mustafa was restless since I've been away so long. I gave him a good workout this morning."

"Mustafa?"

"One of my horses. You'll meet him later. He's one—"

"You slept with me last night," she interrupted quietly.

His knife was a long time making contact with the edge of his bread plate as he lowered it slowly. His eyes sliced up to meet hers challengingly. "Yes, I did."

"I thought you agreed not to."

"I agreed not to make love to you."

She forced down the knot in her throat and toyed with her spoon. "Did you? I don't remember anything after falling asleep in the car."

"You don't remember me carrying you upstairs?"

"Only vaguely."

"You don't remember me undressing you?"

"No."

"Taking off your underclothes?"

"No."

"Touching you?"

"No."

"Kissing you?"

Her throat got even tighter. "No."

"Or you kissing me back?"

"I didn't."

He smiled lazily. "Oh, yes, you did. Rather passionately, in fact."

The bloom in her cheek matched the one lying beside her plate. That telltale blush, combined with his deliberate avoidance of her question, angered her. "Did you make love to me?"

He leaned forward, shrinking the distance between them. "Only my brain had carnal knowledge of you last night, Caren. My body went unrequited. It's under a tremendous amount of stress this morning, and unless you want to gamble on my losing control of it, I suggest you stop questioning me about it and close this topic of conversation."

He let that sink in as she squirmed in her chair; then he continued, "As I was saying before you unwisely interrupted, I'd like to show you around the property today. For the time being, you can ride dressed as you are." He assessed her casual slacks and lightweight sweater. "But soon we'll have you outfitted properly."

She wanted to ask him why he would bother, but she didn't. He went on to tell her that Daisy would always be available if she had any questions or problems.

"This will all take some getting used to," she said.

Taking her hand, he drew her to her feet. "I think that's true of any newly married couple."

"It's not just married life. It's everything. I'm accustomed to getting up every morning and fighting rush-hour traffic to get to work. Having a housekeeper to wake me with a cup of coffee and draw my bath is a novel experience."

A swift kiss was brushed across her lips before she could avoid it. "I have every confidence that you'll adjust." He led her out the massive front door, across a brick front porch, down the steps, and onto a half-moon-shaped driveway that was lined with perfectly manicured boxwoods. His long stride was taking them toward the outbuildings to the right of the house.

"Wait, Derek," she said, pulling on his hand and laughing. "I'd like to see what the house looks like first."

He stood by proudly while she filled her eyes with the Georgian mansion. Its faded red bricks gave it an air of genteel stateliness. The shutters were hunter green and fixed to windows trimmed in white. All the windows on the front of the house were beveled, and they sparkled in the late morning sunlight.

English ivy clung to the north wall, completely covering that side of the house. Two chimneys bracketed the roof, which was steeply pitched and dotted with five gable windows. The main house was three stories, with two-story wings extending from either side.

"Derek, it's beautiful," Caren murmured in the hushed tones of one viewing a museum piece.

"It is, isn't it? I loved it the first time I saw it."

"Did you find it in mint condition?"

"Hardly. I worked piece by piece for years to get it where it is now."

"You've done well. It's fantastic. Are those the Blue Ridge Mountains?"

"Yes. We're in Albemarle County, about twenty miles from Charlottesville."

The grounds were just as spectacular as the house. Rolling lawns spread out on all sides. The landscape was decorated with mature trees. In the distance Caren spied a white fence that extended as far as the eye could see. Cultivated fields stretched far in one direction, heavily wooded hillsides in another, and in yet another sprawled acres of verdant pastureland, the thick grass waving like an emerald ocean.

Caren was held speechless as she stood in one spot on the gravel drive and turned three hundred and sixty degrees. Then, almost angrily, she faced Derek and exclaimed, "You call this a *farm?*"

Eleven

He only laughed and looped his arm around her shoulders. "I hope that means you like it."

The stables he led her to were more like an equine luxury hotel. A score of men, all wearing matching shirts with an insignia embroidered on the breast pocket, were busy grooming, feeding, or exercising the magnificent horses. The animals were treated like pampered pets. Several horse trailers, with the same insignia painted on their sides, were parked end to end outside a tack room where all sorts of activity was going on. Caren stared speechlessly. From the house, all this industry was invisible and unobtrusive.

"Did I fail to mention that our main enterprise here is Arabian horse breeding?" Derek asked when he noticed her astonishment.

"I think your words were 'breed a few horses,'" she said dryly.

She knew only enough about show horses to know that they were incredibly expensive to maintain. She couldn't begin to count the number of thoroughbreds stabled in Derek's barn, which seemed to stretch for a mile down a center corridor.

Just as they exited the brick building, a groom came forward with two horses. Their beauty and high-stepping pride caused Caren to catch her breath. Their coats were sleek and shiny as satin. Their tails were held in a high loop over their rumps before they cascaded down to sweep the ground. Their hooves had been blackened and highly lacquered. Their heads were narrow and aristocratic, their ears small and pointed. Intelligence gleamed in their eyes. The thick manes had been brushed to a glossy luster.

Derek went to a black stallion and cupped his long jaw with a loving hand. "Caren, meet Mustafa." The stallion tossed his head in greeting.

Caren was awed. "He's magnificent, Derek. I don't know much about Arabians, but he's perfect, isn't he?"

"Last year he was honored with the Supreme Legion of Honor. His name means elect, or chosen. I'd say it suits him well." He patted Mustafa's nose. "And this," he said, taking the reins of the copper-colored mare from the groom, "is Zarifa, the graceful one. She's yours."

"Mine!" Caren exclaimed. "But I can't—"

"You don't like her? Would you rather have another?"

"No, it's not that. It's just…well, I'm not up to riding a horse so…so…expensive," she ended in a small voice.

Apparently the animals were accustomed to

Derek's spontaneous bursts of laughter, for they didn't flinch when he threw back his head and roared. "We'll work on your equestrian skills and make you worthy. Come on, they're itching to show off for you."

He helped her mount, making a stirrup with his hands and boosting her into the saddle. Caren took the reins as she'd been taught to do that summer her mother had somehow scraped up enough money to send her to camp.

Derek mounted and led her toward one of the bridle paths that snaked through the nearby woods. She and the mare established an instantaneous rapport. Zarifa's name fitted her perfectly, for she was as dainty in her gait as a ballerina on stage.

"How are you doing?" Derek asked, reining in a half-hour later.

"She's fabulous. I love her," Caren replied, leaning forward and patting the mare's high neck. "But I don't think you and Mustafa are usually this tame, are you?"

Derek grinned. "Do you jump?"

"Lord no. But I'd love to see you. Go ahead."

He needed no further urging. With a simple command, a mere kissing sound of Derek's lips, Mustafa virtually leaped off the ground and into a gallop. As Caren watched, man and horse streaked across the open pasture.

Powerful muscles rippled in Mustafa's flanks. His mane furled in the wind and his tail was like a banner waving behind him. Derek's hair was swept away from his face, revealing the angles of his face as they raced along. Then, like one being, man and beast cleared the fence with room to spare. For a small eternity they seemed to hang in space, to take flight, to defy gravity.

Such coordination between man and animal was magic, mystical, as ancient as the legends associated with the proud breed of Arabians. As they landed, Mustafa's hooves kicked up clods of turf as though to prove he wasn't a myth.

When they came trotting back around the fence, Caren was smiling. "Show-off." Though her tone was sarcastic, Derek could tell she was impressed.

"I'll teach you how."

She shook her head. "I don't think I'll be ready for that for a long time." She was painfully reminded that her stay here was temporary, but she eased the moment of tension by saying, "Mustafa seems to fly."

"Drinkers of the wind."

"Pardon?"

"Drinkers of the wind. That's how the Arabians are referred to."

"How poetic. But then, they move like poetry."

"Yes, they have a mystique about them. The ancestors of these two horses can be traced back for centuries. Their names were recorded on scrolls. They come from aristocracy."

Just as you do, Caren could have added. "How long have you owned Mustafa?"

Derek leaned forward to rub the stallion's glistening coat. "You can't own an animal like this. He belongs to the sky, to the wind, to the moon." He was reflective for a moment, then said, "I've taken care of him for seven years. I bought him as a five-year-old. He's sired some very special animals. Several out of Zarifa." His eyes were twinkling wickedly as he added, "I think she's his favorite dam."

"Though he has many others," Caren countered softly. "I doubt he'd be willing to give them up."

Derek's eyes probed hers for a long, silent moment while only the wind dared move around them. "Are you ready to go back?" he asked at last.

"Yes. I don't want to get saddle sore my first day out."

Daisy served them a salad lunch on the back terrace, which overlooked the purplish outline of the mountains. Afterward Derek showed Caren through the house until she was well acquainted with the floor plan. Then he told her he had paperwork to catch up on. "There's a whole library of books on Arabians, if you're interested."

"I am," she said quickly, following him into a room in one back corner of the house that served as his office.

He supplied her with ample reading material. She curled up in a leather chair while he went to his desk. He dictated letters into a recorder, made notations in ledgers, studied a stack of receipts, used the telephone twice, and wrote out several checks from a large business checkbook.

This was a new Derek, one she'd never seen. As

was evidenced by the careful way the stables were staffed and run, he was as meticulous in business as he was in everything else. His brow was furrowed as he studied a piece of correspondence. A long index finger lay along his cheek, pointing to the outer tip of his eyebrow. His thumb was hooked under his jaw. The other fingers were loosely curled over his mouth.

It was terribly easy to love him. She loved him so much her heart ached.

He lifted his head and caught her staring at him. "Find anything interesting in the books?"

"Yes, it's fascinating." She had learned that an Arabian like Mustafa or Zarifa was valued in the multiple millions. "How many Arabians do you have, Derek?"

"Thirty-two at present."

"And the rest of the farm? I haven't seen it all, have I?"

"No." He laid aside the letter he'd been reading, sensing that she wanted to talk. "I raise winter wheat mostly, some peanuts, some soybeans. I stopped cultivating tobacco several years ago because of all the adverse effects attributed to smoking cigarettes." He stood up and came around the corner of the desk, propping his hip on its edge and crossing ankles and arms in one fluid motion. "I don't do the actual farming. I have excellent people who work for me. They, of course, get a percentage of the profits."

Running an estate of this size must require hundreds of thousands of dollars a year. But what was that measured against millions? Such wealth flabbergasted her, frightened her, and in an unreasonable way angered her. Was it fair for one man to have so much when others had so little?

Taking one of the books with her, she rose. "I think I'll lie down till dinner, Derek."

He pushed himself away from the desk, came to her, and wrapped her in his arms. "All right. You're not ill, are you?"

"No, nothing like that. Just tired."

"After yesterday, I don't doubt it." He tilted her head up with a finger beneath her chin. His lips flirted with hers. Back and forth, once, twice. Everything in her sprang to life. But he only kissed her once, lightly, chastely, before setting her away from him. "I'll see you at dinner."

The nap helped some. At least when she looked in the mirror, the sleep-bestowed rose in her cheeks was something to admire. She looked with distaste at the dress she had put on. It was a good dress, but Derek had seen her in it three times. Three times in only a week.

She glanced into the closet where Daisy had neatly hung her clothes and took inventory. Even with all the clothes left behind in Georgetown, her wardrobe was depressingly scanty.

Instinctively she had guessed that dressing for dinner was expected. She was glad she had. For when she joined Derek in the front parlor he was dressed in slacks and a sport coat. He was playing the grand piano.

"I poured you a glass of white wine," he said, not

stopping his playing, "but if you'd like something else—"

"No, that's fine." The chilled glass had been set on a table near the piano. He slid over on the bench and nodded with his head for her to sit beside him. "I didn't know you played," she said.

"My mother insisted I take lessons. Do you?"

"My mother insisted I take lessons."

He laughed and finished the piece with a flourish in the treble clef. As he leaned sideways, his arm nudged her breasts. "How about a rousing version of Chopsticks?"

Smothering a sigh of pleasure, she said, "Great." She positioned her hands over the keys.

"Wait! I need sustenance." He took a sip of his highball, bourbon and water she thought, and flexed his fingers. "Ready? Go."

"Wait! Unfair. I wasn't ready."

"Okay. Now?"

"Now!"

By the third time through, the tempo had increased until their fingers were flying and they were laughing so hard they missed half the notes.

"Stop, stop, please. I'm getting a charley horse in my pinkie," she cried. She threw back her head and breathed a huge sigh of relief when they brought the tune to a pounding conclusion.

But her next breath was a gasp. Derek had taken advantage of her exposed throat. Bending her back over his arm, he leaned down and planted a kiss directly over the V at the base of her neck. Its fervency arrowed straight down her body until it shattered in a soft explosion in the heart of her womanhood. She clutched the lapels of his coat to keep herself on the bench and in this firmament.

"Derek—"

"You smell so good. Like rain; like honeysuckle." His lips wandered at will over her throat, leaving heated kisses. When he found her mouth, it was softly yielding to his spearing tongue. His technique had no rival. He kissed her thoroughly, expertly, until she was sapped of all will. "Hungry?" he mumbled after a final kiss in which their tongues barely touched.

"Hmm."

"Let's go in to dinner then." Like a sleepwalker, she was led into the candlelit dining room.

They ate a succulent roast beef and vegetables cooked to crisp perfection. The atmosphere was serene. She hated to endanger his mellow mood by bringing up the subject her conscience wouldn't let her ignore any longer. Over their pecan pie and coffee, she affected as much nonchalance as possible and asked, "Derek, have you ever fathered a child?"

He didn't move or respond. She was forced to tear her eyes away from the mush she was making of the caramelized pie filling and raise them to him.

"Why do you ask?"

Her lashes fluttered nervously as she lowered her eyes. "It's none of my business, and I don't mean to pry into your private life. I just wondered if…well, you've been with so many women…I thought…"

Unable to go on, she let her stammerings die a painful death.

"No." The answer was long in coming. When it did, it was spoken with such absolute honesty that she raised her head. "Why do you ask?" he repeated.

She might just as well be diving off the cliffs at Acapulco. It would be just as suicidal a plunge. There was no way around it. She had to tell him straight out.

"In Jamaica, I...that is to say, I had a...I had come prepared, but—"

Her eyes were imploring, hoping he would fill in the blanks and relieve her of the responsibility of telling him. But he sat as still as a statue, not blinking his tiger's eyes.

"I didn't expect you to come into my room and carry me off that first night," she said defensively. "I didn't have time to use anything. How many times that night did you...I mean did *we*...I mean..." Suddenly her uneasiness evaporated and she looked at him with exasperation. "You know what I'm trying to say and for God's sake stop staring at me like that!"

"Are you telling me you're pregnant?"

"No! I'm just telling you that we weren't protected against it." A thought occurred to her. "Were we?"

"If you mean have I had a vasectomy, the answer is definitely no. Is the thought of bearing my child so disagreeable to you?"

"I've always wanted to have children," she answered softly. "But with the circumstances of this marriage being what they are, it would be difficult."

"I see no reason to worry about it." He reached forward and laid a hand on her upper arm, dangerously close to her breast. "I can't think of anything lovelier than watching my child nurse at your breast."

She sat unmoving as his eyes met hers. "I doubt if there will be a baby, but I thought you ought to be warned," she said in a husky voice.

His hand moved up another inch and a knuckle began rubbing the side of her breast. "I didn't need to be warned. I could get excited about the idea if you'd stop refusing—"

She could have kissed Daisy for coming in just then and offering to clear the table. Caren excused herself. "I want to read some more about the Arabians. It's fascinating. I'm still very tired. It must be the country air. Or the riding. I'm not used to it yet. I want to go to sleep early," she rambled.

When she left the dining room, she knew Derek's eyes were boring into her back. She had to escape him. The looks that passed between them were too smoldering. They conveyed sexual messages that were better left untransmitted.

She did read for a while. But it wasn't sleep-inducing. In the darkened room, she tossed and turned for what seemed like hours before she threw off the covers and groped her way into the dressing room. Maybe a couple of aspirins would help relax her.

She opened the door and froze. In the softly lit

room, Derek was standing in front of his closet, shirtless, barefoot, in the act of unzipping his trousers. He turned abruptly when he heard her.

She stood poised on the threshold, a vision of dishabille in her sheer nightgown, with her hair tangled around her shoulders.

"I'm sorry. I didn't hear you come up," she said huskily. The lamplight seemed to pick up every single hair in that curling mass on his chest.

"Is something wrong?" Leaving the trousers undone and lying loosely about his narrow hips, he came toward her, concern wrinkling his brow.

"No. I'm just restless. I thought an aspirin…"

"You look incredibly sexy, Caren." His hands slid under her breasts, under her arms to the middle of her back. They brought her against him from breast to toe. "Incredibly, deliciously, mouthwateringly sexy." His mouth sealed hers hotly.

He was beautiful. He was man. He smelled of lime and wind. He tasted uniquely like Derek. She was hungry for him, so hungry. Everything soft in her yearned for his hardness. The curved muscles of his chest pressed into the pillows of her breasts. Even the faint rasp of evening beard stubble against her chin elicited thrills that chased each other through her body. Her mouth squeezed around his tongue. He groaned and pressed deeper.

One of her hands laced through the long hair at his nape. The fingers of her other hand dug into the fleshy part of his chest. The heel of her hand ground against the tiny, taut nipple.

His hands slid down the silkiness of her nightgown to her derriere. He pulled her against the heat of his sex.

"I ache for you, Caren. God, I want you." Prying her hand from his chest, he guided it down his furred torso to the fly of his pants and slipped it into the open zipper. "Feel me wanting you."

The soft cotton briefs didn't begin to contain his desire. Her fingers encountered the tightening bulge and shrank away from it. "Please, please," he grated against her lips, swollen from their previous kiss. "Please, Caren, touch me."

Her palm. Her fingers. Timid. Then bold.

He was hard, thick, warm.

"Caren, Caren love," he groaned into her mouth. "Tighter, yes, oh yes, yes, that's it." The incoherent chant went on until his mouth ravaged hers, as greedy as her hand.

Caren was mindless save for the passion pouring through her like a tidal wave. Her breasts ached; the nipples were beaded with longing. The mound of her womanhood throbbed, needing to be filled.

"Caren," Derek panted. His hands slid beneath the hem of her nightgown and raised it above her thighs as he caressed his way up. His fingers wove through the nest at the cleft of her thighs and encountered dewiness. He caressed. She called his name in yearning and denial.

Finally wrenching herself away from him, she took several stumbling steps backward. Her hair went sailing wildly about her head as she shook it strenuously. "No," she panted. "I can't."

His chest heaved in and out with his labored breathing. "Like hell you can't," he said in a thick voice, taking a menacing step toward her.

She backed up farther and stretched out a hand to ward him off. "You agreed to the conditions of this marriage, Derek. You did!"

"To hell with the conditions of this marriage. You're my wife. I want you."

And therein lay the reason she denied him. He wanted her. She loved him. There was a vast difference.

Her love would be eternal. But how long would he want her? Until tomorrow morning? Next week? At what point would he leave her? On what day would he announce that it was time for them to get the divorce that would be so convenient for him and devastating for her? She couldn't afford to love him, to give her all to him, and then have to give him up. Not again.

"You said you wouldn't force me," she said desperately as his angry advance brought him nearer. She didn't fear that he'd physically abuse her. Her fear was that he'd destroy her resolve.

Abruptly, he lunged for her, yanking her hard against him with an impetus that knocked the breath from her. He caught her jaw between his hands and tilted her head back. His eyes were like agates glowing in the dark.

"I should," he said with a tight-lipped control that

frightened her more than his rage. "I should strip you naked and spread your thighs and force you to accept what you so foolishly deny yourself. I should love you until you're addicted, until you weep when you can't have me. But I'll be damned before I'll give you all the satisfaction that would go with it."

He released her so suddenly she swayed and gripped the edge of the dressing table for balance. He stormed into his bedroom, slamming the door behind him.

Things were considerably more strained between them after that night. In front of Daisy and the staff, they were polite. In private, there existed between them a truce. One of the peacemaking conditions was a tense silence.

He didn't touch her unless necessary. He insisted that they ride each morning after breakfast. He told her it was to improve her skills. She thought it was to keep up appearances.

She found she missed those flirtatious remarks he could work into the most innocent conversations. Missed too, were the quick, light kisses he was prone to surprise her with. She wouldn't think about the slow, lingering ones.

If his affection was reined, his generosity was not. He presented her with a car, a slick, white sports model whose dashboard was a maze of flashing lights as intimidating as a computer terminal. She tried to refuse it.

"You need something to whip around in," he

stated firmly and finally before tossing the keys to her. Without another word, he turned his back and stalked toward the stables. That was that.

Clothes came next. An entire wardrobe. Daisy summoned her to the foyer and introduced her to a harried gray woman with a pencil behind her ear and a tape measure around her neck. The clothes that were hauled upstairs for Caren to try on were exquisite.

"A size six, right?" the seamstress asked briskly. She was employed at the boutique where Derek had ordered the clothes.

"R-right?" Caren glanced inquiringly at Daisy, who seemed unfazed.

She was fitted with clothes for every occasion. The choices were hers to make. At first she was conservative, knowing she must be running up a fortune of a bill.

Diplomatically, Daisy stepped forward and whispered. "Caren, you're not buying enough. Derek said for me to see to it that you fill up the closet."

By the time the seamstress had breezed out late that afternoon, Caren had been clothed from the skin out, with accessories to go with everything. Very few things needed to be altered. Those that did would be delivered later.

The following morning she appeared at the stables dressed in fawn-colored jodhpurs and a white silk shirt with wide, loose sleeves banded at the wrists. The riding boots were shiny and supple. Her hair was tied into a low ponytail with a black velvet ribbon. Kid gloves as soft as butter were on her hands.

Derek assessed her unemotionally and said curtly, "That's a definite improvement."

She wanted to slap him with her quirt. Instead, she gripped a handful of Zarifa's lush mane and swung into the saddle without assistance. She raced off, giving the mare her head. As they approached a low fence, she let the trained mare take it, squeezing her tear-laden eyes closed until the hoofs struck the other side.

Derek came pounding up on Mustafa. He grabbed Zarifa's reins and jerked the mare to a halt. "That's a damn good way to break your neck," he shouted angrily.

"I thought you wanted me to jump," Caren shouted right back.

"Then you need to learn how properly."

"So stop yelling and teach me."

Thus began her lessons.

But the lessons could only take up so many minutes each day. The remainder of the time she was idle, roaming the house like a homeless specter, looking for something to occupy her. One afternoon she ventured up the stairs that led to the attic. When she pushed the door open, she was met with a choking cloud of dust.

The attic was floored and ran the length of the house. The ceiling was slanted, but an adult could walk its breadth without stooping over. It was the only room on the estate that wasn't immaculate.

Sneaking down to Daisy's supply room, she loaded herself with brooms, dustpans, rags, and other cleaning implements and headed back up the stairs.

An hour later she was interrupted by a furious "Just what the hell do you think you're doing?"

She whirled around. Derek filled the doorway, a contrite Daisy cowering behind him. "I had to tell him, Caren. I knew he wouldn't want you up here doing all that cleaning and—"

"Enough, Daisy," Derek barked. She slunk off down the stairs, leaving them alone. Dust motes spun in the sunlight filtering through the foggy windows that her cleaning rag hadn't gotten to yet.

She propped herself on the broom handle and faced him belligerently. With her hair tied up in a scarf and a smudge of dirt on her nose, she looked so adorable that Derek didn't know whether to take her in his arms and kiss her till she fainted, or to bend her over his knee and paddle her cute jean-clad butt.

"Well?"

"What does it look like I'm doing?" she snapped. "I'm cleaning the attic."

"Caren," he said with diminishing patience, "I have employees who can clean attics. I don't need my wife to do it."

"Well, maybe your wife needs to do it. Maybe she feels like she should earn her keep, pay for the cars and the clothes and the food, etcetera."

He eased himself away from the door frame in one of those deceptively lazy movements that she knew masked a rising temper. "What's that supposed to mean?"

"It means that I'm uncomfortable living like this."

"Like what?"

"So affluently. Derek, I've always worked. I've never had money to waste the way you do. You may feel perfectly justified living high on the hog while people in our country are starving, but I don't. You can buy cars and designer clothes and toss hundred-dollar bills to any teenage girl who flutters her eyelashes at you, but I'm not that frivolous."

A seething silence followed. Finally he said, "Are you finished?"

"No."

"I meant with your sermon, not with your cleaning. *That* was finished the moment I stepped into this room."

"I've said all I have to say."

He stepped aside and let her know with a baleful glare that she was to leave the attic and that there would be no argument about it. He locked the attic door behind them and pocketed the key.

Several days later she was passing one of the long hours of the afternoon by sharing a cup of tea with Daisy in the kitchen. Daisy was up to her elbows in bread dough when the doorbell rang.

"I'll get it," Caren said, jumping from her stool, glad for the distraction.

"Hello," the woman on the threshold said uncertainly. "I'm Sarah Caldwell from the Shenandoah

Valley Orphanage. Is Mr. Allen at home?'' The woman was midfortyish, stylish, handsome.

"He's at the stables," Caren said, perplexed. "I'll send for him. Please come in." She ushered the woman into the formal parlor, picked up a telephone extension, and asked that Derek be notified of his visitor. When she hung up, she faced the woman nervously. "I'm Caren Bl—uh…Allen."

"Oh, Mr. Allen's bride. I should have guessed. I read in the Washington papers that he had recently married."

They talked about the encroaching autumn and how the mornings and evenings were becoming cooler. Derek came striding in several minutes later. He smelled of the outdoors, of sunshine, leather, and sweat. With his wind-tossed hair, jodhpurs, and boots, he was ruggedly appealing. Caren could forgive Ms. Caldwell her covetous stare as Derek shook her hand and took a chair in front of her.

"You've come for the check, I presume."

"Well, yes. If it's convenient."

"I've already made it out." He went to a small secretary in a corner of the room and pulled open the narrow drawer. Taking out an envelope, he passed it to Ms. Caldwell.

"I can't tell you what these contributions mean to us, Mr. Allen. Last year your check for a hundred thousand kept our infirmary operating with our own staff doctor and nurse."

"I'm glad to hear that."

Sarah Caldwell directed her eyes to Caren, who

thought she might be physically sick as a result of self-disgust. "You must be terribly proud of all your husband does for charity, Mrs. Allen. Of course, the orphanage is just one of many causes he supports. I served on the Hunger Fund committee for—"

"If that's all, Sarah," Derek interrupted quickly and got to his feet. "Please excuse me, but I must get back to the stables." As kindly as he could, he helped Ms. Caldwell from her chair and escorted her to the front door. Caren murmured a goodbye. When Derek came back into the parlor, it was to find her softly weeping in her chair.

"Caren!" He crossed to her rapidly, dropping to his knees in front of her. "What is it?"

"I'm so ashamed," she whispered, unable to lift her eyes to his. "I thought... Oh, you know what I thought. I should have known better. I'm so sorry for everything I said."

He lifted her head and dried her tears with the pads of his thumbs. "You're forgiven. I *do* live high on the hog." A smile tugged at the corners of his lips.

Caren longed to lean forward and press her mouth to his. Instead she asked, "Why didn't you defend yourself the other day?"

"Because you might have thought I was grandstanding. Besides, real charity is doing something benevolent that no one ever knows about."

"You're a much nicer man than I gave you credit for."

"No," he growled, "I'm rotten. Especially as far as being a good husband goes." He searched her teary eyes. "Are you awfully unhappy here, Caren?" His gaze was so intent, she could almost believe it would break his heart if she said yes.

"Not unhappy. How could anyone be unhappy in such a lovely house? But I'm not busy enough, Derek. Would you oppose the idea of my finding a job in Charlottesville? Even part-time?"

"Ali Al-Tasan's wife does not work."

She sighed. "I thought so."

The subject was closed. Though she felt better about Derek's lavish spending, knowing now that he shared his wealth generously, she still moped around the house feeling useless.

Derek hired someone to clean the attic. For days workers trooped up and down the stairs, but the door was always closed to her. She thought they must be doing a heck of a job for all the equipment they hauled in and all the hammering and pounding and tromping going on overhead.

Early one morning, Derek came to wake her. Surprised, she sat up in bed, letting the covers slide down her chest. After that first night, he had never come into her bedroom.

"I have something to show you," he said with the eagerness of a boy with a secret to tell.

"But I'm not... Now?"

"Now."

Grabbing her hand, he hauled her out of the tangle of covers and without pausing for her to put on a robe or slippers dragged her upstairs to the attic. He pushed the door open and moved inside.

Caren gazed at the room with amazement. She took in everything at once, then slowly let her eyes drift from one incredible sight to another, trying to digest what it meant.

At last she turned to him. "How did you know?"

Twelve

"Kristin let the cat out of the bag. Remember the night we took her out to dinner, she said, 'Oh, Caren, you can go back to sculpting.' I tucked that piece of information away, recalling a rather awesome sea monster I once stepped on and squashed."

"The other day when you seemed so depressed over your idleness, I called Kristin to ask just how serious you were about art. She told me you were a dedicated student before your mother's death."

"When she died and I assumed responsibility for Kristin, I had to turn to a more practical occupation."

"So Kristin said. I think she felt guilty about that. A starving artist can survive, but a starving artist can't support a teenaged sister. She was excited when I told her what I intended to do and gave me a list of things every sculpture studio should have."

"I thought you were having the attic professionally cleaned." She was no longer afraid it was a mirage she was seeing and stepped farther into the converted attic.

"That's what you were supposed to think. You were rather peeved when you noticed the door was unlocked to anyone but you, weren't you?"

Over her shoulder she cast him a wry look. "I thought it was your way of keeping me in line."

He laughed. "Well, now that you know better, how do you like it?"

Sections of the roof had been removed and replaced with skylights. There would never be a scarcity of natural light. The walls were lined with worktables. The drawers were filled with tools, and the cabinets contained enough supplies to keep her busy for months.

"You'll probably want to rearrange everything to suit yourself. I have some knowledge of art, *finished* art, but how one creates it is beyond me."

"Don't expect too much from me," she said uneasily. All this must have cost a fortune. She hoped he wasn't expecting her to produce masterpieces.

Coming to her, he clasped her shoulders and turned her around to face him. His hands were warm on her bare skin. She became aware of her sheer batiste nightgown. But he was looking down at her with another kind of affection.

"Caren love, I don't care if you fashion ugly ashtrays we'll have to sell in garage sales, or if you want to make mudpies, or if you turn out nothing. I just want to see you smile again."

"Have I been that sullen? I'm sorry."

"You've been unhappy. For that I'm sorry. I truly

thought when I offered you marriage that it would be best for you.''

She gazed up into his tiger eyes. ''I can't be a pet, Derek. You told me yourself that you couldn't actually own a creature like Mustafa, that he belonged to the sky. You can't own a human being, either.

''As marvelous as this house is, it could become like a cage unless I feel some sense of worthiness. Daisy won't let me lift a feather duster. She won't let me cook. The grounds are taken care of by an army of workers. I have nothing to do. Even the horses in the stable have more responsibility than I.''

A golden gleam of light burst from his eyes. His voice was as raspy as the wind that rustled the leaves in the tops of the trees outside the gable windows. ''You know what their responsibility is. Breeding.'' One hand moved to her cheek. ''If you want to take part in that, all you have to do is let me know. Of course, there would have to be some changes in sleeping arrangements.''

She edged out of his warm clasp before she surrendered to the lulling cadence of his words and fell against that broad chest. She was mildly surprised, and vastly disappointed, when he let her go.

Her eyes roamed the transformed attic. It looked like a permanent installation. She would love to believe that it was. But they both knew it wasn't. She wondered what he would do with this room when she was no longer in residence. Lock it up again? Let it collect dust?

"With all the supplies you've bought, I'll have plenty to do now."

"What will you start on?" he asked, dropping onto a high stool.

"Limbering up my fingers," she said, laughing. "It's been years since I've had access to a mass of clay." Her hands drifted over the array of tools neatly lined up on one of the tables. She could almost feel the texture of cool, moist clay against the pads of her fingers. How she had missed it.

When she had suggested to Wade that she would like to enroll in a class just to keep from getting rusty, he had asked her what the point of that was. As usual, she hadn't questioned him, hadn't even thought of going against his wishes. She had doubted she would ever again know the joy of coaxing a shape out of something shapeless. Gratitude squeezed her throat, and she turned to her husband, who had given her this gift.

Derek was watching her closely, not a single muscle moving. Even when she padded toward him on her bare feet, he didn't move. "It was wonderful of you to do this for me. Thank you, Derek."

Bending at the waist, she leaned over and laid her lips on his. Hers were slightly parted. His more so. She kissed him, but briefly. When she started to pull away, her lips seemed to have a mind of their own. They clung. And clung longer.

Derek still didn't move, not to put his arms around her, not to make close contact with her body, which she knew was still warm from bed and rosy and quite visible beneath the sheer nightgown. Was her kiss so bland and unexciting that it didn't stir him at all?

Daringly, she pushed her tongue forward and barely dampened his lower lip with it.

Then he moved.

All of him at once, in one fluid motion. His head tilted to one side; his mouth slanted over hers possessively. He came to his feet, bringing their bodies so close that his actually slid up hers until he towered over her. One arm went around her, hauling her against him.

Her neck became boneless and her head fell back against his upper arm. His free hand spanned her rib cage, pressing, pressing, hotly.

There was no hesitation in his kiss. Passion that had been pent up for weeks had finally been given vent. It poured out of him and into her like sweet golden syrup.

His hand crept up her ribs until his thumb met the soft undercurve of her breast. It seesawed back and forth tantalizingly.

But it never touched the crest that readied itself for his caress.

Derek wanted her. Every cell in his body was aching to take her. But he wouldn't. Now now. Not yet. She might come to think of this as a trade-off, the art studio for sex. He didn't want that.

She continued to be a puzzle. All the women he had known loved to be cosseted, loved to be lazy. Here she was, wanting to work. Would he ever know all of her? He hoped not. Each new day was something to look forward to because it revealed another aspect of Caren to him.

Even though his body was protesting his enforced abstinence more strenuously every day, life was more exciting than it had ever been.

Gradually he released her, bringing her upright first and giving her time to steady herself before he lifted his devouring mouth from hers. He dropped his hand from her breast. The other came up to stroke her cheek,

"If I'd known you were going to kiss me like that, I'd have built this studio long ago," he said softly, gazing into her limpid eyes.

After that, their relationship underwent another change. The atmosphere in the house was markedly more relaxed. There were frequent affectionate pats and kisses, but Derek made no effort to increase that affection to passion or to get her into his bed.

Caren alternated between relief and disappointment. Derek was still the most attractive, exciting man she had ever met. Every time she thought of him on the beach in Jamaica or striding into the chamber in the State Department, the kaffiyeh on his head, her heartbeat accelerated.

But here, on this estate he euphemistically referred to as the farm, he was in his element. He was demanding of his employees, but they respected him because he demanded just as much of himself. Caren was coming to see him as a caring human being. She was coming to know Derek Allen the man.

Still, she watched for the Tiger Prince to emerge.

One evening they were surprised by a telephone call from Al-Tasan and Cheryl. Al-Tasan was returning to Saudi Arabia after a series of successful conferences in Washington. Caren and Derek had been following them on the newscasts.

Caren had a brief conversation with Cheryl in which the older woman politely inquired into Caren's well-being. Derek spoke longer with his father. After he hung up, he turned to Caren and said, "He's meeting Mother in Geneva in October and he's asked us to come along. Would you like that?"

Dumbfounded, she stammered, "Y-yes, of course."

"He says he wants to get to know you better," he teased, lightly pinching her nose. "Hamid and his wife will be there too. I'd like you to meet him."

"Your older half-brother?"

"Yes."

"Father asked me if you were pregnant yet."

She covered her dismay by plumping a pillow on the sofa. "I hope you told him that was none of his business."

"He considers it his business."

"What did you say?"

"I said no." There was a question lurking in his eyes, and Caren looked away.

"That's right. I've had a period. I'm not pregnant."

"So it didn't happen in Jamaica," he said reflectively. She could have sworn there was a trace of regret in his tone, but she let the subject drop. As they went into the dining room for dinner, she asked, "Where does Cheryl live when she's not with your father?"

"On Long Island. She has a terrific house on the Sound. We'll visit her there sometime. Maybe take Kristin along. She'd love it."

"She just sits there and waits until your father crooks his finger for her to come running to him anywhere in the world?" Caren asked singlemindedly.

Derek's smile faded. "She understands."

Caren was glad Cheryl understood, because she certainly didn't. But she wasn't going to shatter her fragile friendship with Derek by discussing it further.

The next evening Kristin called. To Caren the telephone calls lent a permanence to the marriage. Everyone considered Derek and her a unit, an established couple. It made her uneasy. The break would be just that much harder to explain. Yet when the lease on her apartment ran out and she asked Derek what she should do about it, he had said, "Let it expire." Everything she owned in the world was now under his roof.

Kristin was bubbling with excitement.

"Two things," she said importantly when Derek, on another extension, asked her what she was so giddy about. "First, remember the boy? You know the one, Caren. You can tell Derek about it later. I'd *die* of embarrassment if I had to talk to Derek about a thing like that. Well anyway, he called back and invited me to go to a concert and reception his school is hosting as soon as the fall semester starts.''

"Terrific!" Caren exclaimed. "I knew he'd come around.''

"If he hadn't he certainly wasn't worth losing sleep over,'' Derek added.

"And second, this friend of mine,'' Kristin rushed on, "invited me down to her folks' place in Florida for two weeks between summer and fall semesters. Can I go, *please?* Derek, I know I promised to come to the farm and see the horses and all and, wow, I *want* to. But you guys are still on your honeymoon and all, and—''

"How can we possibly compete with Florida?'' Derek interrupted her.

"Then I can go?" she shrilled.

"Just a minute,'' Caren intervened. "Do I know these people?''

"Oh, Caren, they're real *nice.* Her mom said she was going to call you and make everything all right, you know. But can I go? I've worked so hard, taking courses through the summer. I know it was my decision, but it's been tough going straight through like this without a break. Can I, please?''

"Caren?" Derek asked from his extension.

"I suppose it will be all right, but I want to talk to the girl's parents first.''

"Gee, thanks, Sis. I love you, I love you.''

"And we'll expect you for Thanksgiving. No excuses, brat,'' Derek said sternly. "I'll send you a check for the trip tomorrow.''

"But they're paying for everything. I was asked to go as their guest."

"We can't have a member of this family looking like a pauper, can we? Buy some nice things to take with you."

Kristin screeched again, and when they asked her about the upcoming finals, she could barely contain her jubilation long enough to tell them.

For the rest of the evening, Caren was pensive. With everything he said and did, Derek indicated that the marriage would remain intact—the reference to a child, the relinquishing of her apartment, the planned trip to Geneva, the studio he had built into his house, the word "family" being slipped so naturally into his dialogue with Kristin, his brotherly attitude toward her.

Could it be...

No. She couldn't let herself even ponder it. One of these days, he'd grow restless. He was a man accustomed to having a woman when and where he wanted one. He had been without for weeks. Soon he would become anxious for the life he'd led before their marriage and would ask for the divorce.

Every day she found another reason to love him. Every day her body longed more for his. If she gave him the slightest hint that she felt that way, made the most subtle gesture, she knew he would take her to bed immediately. His gaze, burning and intent, was often on her. When she least expected it, she would turn and find him watching her with a hungry look.

It happened that night. He had been playing the

piano, and when she glanced up, rousing herself from her musings, his eyes were on her. "You've been awfully quiet. Worried about Kristin's trip?"

"No. I'm sure it will be all right." She got off the sofa and went to the window.

"The boy that she'd *die* of embarrassment telling me about, what was all that?" He ended the piece and came to stand beside her.

"The usual. She liked him, but he wanted to make out and was putting pressure on her to come across with the goodies."

"Men! They're all villains." When she looked up at him, his eyebrows were bobbing up and down and he was twirling the tip of an imaginary mustache.

"How well I know."

Growling lecherously, he swooped her close to him and bent her low over his arm. "Come across with the mortgage payment or I'll toss your old sick uncle out in the cold and take you, you damsel in distress you."

She shrieked, and he kissed her with farcical passion. Their lips were closed and they were laughing so hard it really couldn't be classified as a kiss.

Until they got one taste of each other. Then their comical kiss became serious. His lips hesitated. Pressed. Pressed again. Held.

He drew her up. She took a step closer, lightly laying her hands on his chest. Their mouths met and melded. She heard his rushing breath, felt the gathering passion in his body, and knew that if she didn't stop it now, she wouldn't be able to.

Stepping away, she tried to smile as though continuing the joke. Her lips were shaky. "I'd better go see if I can scrape up that mortgage payment. Good night, Derek."

"Good night."

She left him. She didn't want to. Yet she couldn't surrender to her impulses. If she did, she would never be able to bear their parting.

Each morning they continued to ride together. He gave her jumping lessons. She and Zarifa were taking low jumps with ease now. Every afternoon she worked for several hours in her studio. At first she just played, reacquainting her fingers with the feel of the clay, her favorite medium. Gradually she began to work on more complicated shapes until the talent she had been born with resurfaced.

One day, on a sudden inspiration, she began a new project, more complicated than any of the others. It became an obsession. For days she toiled over it, working off the sexual tension that had her strung as tight as she could go. Sometimes she thought she would die if Derek didn't touch her. But he rarely did now. She was left in a perpetual state of longing.

After spending hours on the project one afternoon, she was exhausted, but pleased with her progress. Exhilarated, she decided to take Zarifa for a ride before dinner.

As she was making her way into the stable, Derek was coming out. "Are you going riding?" he asked, eyeing her slender shape in the jodhpurs.

"I worked hard this afternoon and need to iron some kinks out of my neck."

Her blouse was soft and sheer. As the wind molded it to her breasts, Derek detected the lacy demi-cups of her brassiere and the faint shadows of her nipples. Inwardly he groaned.

How long could he be expected to hold out? His desire escalated by the hour until he thought he might explode if he didn't have again what his memory wouldn't let him forget. He even forced himself not to touch her too often for fear of losing control.

"Mind if I come along?" he asked huskily.

"No."

His clothes were slightly rumpled; he'd worked in them all day. He had unbuttoned several of the buttons down his chest to reveal the thick carpet of brown-gold hair, damply curled now with perspiration. The salty tang of a man who had worked hard outdoors filled her nostrils, and she wondered what the skin of his throat tasted like right now. It would be warm and damp against her lips. "I'd like the company," she said in a low voice.

Five minutes later they were on Mustafa and Zarifa and were chasing through the twilit evening. A perfect crescent moon was just coming up over the treeline. There was plenty of remnant daylight, so their ride wasn't hazardous.

Still, with the wind tugging at her hair, the powerful animal beneath her, the rugged man at her side giving his own mount his head, Caren experienced a sense of freedom she hadn't known for weeks.

The success of her project in the studio gave her a feeling of recklessness. Her eyes were full of the moon. She was drunk on the scent of the man, the horses, the smoky flavor of Indian summer.

So when the fence came into view, she knew she was going to take it. She and Zarifa were one, moving together in perfect harmony. They had the speed, the power. They could fly!

"Fall back, Caren. I'll take the fence and circle around."

She ignored Derek's instructions and bent down low over the saddle. "Come on, girl. We can do it," she whispered into the mare's pointed ears.

"Rein in. You're getting her too close," Derek shouted. Then he fully realized her intention. "No, Caren, it's too high," he yelled over the thudding hoofbeats of their horses. "You've never jumped a fence that high. Dammit, I said to fall back!"

But she only nudged her heels deeper into the mare's flanks and closed her ears to Derek's virulent cursing. The fence loomed nearer. Her spine prickled with fear. It was high! But it was too late to rein in now. Besides, Zarifa knew what she was doing. All Caren could do at this point was hold on.

She had time to draw in one deep breath before she and the horse went sailing over the fence. It seemed an eternity before they landed safely on the other side. But as soon as they did, Caren let out her breath in a long, relieved gust and began to pull the reins in.

She knew Derek must be close behind her, but

when she pulled Zarifa to a halt and wheeled her around, she didn't expect to see him and Mustafa bearing down on them, his face as fierce as a spiteful god's. He reined in so abruptly that Mustafa reared, pawing the air. Caren shrank from the might and fury of both the man and the beast.

"For that stunt I ought to paddle your butt till you can't sit down for a month."

"I'd like to see you try! And that wasn't a *stunt*. I was in control the whole time."

"Well, you just lost control, lady." Leaning over, he swatted Zarifa on the rump and spoke a command in soft Arabic. The mare obeyed immediately. Turning toward the stables, she headed back at a docile trot, regardless of any instructions Caren gave her to the contrary.

Caren was seething with rage and humiliation by the time they reached the stables. She dismounted in huffy silence. Derek tossed the reins of both horses to the groom who rushed out to take them.

Caren was already halfway to the house when she was brought up sharply by Derek's hand digging into the back of her waistband and grabbing a handful of the seat of her pants.

"Just a minute."

"Let me go!"

"I'm not finished with you yet."

"The hell you're not." She wiggled free, but faced him like a spitting cat. "Don't you ever, *ever* talk to me that way again."

"What way?"

"Shouting at me what to do or what not to do."

"You could have killed yourself!"

"But I didn't!"

"That's beside the point."

"Then tell me the point."

"You disobeyed me. When I give a command, I expect it to be obeyed."

Her mouth fell open. "Command! Obey! Well, forget that, mister. You may order other people around. You may have women all over the world eating out of your hand, bowing and scraping, ready to do a belly dance at a signal from you. But not me." She punched her index finger into her chest several times for emphasis.

"I am an independent person. And if I want to jump fences, or shave my head, or become an astronaut, or dig ditches, I don't need your permission to do it, Prince Al-Tasan. So forget my ever salaaming to you. I'm your wife, not your slave."

With that grand exit line, she spun on the heel of her boot and marched toward the front door. She heard his decisive footsteps in the gravel a split second before he caught her upper arm and pulled her around.

"My wife, is it? Well, by God, it's time you started acting like a wife."

He swept her into his arms, imprisoning her against his chest. He climbed the steps and strode across the porch and through the front door. Daisy, having heard the commotion outside, was standing in the entrance hall with a dripping spoon in her hand and an open-mouthed expression on her face.

"We won't be having dinner tonight, Daisy," Derek said tightly. "But I imagine we'll want an enormous breakfast."

He took the stairs two at a time and burst through the door of the bedroom Caren had seen only once, that first day when he had taken her on a tour of the house.

"I hope you like it," he said as her eyes widened in alarm. "But if you don't, that's tough. Just get used to it. This is where you'll be sleeping from now on."

He dumped her onto the bed. She landed on her hips and rolled to her back in time to see him yanking open the buttons of his shirt and peeling it off. He flung it away.

Then he fell on top of her, trapping her startled face between his hands and capturing her speechless mouth with his lips. He kissed her long and hard and deep. His lips were bruising, his tongue rapacious.

The kiss electrified Caren. Automatically, instantaneously, she raised her knees. The heels of her boots ground into the mattress. He lifted himself up and resettled himself between her open thighs, all without releasing her mouth from that kiss that branded her his.

Supporting himself on his knees and using both hands, he ripped her blouse open, exposing the heaving breasts that rose full and creamy over the lace cups. His mouth came down on them, hot and rampant. Madly, blind with passion, he clumsily worked the satin straps off her shoulders. Still impeded by the scrap of lace, he slipped his hands into the cups and lifted her breasts free.

He took one nipple between his lips and sucked it inside. Then, lifting his mouth away, he drew circles around that sensitive bud with his tongue. He loved it again, drawing on her so sweetly that she wept. Tears streamed down her face because it was so good, so gratifying, so much of what she had wanted and had stupidly denied herself.

Her hands tunneled through the shiny mass of his striped hair until she cupped his head in ten hard, grasping fingers. She clasped him to her breasts, never wanting him to stop that heavenly torment.

But it wasn't enough, and his appetite was voracious. He fumbled with her belt, then the fastener of her jodhpurs, until his groping hands found satin panties and skin just as soft and warm beneath. A soft tuft of hair. Then her. Wet, warm, welcoming.

Caren's breath hissed suddenly when his fingers slipped inside. She caught her lower lip between her teeth, but there was no stopping the shiver that ran from the crown of her head to the tips of her toes.

She arched against him at the same time that her nails raked down his chest. They skimmed the hard, flat plane of his stomach, then grappled with his belt and zipper.

When he filled her hand this time, there was no cloth between her flesh and his, for she had shoved down his clothing, frantically and brought herself close, close, until...

"Oh, sweet—"

"Derek, Derek."

After that first eruption of passion, their lovemaking gentled. Weakened, dampened by a sheen of sweat, he moved off her and cradled her against him.

"Are you all right?" he asked at last.

"Wonderful."

"Did I hurt you?"

"Of course not."

"I was in a hurry."

"So was I."

"I've wanted you for so long."

"I've been a fool."

As she said the words, she realized just how big a fool she'd been. If Derek could give her this much joy, why deny it to herself? Even if it were temporary, why not take what he offered now? The memory of it would sustain her for the rest of her life.

But not wanting to think beyond the moment, she let her lips move up his neck, over his jaw, and to his mouth. She kissed it lightly and left her lips there while she whispered, "You're not very chivalrous. You didn't even take your boots off."

"You didn't take yours off either."

They laughed at their ridiculousness, then undressed slowly, making of the soiled, damp—and in Caren's case, ripped—clothes a pile that would no doubt bring a frown to Daisy's face. When Caren remarked on it, Derek laughed.

"Are you kidding? She's been after me for weeks to treat you better so that our 'bedroom problems' would be worked out."

Their nakedness in the dusky room brought on another wave of desire, but this time they didn't rush. Caren basked in his loving attention, reminded of the sunny days and starry nights in Jamaica, when they were governed only by their senses.

His hands and lips explored her in delight. He caressed and stroked and tasted until she voiced her mounting passion with unintelligible murmurings and low purrs. She felt his lips whispering against the petals of her femininity, pressing Arabic accolades into the quivering flesh before gently applying his tongue.

After a finale that left them both replete and breathless, they went into the bathroom and sank into the silky warmth of a bubble bath. The marble tub had jets that sent the water swirling around them to rejuvenate tired muscles.

He filled her again, rocking her body over his as her thighs straddled his hips. "I'll never have enough of you, Caren love. Never," he rasped against her breasts as he held her tight and released his passion again.

The bath left them blissfully languid, their bodies weighted with a delicious lassitude. They slept, curled together, touching as much of each other as possible. And once during the night Derek awoke to find her making precious love to him. He groaned in ecstasy, threading his fingers through her hair, which swept his middle.

Whispers in the dark. Seeking hands and lips. Giving to each other.

Fourteen hours after the door was closed behind them, it was opened. Derek, fresh from a shower, impolitely bellowed down to Daisy that they were ready for breakfast.

Apparently Daisy had had it ready and waiting. Less than five minutes later, she entered the room, beaming happily. But she looked no more happy than the woman languishing on the heap of pillows, wrapped in her husband's terry cloth robe and a smug smile.

When Daisy quietly closed the door behind her, Derek was feeding Caren bites of bacon and she was licking his fingers clean after each bite.

"I have something to show you," Caren said as they finished their breakfast. Derek moved the tray aside.

"Goody, goody." He nudged the lapels of the robe aside for a better view of her nakedness.

"Not that," she said, playfully slapping his wandering hand from her breast. "It's something in the studio."

"You keep that place under lock and key."

"Artists are very sensitive about anyone viewing their work before they're finished," she said loftily.

He smiled, thinking she looked adorable bundled

in his robe, smelling of soap and woman. "But you want to show me something? I'm honored."

"It's supposed to be a surprise, but I can't wait."

"Come on, then."

Together they took the stairs, and she led him inside. Going straight to a draped block standing in the middle of a table, she pulled the cloth off. Clutching it to her chest, she watched him anxiously.

Derek stared at the piece of artwork: it had movement and grace; it had original style; it had the proud personality of the subject stamped all over it.

"Mustafa." Derek's soft whisper filled the room. He came forward until he was standing over the sculpture of the stallion, staring at it with awed appreciation.

"It's not finished, of course. This is just the clay model. I want to cast it in bronze."

He turned to face her, and she saw them, twin tears, one in each eye, making them more jewel-like than usual. Those two heavy tears glistened and grew in volume until they looked too large for his eyes to hold.

They were her undoing.

Laying a hand on his forearm and meeting his fervent gaze, she spoke aloud the only thought in her heart at the moment. "Derek, I love you."

Thirteen

❧~⊙⊙⊙~❧

The days were enchanted; the nights magic.

Caren moved through them in a cloud of happiness. When she wasn't with Derek, she thought about him. When she was with him, they were making love in one form or another, with their bodies, with their words, with their eyes.

By day, Derek was an American horse breeder who went about his work managing his farm and handling its various enterprises. By night, he was the Tiger Prince, transforming their bedroom into a sensual den. He didn't go so far as to change it as he had the bungalow in Jamaica. But his lovemaking was ever exotic, a festival of sight and sound and scent, a banquet for her senses.

She started to spend time in the stables and his office, learning about the business of breeding Arabians. Now that she shared his bed, it seemed appropriate that she share other aspects of his life as well. Derek did nothing to discourage her interest. Indeed, he was delighted with it and answered her intelligent questions patiently and in detail.

They spent hours on horseback. He graduated her to another level of training, after admonishing her again on her recklessness. She promised not to be so impulsive and sealed her promise with a kiss.

She didn't neglect her artwork. Every day she spent hours in the attic studio working on the statue of Mustafa. She wanted it to be as perfect as she could make it. A dozen times Derek tried to convince her that it was finished, that it couldn't be improved. She argued that it wasn't and that it could.

"How will you know when it's finished?" he asked late one afternoon. He had driven to Charlottes- ville that day on business and had just returned to find her hard at work in the attic.

His suit coat was held over his shoulder by a crooked index finger. She had on a sloppy pair of jeans and one of his shirts, which Daisy had procured for her out of a box destined for charity. The sleeves were rolled to her elbows. Her ponytail was scraggly and her brow was corrugated with concentration as she bent over the sculpture.

"I'll know," she said distractedly, and she pinched the clay between her stubborn fingers.

"You know," he said, dropping his coat onto a stool and advancing into the room, "I might begin to get jealous."

"Of my work?" Having glanced up at him, she could tell he wasn't serious.

"Yes. You spend a great deal of time looking at those lumps of clay."

"And a great deal of time looking at you, too."

"Maybe we should combine the two occupations. Have you ever thought of using live models?"

She straightened and wiped her hands on a damp towel before covering the sculpture, instinctively knowing that work for the day was over. Her husband was demanding her attention, and she was all too ready to give it to him. "Are you volunteering?" she asked coquettishly.

His grin was lazy and full of implication. "You know I have very little modesty."

"Very little?"

"Okay, none. I have no qualms about being naked."

"Yes, I know. That's part of your Eastern heritage, I believe. You have none of the traditional Puritan inhibitions most Americans have regarding their bodies."

"Complaining?"

"Absolutely not. I rather like you naked."

"Yeah? Then you'd like me to model for you that way?"

"Wait a minute," she said, holding both hands up, palms out. "There'll be no jumping to conclusions here. I was speaking as a wife, not as an artist. Viewing you as a model is something else entirely. Before you model for me, I'd have to see how well you're... equipped."

A spark leaped in his eyes. It's origin was sexual. "What do I do, audition?"

"Yes."

"How?"

"You start by taking off your clothes."

"Strip?"

"On a purely professional level, of course. We'll go from there."

His eyes never leaving hers, he reached far behind him and swung the door shut, locking it with a sound click. "That shouldn't be too difficult."

His necktie had already been loosened. He worked free the knot, slid it through the tunnel of his stiff collar until it popped free, then tossed it onto the same stool where his coat lay. The starched linen shirt came off with dispatch. As always, the sight of his bare chest touched off tiny flames in Caren's stomach.

"That won't quite do, Mr. Allen." He had stopped with his shirt. "I need to see—" she paused significantly "—everything."

"I understand," he replied humbly as he bent down to take off his shoes and socks. She liked his feet. They never seemed pale and sickly for lack of sun, but were as toasty brown as the rest of him.

Caren's eyes were riveted on his dexterous fingers as he unbuckled his belt and whipped it through the loops. His hands paused not at all before unfastening the snap of his trousers and sliding the zipper down.

His eyebrows arched inquisitively, and with supreme politeness he inquired, "In stages or all at once?"

"It doesn't matter."

"Which would you prefer?"

"Please, make it easy on yourself," she replied through a mouth gone suddenly dry. Sex with Derek was never dull or routine.

He pulled down the tight pair of briefs along with the slacks. When he threw them aside and straightened to face her, he was splendidly naked, as perfect as a young god.

For long minutes her eyes feasted on him, taking in the breadth of shoulders and chest, the tautness of stomach, the narrowness of hip, the length and leanness of thigh, the pride of manhood. His body hair was like a gold net stretched over it all, fleecy and thick at his chest and loins, a mere dusting on his limbs.

"Turn around."

He obeyed, pivoting slowly. His arms, muscled but not bunched, were held slightly away from his sides. His back was smooth and sleek, with a supple spine that flowed gracefully into the valley between his hard buttocks. Slowly he came around to face her again.

"Well? Will I do?"

Her heart was thudding with arousal. She wanted him, and if the gleam in his eyes was any indication, it had been a long day for him too. Still, the game had its merits. "You must understand, Mr. Allen, that I don't work by sight alone."

"No?"

"No."

"What else, then? Oh, wait. I think I know." He took the steps necessary to bring himself within arm's length of her. "You work by touch."

"Exactly."

"I can't tell you how much getting this job means to me," he whispered raggedly. "You may touch me all you want."

"Your cooperative attitude is being noted. A willing spirit on the part of the model is important."

"If my spirit gets any more willing, your part is going to get stabbed," he said out the side of his mouth.

"I beg your pardon?" she asked as if she hadn't heard, biting back laughter.

"Nothing. Proceed."

She laid her hands on his shoulders. "Nice and hard. As are your arms," she said analytically, sliding her hands down his biceps.

"Speaking of hard…"

"Yes?" She glanced up innocently.

"Never mind."

"Please, Mr. Allen. We must remain open and honest with each other. Say what's on your mind."

"You do intend to examine all of me, don't you?"

"Why, yes. It's necessary."

"Do you have any idea how long it's going to take?"

"Are you in a rush?"

"Uh, somewhat, yes."

"I'll keep that in mind."

"How about my chest? Will it suffice?"

She tilted her head to one side as though considering him. "Yes, I think so. Your pecs are good."

"So are yours."

"Hmm? Did you say something? I'm having a hard time hearing you." He groaned when she pressed her palms over the curves of his breast. "And you've got nice nipples. Nipples are important."

"I've always thought so myself," he grated as she feathered them with the tips of her fingers. Reflexively his hands came up to clasp her on either side of her waist.

"Mr. Allen, I don't think you understand."

"I don't think you do either."

"It's the artist who works by feel, not the model."

"Says who?" His hands were framing her breasts in the wide V's between his thumbs and index fingers.

"Says the artist."

"That's hardly democratic."

"Nevertheless, that's the rule."

"Well, then the artist had better be advised not to go without a brassiere, because the model can see her breasts."

"I'll take that under advisement." She shuddered as he tempted a stunning response out of her nipples with the circling pads of his thumbs.

"What about the rest?"

"The rest?"

"The rest of me."

"Oh, well, let's see." Her hands slipped under his arms and spread wide on the middle of his back. Her fingers tiptoed over the smooth expanse. "Nice, very nice. Good skin texture." She cupped his buttocks in her palms and pressed him against the fly of her jeans. "Good buns."

"Thanks," he panted.

Slowly her hands caressed their way around him until they found his sex. "Why, Mr. Allen. You apparently have the wrong idea. I won't be doing any statues of the fertility gods. That's a bit too pagan for my taste. The nudes I'll be doing will be..."

"Good Lord, Caren, sweetheart...ahh... darling..."

"...will be artworks glorifying the human body in its natural state."

"With what you're doing to me, this *is* the natural state... Oh, sweetheart...believe me. I'm about to—"

"They'll be studies in a purer form, you understand."

"Will you take me or not?"

She took him.

Minutes later they lay, not very comfortably, on one of her worktables. Somehow in their stumbling haste to reach the table, she had managed to get rid of her jeans and underwear. Derek's old shirt lay around her like a molted skin, one sleeve on, one off. She looked blissfully debauched.

"It was never like this before," she said, idly tracing her initials in his chest.

"What?"

"Sex. With Wade. It was never spontaneous and fun."

"You were having fun?" he asked, cocking his head to one side to look down at her. "All that scratching and biting and moaning is your idea of a good time?"

Blushing hotly, she buried her face in the furry warmth of his chest and joined his chuckling laughter.

"Thanks for telling me that it's different for you with me," he said quietly after a moment. Raising her chin with the end of his finger, he kissed her softly on the mouth.

"I wanted you to know. You're very special. I hope I never get used to the crazy things you do."

"You mean like bringing a guest home for dinner and leaving him to his own devices while I'm making love to my wife in the attic? Crazy things like that?"

She sprang up, balancing herself by bracing a hand on his sternum. "*What?* You're kidding, aren't you?"

His expression was boyishly guilty. "'Fraid not, honeybun. Met a friend from Texas today in Charlottesville. It would have been plumb inhospitable not to invite him home to din-nuh to meet my new wife," he said in a passable Texas twang. "I left him with one of the grooms to too-uh the stables while I came to fetch you. Then he was going to find the ba-uh and fix him a big buh-bon with just a splash of branch wat-uh and wait for us to come down."

"Are you…" She scrambled up and began gathering her discarded clothes. "Derek, are you telling me the truth? Is this for real? What will he think?"

"He'll think we were doing just what most new-lyweds would do after spending a whole day away from each other," he teased, grabbing a handful of her fanny as she wiggled into her jeans.

"Oh, my Lord." She crammed her feet into her moccasins.

"But we'd better not keep him waiting too much longer, or he'll begin to feel left out."

Casting him a fulminating look, she yanked open the door and hastily made her way to their dressing room.

Forty-five minutes later, as Caren entered the front parlor to meet their guest, the only evidence of her earlier agitation was the high color in her cheeks. Derek had rushed through his shower, so he was already there, sipping a drink, engaged in conversation with the heavyset man who surged to his feet when she came in.

"So this is the little lady. My, my, boy, you've done yourself proud. She's a beauty." He barreled forward on stocky legs. "Bear Cunningham, ma'am," he said, taking her hand in a bone-crushing handshake and pumping it heartily.

"Caren Allen," she said, introducing herself. "I'm sorry I'm late coming down. Derek didn't tell me we had a guest, and I was…uh…busy."

"In her studio," Derek added, winking at her surreptitiously. "She demonstrates boundless enthusiasm for everything she does in there."

Bear Cunningham was loud, brash, and impossible not to like. As she sipped the chilled white wine Derek poured for her, she fell into easy conversation. Her days in the State Department had given her plenty of opportunities to attend cocktail parties on Capitol Hill. She was accustomed to making small talk with strangers. This was their first guest since their marriage, and she felt a warm glow of satisfaction spread through her when she noted the pride in Derek's eyes.

She was wearing one of the new dresses she had selected, but which she had never had occasion to wear before. It was a vivid green silk that deepened the chocolate color of her eyes and made her hair shine with honeyed highlights. The pink coral jewelry she'd chosen to wear with it complemented her complexion. She knew she looked attractive and also knew that the main reason for the flow surrounding her was her love for Derek.

Dinner conversation revolved around Arabians.

"Bear has a ranch near...Weatherford, isn't it?" Derek said.

"Yep. Know Texas, Caren?"

"I'm afraid not." They had been on a first-name basis since shaking hands. "I've never been there."

"You git this sorry husband of yours to bring you down. Y'all can stay with us. That'd tickle Barbi to death. She'll fly you around in her plane."

"Barbi is...?" Caren let the question trail.

"My wife. Couldn't make this trip. Some function or another she was involved in. But we love to have comp'ny. Y'all come down anytime."

From what she gathered, the Cunningham ranch was four times the size of Derek's estate in acreage, but the stables weren't as impressive. The millionaire was working on remedying that. Thus this buying trip to Virginia and Kentucky.

"You know anything 'bout horses?" he asked Caren as they moved into the parlor, where Daisy suggested they take their coffee.

"I'm learning. And I have an excellent teacher." She sent Derek a loving glance.

"She is learning about our operation here, but she has a talent all her own," Derek said proudly. Suddenly setting his brandy snifter aside, he got out of his chair. "Hold on, Bear. I want to show you something."

"Wait!" Caren exclaimed, guessing his intention. "What are you doing?"

"I'm going to show him your sculpture."

"Oh, Derek, it isn't finished."

"It's magnificent."

He dashed up the stairs without listening to any more of her protests. Conversationally she asked Bear where Weatherford was, and he launched into a boastful speech on Texas geography. She fidgeted, hoping Derek wouldn't make a fool of them both. Was the sculpture really good? She was no judge of her own work. And his affection for her could have colored his opinion.

When Derek returned, respectfully bearing the sculpture like an offering to a pharoah, Bear heaved himself to his feet. He chomped on his fat cigar for several moments before he said. "Well I'll be damned. Pardon the French, Caren. That's your stallion Mustafa, ain't it?"

Derek beamed at Caren. "See? I told you it was magnificent."

Self-consciously she brushed the skirt of her dress. "It's my first piece of work in a long time."

"Hell, I think it's great!" Bear boomed. "Can you do me one?"

Caren's head snapped up. "Pardon? You want a sculpture of Mustafa?"

"Hell no, of Fancy Pants. That's Barbi's Arabian mare. Treats that horse like a queen. I've been wonderin' what I was gonna get Barbi for Christmas. Hell, she's got two of everything Neiman-Marcus sells. Would you do me a stachoo like this if I sent you a pitchur of Fancy Pants?"

Caren was struck dumb. She had never considered doing commission work, but the idea excited her. "I don't know. I guess I could." She looked at Derek. His face remained impassive, but she could tell by his dancing eyes that he was enjoying himself immensely and favored the suggestion.

"Is it money? How much you want?" Bear asked with the firm resolve of a man for whom money was no roadblock to having what he wanted.

"How much?" Caren hesitated. "Uh…" How much? Ten dollars? Fifty?

"I wouldn't let her do it for under ten thousand." Derek spoke from across the room, where he had gone to replenish Bear's glass of bourbon. "She spends a lot of time in the studio as it is. I don't like sharing her. It'll have to be worth her while."

"Well, I don't know," Bear hedged, scratching his head.

Caren thought Derek had surely lost his mind. Flabbergasted, she began to apologize, "Mr. Cunningham, Bear, I—"

"Don't seem like ten's enough to me," Bear said. "How 'bout twelve?"

"Yes!" Caren gasped, just recovering her voice after being shocked by Derek's gall. Twelve thousand dollars! "That...that will be sufficient. Send me the picture of Fancy Pants, and I'll get started as soon as I finish Mustafa."

"Will I git it by Christmas?"

"I promise. And don't send me any money until you've seen the sculpture and are satisfied with it."

Bear looked covetously at the sculpture of Mustafa. "I'll be satisfied, and Barbi'll pee in her pants. Pardon my French, Caren."

He left a half-hour later. As soon as the door closed behind him, Caren whirled on Derek and hissed, "Ten thousand dollars? Have you gone mad? Where did you get the nerve enough to ask for ten thousand dollars for a sculpture not two feet high?"

His answer was a rib-crushing embrace and a scalding kiss. "I couldn't live through one more minute without a taste of you,'' he whispered in her ear when he finally lifted his lips from hers.

''You're changing the subject.''

''What subject?''

''Derek,'' she said with aggravation, pushing him away. ''What if I'm not good enough? What if the statue of Mustafa was a fluke. What if—''

He laid a silencing finger on her lips. ''Then you'd better get in hours of practice. Bear's got a mouth as big as the state that spawned him. He'll brag about his sculpture of Fancy Pants to everybody he meets in horse circles, and he's a friendly fellow,'' Derek warned. ''My guess is that before you know it, you'll be swamped with commissions. You'll be turning down more than you accept.''

''But ten thousand dollars,'' she said, leaning against him weakly.

''Twelve,'' he reminded her, ruffling her hair affectionately.

''Derek, I barely made that in a year working at the State Department.''

''It's all relative, my darling. These people own some of the most spectacular animals in the world. They couldn't afford to unless they were incredibly rich to begin with. They have money to burn. The more you charge them, the more they think you're worth.''

''The money would be nice to have. Not for me, of course,'' she added hastily. ''But for Kristin. I could put it into a trust fund for her.''

And start a nest egg for me should I ever need it,

she thought to herself. In the past few weeks, things had been so marvelous between them that she hadn't thought much about a divorce or life without Derek. He gave no signs of growing tired of her. But the possibility lurked on the outskirts of her mind like some terrifying monster. She hugged him tighter, almost desperately.

"The money will be yours to do with as you wish." He tilted her head up for his kiss. "Just as I am."

His prediction proved correct. They attended an Arabian horse show in Richmond. Bear was there, taking Caren under his wing and introducing her as if she were his discovery instead of Derek's.

The Allen stables made an impressive showing, with two of their three entries taking home trophies. Derek was offered unlimited amounts for stud fees, besides the offers he got to sell the horses outright. The former he accepted, the latter he refused.

"But it's not my horses who have stolen the show," he told Caren, kissing her ear. "It's my wife. How many people have asked you to do sculptures of their horses?"

"Seven. One even asked if I'd do one of the family dog, too."

"If you weren't so lovely, people wouldn't be nearly so eager to meet you and talk to you."

"You think so?" she asked flirtatiously. They were strolling through the stables, looking at the Arabians temporarily stalled there.

"Think you're lovely? I certainly do."

He gave her no reason to think otherwise. He introduced her to his friends, behaving as though their marriage had been a love match rather than one of convenience. The envious looks cast in her direction by restless wives and single women told her his act was convincing. He convinced her, too, with his tender, passionate lovemaking in their hotel suite each night.

The only thing that disturbed her was the way his friends reminded him that they hadn't seen him around.

"Where have you been keeping yourself, Derek?"

"Have you been abroad?"

"Did you go to Cannes this summer as you'd planned?"

"What about Monte Carlo? Are we still on for the spring?"

"Are you going to Cortina for Christmas again this year?"

He answered their curious questions in a desultory fashion while Caren precariously clung to the hope that he didn't miss the jet-setter lifestyle.

When they returned home, she settled down to work on her sculptures, though she didn't sacrifice time with her husband. He seemed to enjoy her presence by his side in the stable or admiring him from her perch on the white rail fence as he exercised one of the horses.

One morning they were returning from their ride when they noticed a car in the drive.

"That's Mother's car," Derek exclaimed happily, lifting Caren off Zarifa. Together they walked into the house.

Daisy had already provided Cheryl Allen with a cup of coffee, but it had gone untasted as she sat in one of the wing-backed chairs in the parlor, staring vacantly into space.

When they came through the arched doorway arm in arm, she roused herself. Her smile was forced. Her eyes were red and puffy from crying.

"Mother?" Derek asked, alarm squeezing his chest painfully. He knelt in front of her. "What's the matter?"

She clasped his face between her hands. Tears slipped unheeded from her eyelids. "Hamid. He was killed in France."

Caren covered her mouth with her hand to trap an anguished cry. Derek had spoken often of his half-brother. He felt a tremendous affection for him despite their different upbringings. He had been looking forward to the trip to Geneva, if for no other reason than to see Hamid.

"How?" he asked roughly.

"In a car race. You know that racing car he had. He was driving it. There was a wreck and fire..." Her voice dwindled to nothing as she raised a handkerchief to her eyes.

"Father?"

Cheryl composed herself. "He's taking it very hard. I've talked to him almost hourly since he received word. Hamid's wife was with him. She's escorting the body back to Riyadh."

Derek's head fell forward in grief. His mother stroked his hair. "I want to be with Amin, of course, but that's impossible. He knows it. So do I."

"I'll go immediately."

"I was hoping you'd say that. I've already called for a car and driver to take you to Dulles Airport. You can get a flight there faster than in Richmond. Amin needs you, Derek. Desperately. He is inconsolable."

An hour later, he was ready. Daisy had anticipated his needs. She had already begun to pack for him as soon as Cheryl told her the purpose of her visit.

Caren moved in a stupor, wishing she could find something useful to do. She had never felt more inadequate in her life.

The man who walked down the stairs with his suitcase in one hand and an overcoat over the other arm was a stranger. Dressed in a severe black three-piece suit, a kaffiyeh anchored to his head, he looked like anything but the husband she knew and loved. His eyes were remote, as was his voice.

"Mother, will you stay with Caren until I return?"

"Of course."

"I'll give Father your love."

"He knows he has it. I suffer for him."

Derek kissed Cheryl's pale cheek, then turned to Caren.

"I'm so sorry, Derek. For you, Hamid's wife, and the sheik. Please extend my sympathy to them."

He nodded. "Goodbye." His kiss was cool and dispassionate.

Everything inside her seemed to congeal as she watched him walk purposefully toward the waiting black limousine.

Fourteen

—❧❧❧—

Caren wasn't under any delusions. She knew the repercussions Hamid Al-Tasan's untimely and unpredicted death would have on her life with Derek.

Derek was Amin Al-Tasan's second son. Now that the heir apparent was dead, Derek would be expected to assume that role. The sheik would have great expectations for his son Ali.

Amin Al-Tasan had done what his father had expected of him. He had divorced Cheryl under Islamic law and married an Arab. Al-Tasan would expect no less from Derek. Even though the sheik had other children, Derek was next in line. Tradition and obligation were important to men like Amin Al-Tasan. They transcended everything else.

Caren and Cheryl shared dinner in the dining room the evening after Derek's departure. The mood was bleak and their conversation was forced and stilted. Cheryl was sick with worry over Amin. She wanted to be with him, but knew this was one instance when her presence was forbidden. They retired to their rooms upstairs as soon as they had finished the meal neither of them tasted.

That night, sleeping alone in the bed she now shared with Derek, Caren dreamed. Her body bathed with sweat, she awoke with a start. Her breasts were heaving. Miserable, she covered her face with her hands and wept. The sobs wrenched her body until it was sore.

The next morning when she came down to breakfast, Cheryl looked at her with concern. "You look pale, Caren. Didn't you sleep well?"

She shook her head as she poured a cup of coffee. "No. I had a dream. About Derek." She felt unreasonably compelled to talk about it and began describing the dream to Derek's mother, who listened sympathetically.

"I saw Derek." Caren smiled softly. "You have a beautiful son."

"Yes, I know," Cheryl replied without conceit. "Go on. Why did the dream disturb you?"

"I saw Derek clearly. The golden streaks in his hair and eyes were shining unnaturally bright. But as I watched, he became more dreamlike. Faint and elusive. His image blurred, became transparent. And all the time, he was slipping away from me, moving farther and farther away until I couldn't see him anymore."

She fell silent, unable to voice what both women knew to be a fact. The dream was prophetic. Derek was slipping away from her. He would no longer belong to her. He would become part of a world, a culture, a religion that was foreign to her and in which she had no place.

The gloomy atmosphere in the house prevailed. Cheryl and Caren did their best to pretend that everything was normal, but their efforts at cheerfulness were futile. Eventually they gave up trying to entertain each other, but a bond grew between them. They shared heartache, each for a different reason.

Caren continued to ride every day. At times she could almost imagine Derek riding beside her, his white teeth flashing at her as he smiled. But he wasn't there, and the gaping hole left in her life was deeper than she would ever have imagined it could be.

When Wade left her, she had suffered, but it was nothing compared to this living death that life without Derek was. He had taken her heart with him when he left.

The first week of Derek's absence dragged by, each hour seeming like a day. She spent long hours in her studio working on her sculptures. One afternoon it occurred to her why she was suddenly so diligent—this might be all she had left. Kristin's and her future might depend on how successful this enterprise became. She had a good start, but the business would have to be carefully cultivated. She couldn't afford to let it slide now.

"Caren," Cheryl said, tapping lightly on the attic door. "May I come in?"

"Certainly," Caren said, reaching for a cloth to clean her fingers with. The visit was a surprise. Cheryl had made no attempt to see her when she was at work. "I was about to wrap it up for today anyway."

"Daisy made a pitcher of lemonade. I didn't want it, but bless her, she's been so discouraged by our lack of appetite, she needed something to do. I didn't have the heart to turn down the offer. She's baked cookies, too." Cheryl carried in the tray. Caren made space on one of her worktables for it.

"Derek's favorite cookie," Caren said wistfully. She picked up one of the chocolate chip cookies, broke off a piece, studied it with a sad smile on her face. "One evening he ate at least a dozen of these. I warned him that he would get fat if he didn't ration himself." She put the cookie back on the plate without eating it.

"Daisy misses him too," Cheryl said. "We've been like three ghosts haunting this house waiting for the master to return." She sighed as she sipped at the unwanted lemonade she'd poured herself. "I guess that's been the plight of women throughout history, waiting for our men to return from the sea or from wars, while we stay behind and keep home and hearth ready for the day they come back."

"Maybe a long time ago. But now? In the twentieth century?" Caren was shaking her head in disagreement. "Those days are over."

Cheryl looked at her closely and asked softly, "Are they?" Caren's eyes fell away. "Your work is fabulous," Cheryl said briskly, changing the mood. "Derek bragged about it, of course, but I thought that was just husbandly pride talking. He didn't exaggerate. You're quite talented."

"Thank you. I hope I have something to offer that the public wants. Especially now." She hadn't realized that her innermost fear had been spoken aloud until she heard the words leave her mouth. Quickly she raised her eyes to Cheryl's. Her mother-in-law reached out to press one of Caren's hands between her own.

"That's what's bothering you, isn't it? Your future now that Hamid's dead."

"Yes." It was a relief to admit it. She kept her eyes on their clasped hands. Cheryl's ring finger sported a spectacular emerald. It was her only piece of jewelry, remarkable in its solitude. But she couldn't treasure it any more than Caren did the gold band on her own ring finger.

"What do you think will happen? Will Derek's father want him to step into Hamid's place in the Arab world?"

"I would imagine so, wouldn't you?"

"Yes." Her voice was an undignified croak. She hoped she wouldn't disgrace herself by crying.

"He is, after all, next in line to rule Amin's sheikdom."

"I know."

"He's a natural leader. He's popular, well-liked, and respected in the Arab world even though he's always shown a marked preference for the West."

These impressions of Derek weren't exclusively Cheryl's. Caren shared them. But each of Cheryl's words was like a hammer blow striking the nails of her coffin.

"What will you do if Derek aligns himself with his father?"

Caren got off her stool and began to wander around the studio, needlessly straightening her tools, redraping damp cloths over her clay models. She was arranging her thoughts, rearranging them, but always she came to the same conclusion.

"I couldn't live as you do, Cheryl. I'd never be a slave that Derek could whistle for."

Rather than taking offense, Cheryl laughed delightedly. "Do you think that's what I am, Amin's slave? Well, I suppose to some people, particularly an enlightened young woman like you, I would appear to be."

"He practically dragged you into that hotel bedroom the day Derek and I got married," Caren said heatedly.

Cheryl laughed. "Yes, well, you see, that morning we were in bed when he got the call about the situation you and Derek were in." She grinned naughtily. "Understandably, he wasn't in the best of moods. He was merely anxious to finish what we'd started earlier."

"Oh," Caren said, blushing.

Cheryl smiled warmly, almost sympathetically. "I'm not enslaved by anything but love, Caren. Actually, I have more freedom than most women in the world. I have a beautiful house—I do as I please."

"Except when Al-Tasan beckons you to come anywhere in the world to meet him," she argued.

"I go because I *want* to, not because he commands it."

Caren stared at her in bewilderment. "Doesn't it bother you that he has another wife, that he's had children by her?"

A shadow drifted across the otherwise serene face. "Of course it does, Caren. I wouldn't be human or female if it didn't. The only regret of my life is that I couldn't have more children. Amin and I agreed years ago that Derek's life would be complicated enough. We couldn't inflict that kind of ambiguity on any other children."

She came to where Caren was standing near one of her worktables. "I love Amin; I have since the moment we met. And I know he loves me. His wife in Riyadh may have his name, his children, but I have his heart. There's never been any doubt in my mind that I am the woman he considers his true wife, his soulmate.

"Otherwise, he would have deserted me years ago when his father demanded the divorce. He could have taken Derek, and I would never have seen my child again. He loved us both too much to do that."

"But you and Derek have suffered so much."

"It hasn't been easy for Amin either. He's compromised many times to make things easier on me. I stay in the background, and he protects me from publicity. There are many people around the world who wouldn't understand our relationship. They would see me as a kept woman, the mistress of a rich and powerful man. I accepted that a long time ago. I can't worry about it.''

She gazed through the clear skylight overhead where the first red-gold streaks of sunset slanted in. Caren knew Cheryl wasn't seeing the sky. She was seeing her loved one's face. "He needs me; powerful as he is, world leader that he is, Amin needs me. So when I can, I stay close to him. I do what is necessary to make him happy because I love him.''

Spontaneously and unselfconsciously she hugged Caren to her. "Do you love my son?"

Caren accepted the comforting embrace she had needed for days. "Yes. Very much.''

"Then somehow the two of you will work it out. You'll see your way through this.''

They spoke no more about it. At dinner Cheryl was more relaxed with Caren than before. She told her stories of her travels with Amin and anecdotes about Derek as a boy.

But if Cheryl was more relaxed, Caren was more troubled. She put up a good front for her mother-in-law, but when she retired to the master suite that night, she fell across the bed and dissolved into tears.

What was she to do?

Cheryl's happiness with her station in life was obvious. She had chosen it years ago. But Caren wouldn't ever be satisfied with being a standby wife, especially after having lived in Wade's shadow for seven years.

What had that kind of meek servitude gotten her

but a low self-image and a nonexistent ego? No, never again would she become a fixture in a man's life, an ornament he could pick up and play with when the mood suited him and dispose of just as negligently.

Nor could she make any demands of her own on Derek. It was laughable to think of herself competing with sheik Al-Tasan for Derek's loyalty and love.

Besides, Derek had never spoken of love. Even that morning in the studio when she had quietly confessed her love for him, he had drawn her tightly to him, cradled her head against his throat, and murmured what sounded like love words into her hair while his hands gently caressed her back. But she had never heard the words from his lips in her own language. Never "Caren, I love you."

There was no other course for her to take but to leave.

She would be leaving the house she had come to consider home, the people she knew now as friends, the man she loved. But she wouldn't be waiting here when he returned, waiting for him to say what she dreaded hearing. Walking away would be the most painful thing she had ever had to do. But not as painful as being walked away from.

She would retain her pride and give Derek his freedom. As Cheryl had said, she would do what was necessary because she loved him.

By ten o'clock the next morning she was packed, taking with her only the things she had arrived with.

The note Derek had written her in Jamaica was in her handbag, but she left her wedding ring in an envelope with a letter to him.

Cheryl was in the dining room, having one last cup of coffee with the morning newspaper. She glanced up with a smile when Caren came in. The smile faded when she saw the two suitcases Caren was carrying.

"What—"

"I'm leaving, Cheryl," Caren cut in. "I've left Derek a note on his desk in his office."

"But—"

"I'm taking the car he bought for me. Tell him I'll make arrangements to have it returned later."

"You can't mean this," Cheryl said, rushing to her feet. "Where are you going?"

"I'm not sure yet. Possibly back to D.C., though that idea doesn't really appeal to me. I want to set up a studio where I can work peacefully, some place not too far from Kristin. Ask Derek to please save my correspondence for me. Tell him that I'll move the sculptures out as soon as possible. I'd like to buy the equipment if we can settle on a satisfactory price."

"Derek will be very upset, Caren. Are you sure—"

"He'll raise bloody hell," Daisy said bluntly, having heard from the doorway what Caren planned.

"Daisy, thank you for everything. You've been wonderful to me, and you can't know how much I appreciate that. Now, please, don't either of you say anything more." She clung to the determination not to cry. "I've thought it through. The circumstances of our marriage were...out of the ordinary...to say the least. This is best, believe me. For both Derek and me. I'm just going to say goodbye to Zarifa, then I'll be on my way."

Hurriedly, before the tears could be detected, she turned on her heel and, carrying her suitcases, went through the front door. The luggage was stored in the small trunk of the sports car. She revved it to life and drove it to the stable. When she didn't find Zarifa in her usual stall, she asked a groom where the mare was.

"Out in the south pasture, you know the one, where Mr. Allen lets them graze sometimes."

"Yes, thank you."

Luckily the pasture he referred to bordered the road, so she could drive right to it. Ten minutes later she spotted the mare and several other horses grazing on the fertile grass. Cutting the engine of the car, she squeezed through the slats of the fence and walked toward them. She called to Zarifa as Derek had trained her to do, and the horse responded immediately.

Caren rubbed the velvety space between the huge brown eyes. "I'm going to miss you, Zarifa, my graceful one." The tears that had been threatening all morning finally welled up. She rested her forehead against Zarifa's nose and let them fall. "I'm going to miss *him*," she whispered fiercely.

Derek's eyes were gritty. He'd flown all night. His clothes were travel-wrinkled and his jaw was rough and shadowed with beard. He shrugged off his suit coat as he strode purposefully through Dulles Airport. He'd just disembarked from the jet his father had made available to fly him home. He had been too impatient to wait for a scheduled flight. Now he was on his way to the heliport, where a helicopter was standing by to take him the rest of the way home.

Home to Caren.

At just the thought of her, he began to walk faster, tired as he was. He hadn't called. His father had cursed the poor connections when he telephoned Cheryl daily. Derek didn't want an unsatisfactory telephone line to be his first communication with Caren after his hasty departure. He wanted her body close to his in a warm embrace, her mouth beneath his kiss.

God, he couldn't wait to see her!

His kaffiyeh blew around his head as he stooped under the blades of the chopper and climbed aboard. The pilot greeted him with a deferential nod, and they left the ground as soon as Derek had stashed his suitcase and buckled his seat belt.

It was a beautiful day. He noticed as they flew over the trees that most of them were becoming tinted with the russets and reds and golds of fall. The air was crisp. Maybe this afternoon after he cleaned up and rested a bit, he and Caren could go for a ride. He had had enough of grief and funereal gloom. He would forever miss his brother, but after having laid him to rest, he wanted to celebrate life with his wife.

The trip to Geneva hadn't been canceled or postponed. His father had told him that he, Caren, and

Cheryl could fly there together. Al-Tasan mourned Hamid as well, but he, too, knew that life went on.

Derek grinned to himself. Actually, he knew his father was longing to see his mother. They had a strange relationship. Derek had reconciled himself to it years ago when he was first old enough to understand it. He considered himself lucky. Few children had parents who loved each other as much as his did.

He had often teased his father about his impatience and anxiety when Cheryl wasn't with him. Now he knew that that kind of desperation was no teasing matter. It had shaken him to realize how much he missed Caren, just how much he loved her.

The flight was uneventful and therefore seemed even longer to Derek, who couldn't wait to get home. The pilot set the chopper down close to the house. Derek thanked him, shook his hand, and pulled his suitcase from behind the seat. By the time he set foot on the ground, Cheryl and Daisy were rushing from the house to greet him. The pilot lifted the chopper off.

"Hello!" Derek shouted over the racket of the blades. "Where's Caren?"

His mother flung herself against his chest, hugging him hard. Was she crying? Daisy was wringing a dishtowel in her capable hands and gnawing on her lower lip.

Derek pushed his mother away. Tears had streaked her flawless, unlined cheek. "What kind of homecoming is this? What's the matter?" He glanced toward the house, expecting to see Caren running toward him any second. She had those stairs from the attic to negotiate and—

"She's left, Derek," his mother wailed. "And I think it's all my fault."

Derek gripped his mother's hands. "Left? Caren? What in the hell are you talking about? Mother, stop crying and tell me what's happened."

She sniffed back her tears and gazed up at her son. In his kaffiyeh he reminded her so much of Amin. "She...she came downstairs this morning with her suitcases, saying she was going to leave. Daisy heard." His eyes sliced to Daisy, who bobbed her head in affirmation. "Last night we had a talk about my life with your father, and I said something about doing what was necessary. Do you think she read something into that that I didn't mean?" Her lower lip began to quiver uncontrollably.

"Calm, Mother, calm. What reason did she give you for leaving?"

"No reason. She was talking about cars...and... and what else? Oh, yes, she mentioned something about her studio and buying the equipment from you. She left a note in your office."

"To hell with a note!" Derek barked. "Where did she go?"

"She said she wanted to say goodbye to a horse."

"How long ago?" he asked over his shoulder. Having dropped his suitcase and coat, he was already running toward the stables.

"How long, Daisy? Twenty minutes? Half an hour? I can't remember. We've been so upset."

Derek didn't hear the rest. He was covering the distance to the stable with amazing speed. It was cool, dim, and serene when he dashed through the wide doors. It instantly came to life when Derek bellowed for a groom. Several came running to see their employer, who was usually the picture of composure, more distraught than any had imagined he could be.

"Where's Mrs. Allen? Is she in here?"

One poor soul was forced to step forward like a young David facing Goliath and provide the information he had. "No, sir. She came by and asked for Zarifa. But the mare's in the south pasture. The missus said she would go by there. Do you want to take the truck?" he asked, tentatively offering a set of keys to Derek.

"No. Mustafa can cut across the fields."

With dispatch the stallion was backed out of his stall. He was pawing the ground, apparently as agitated as his rider, who vaulted onto his back without the benefit of a saddle. Taking up the reins of the bridle someone had quickly slipped over Mustafa's proud head, Derek whirled him around. Horse and man shot out of the stable door as straight and clean and sure as an arrow from a bow.

"Goodbye, Zarifa," Caren whispered one last time, saying goodbye to much more than the mare. Turning, she walked through the lush grass toward the spot where her car was parked.

She felt the vibration beneath her feet before she actually heard the pounding hooves. Mystified, she looked around. What she saw caused her to gasp in amazement.

Derek and Mustafa came flying over the far fence of the pasture. Their landing must have been jarring, but the animal never broke the long, enduring stride that kicked up clumps of turf in his wake.

The rider was bent low over the stallion's back. A white kaffiyeh, still secured to his head by a silk cord, flapped in the wind. His shirt, hastily unbuttoned to allow him more freedom, billowed away from his chest, which seemed as powerful as that of the beast beneath him. Hard thighs gripped the flanks of the stallion. He was clutching handfuls of the luxuriant black mane with the same determination that kept his jaws locked in a feral grimace.

Caren's heart soared at the sight of him. He was from the *Arabian Nights*, from *The Sheik*, from mythology. She wouldn't have been surprised if he had been brandishing a lethally curved scimitar.

But just as the surge of gladness at seeing him leaped in her breast, it was swamped with fear. He wasn't slowing down and he was riding straight toward her! The other horses fanned out to give them room.

Uselessly backing away, Caren watched Derek and Mustafa race closer, bearing down on her. She could feel the stallion's hot breath, see the fire in his black eyes, see the lather on his coat, before Derek swerved him to one side, barely missing her. Bending down low, he scooped her up with one arm and positioned her between his thighs. Then he urged Mustafa into another charging gallop.

Terrified by their thundering speed, Caren closed her eyes. She clutched at Derek in an attempt to stay on the horse. But there was really no way for her to fall off, for Derek's arm was almost cutting off her breath, so tightly had he imprisoned her against his thudding heart.

She saw the fence coming and couldn't believe he was going to take it with both of them on the stallion's back. She underestimated both horse and rider. The horse was of the elite. His ancestors had carried warriors into mountainous Spain and fighting bands over scorching deserts. Mustafa's heart pumped royal blood.

And the man. The man was more furious than she'd ever seen him. His whole body was tense with pent-up rage. He would dare anything.

They cleared the fence with seemingly no effort on Mustafa's part. But not until they had left the pasture and entered the woods did Derek lessen the pressure of his knees on the horse's sides and slowly bring him to a halt.

He swung his long leg over and dragged Caren off the horse with him. Every muscle in her body was quivering with fear over the hazardous ride she'd just taken and with anxiety over the expression on Derek's face. That was why the merest pressure of his hands on her shoulders sent her collapsing onto a bed of fern.

She lay on her back, looking up at him with wide,

frightened eyes. The hem of her skirt was riding high on her thighs. Her elbows were supporting her, and the position proved too much of a strain on the buttons of her blouse. They popped open, but she didn't even notice. "Derek?"

His breath was labored. His eyes smoldered with emotions she was afraid to name. He held his arms rigid at his sides, flexing his fingers. His lips had thinned to an almost invisible line. As always, the kaffiyeh made him a stranger to her. An exciting stranger straight out of a fantasy.

He came down on one knee only and wedged it between hers before stretching out fully on top of her and pressing her down. With fists as hard as manacles, he anchored the backs of her hands to the ground on either side of her head.

"You will not leave me, wife. You will not."

The kiss that followed was blistering. Passion, rampant and searing, fueled it. He buried his tongue in her mouth and thrust deeply, repeatedly, again and again. Each deft stroke was like a licking flame that coaxed fire from her veins. The kiss had no subtlety. It was bold, blatant, carnal.

But not subjugating. The kiss was suppliant. Desperate, not dominating.

When he lifted his mouth from hers, his voice cracked emotionally as he repeated his message. He burrowed his head between her breasts. With nose and mouth, he nuzzled the sweet curves, the ripe mounds, the tender crests. With his chin he opened her blouse wider until her skin was abraded with his beard.

His breath, his mouth, his tongue, his words were hot.

"You will not, you will not, you will not…"

"I'll have bruises for a month."

"Bitch, bitch, bitch." The words were muffled, for the mouth speaking them was otherwise engaged.

"Just look at this. That's from your arm. It felt like a grappling hook lifting me off the ground."

Deeply remorseful, Derek inspected the faint bruise along her rib. "I'm sorry." He leaned over her torso to nibble along her rib. Unable to stop there, his lips meandered to the underside of her right breast.

"And this one," she said, pointing to the purplish bloom on her lower hip, "is from when I landed on Mustafa's back."

"Hmm," Derek murmured sympathetically and moved down her body to plant a soft kiss there as well.

"No telling how many will show up tomorrow."

"I'll give each one the same tender loving care." His lips feathered down her hip, then over the soft valley of her belly to her navel, which he leisurely kissed.

"Promise?" She sighed, arching her back with a movement that brought her closer against his mouth.

It was late. Long after he had found her in the pasture, they came riding out of the woods at a much more sedate pace. Decorum and modesty were totally alien after their fierce lovemaking on that bed of fern. She sat facing Derek on the stallion's back. Mustafa picked his own way home. They kissed every step of the way.

By the time they reached the house, they were both mellow, but vibrating with renewed desire. It took all the willpower they possessed to shower and dress for dinner with Cheryl, who hovered over them anxiously even after she had been assured that Caren wasn't leaving and that all was well.

By the time dessert was served, she was convinced, as was the worried Daisy. The couple could barely eat for feasting their eyes on each other. As soon as the dishes were cleared away, Cheryl invited Daisy out to a movie, deliberately leaving the house to the lovers.

Derek and Caren could barely contain their excitement as they raced upstairs, undressed, and met each other in the middle of Derek's wide bed.

Now he was driving her to blissful distraction by brushing his mouth back and forth over her lower abdomen. "What if you're carrying my baby, Caren? I've been doing my damnedest to get you pregnant, if for no other reason than to keep you married to me. Did you think I'd let you escape with my child?"

"It's true I haven't been using anything to prevent pregnancy, but I've had no signs."

"But you could be. My baby could be growing inside you even now."

"Is that the only reason you came after me?"

His answer was in the form of a kiss that branded her flesh and caused her womb to contract. "No."

"Your father let your mother leave with you. She went halfway around the world from him."

"He had no choice. At least by his code of honor he didn't. He was born knowing his duty."

"And you?"

"I have no such sense of duty to the Arabs. I'm American, Christian. I love my father. I love the Arab culture, appreciate its mystery and beauty. But I don't owe it the allegiance my father did. He won't demand it of me, because he and my mother have suffered so much because of his decision. It was the only one he could make. That's not true in my case."

"He won't resent me?"

"No." He pressed his lips into the softly swelling delta. "Of course, a few grandchildren would win you points."

Grabbing handfuls of his hair, she lifted his head. "You rascal. Kiss me."

Slowly he climbed her body, dropping adoring kisses every inch of the way. By the time he reached her mouth, they were starved for each other. His tongue mated with hers, stroked the roof of her mouth.

"I want to stay here with you forever, Caren." His fervent lips found her ear and loved it.

"Don't you miss your other life? You were a play-boy, Derek. A jet-setter. You didn't choose to be a settled, married man. You were coerced into marrying me."

He smiled down at her with that lazy, feline grin that never failed to pitch her insides into chaos. "Is that what you thought?" He kissed her cheek softly. "Caren love, offering you marriage that day was the only way I could see to keep you."

"What are you saying?" She didn't trust her own ears.

"That I loved you from the first minute I saw you. That I went into such a rage when you left that I'll probably never be allowed back in Jamaica for as long as I live. I went on a search for you that rivaled the search for the lost ark. I literally turned that island upside down looking for you before being summoned home by my father on a matter of grave importance. I could have shouted for joy when I learned you were the gravely important matter."

"But you seemed so remote that day, so angry."

"I was pouting. I could have strangled you for leaving me. But at the same time I wanted to make love to you until you admitted that you couldn't do without me either." He kissed her. "If Speck Daniels hadn't helped me out, I would have turned the planet inside out until I found you. I told you you would never outrun me. I proved it again today."

Tears were beading in her eyes and sliding down into her hair. "You won't ever want to go back to your former philandering?"

His hand found the fullness of her breast and its responsive peak. "I was tired of it before I ever met you. I was restless, dissatisfied, looking for something that I knew was missing in my life. I didn't know what it was until I nearly stepped on it on the beach. Now I want to spend every day of my life loving you.''

She smiled, both at his words and at the way his tongue was laving her breast. ''I can't be a meek and submissive wife, Derek. Life with you is the best I've ever known, but I have to have my own life, too.''

Realizing how important this was to her, he raised his head and searched the dark velvety depths of her eyes with his. ''I know that, Caren. You may do as you please.''

''My work?''

''No one is prouder of it than I. If you ask my assistance, I'll gladly give it. But I'll never interfere in the business you're building. It's yours.''

She felt warm and glowing all over. Love flowed through her like fine wine, bubbling out in every pore. ''I love you.''

''I love you.''

''I know. You told me today in the woods.''

''You didn't know till then?'' She shook her head so that her honey-tinted hair shifted like silk over his hands. ''Even if I never said the words in English, didn't I demonstrate it often enough?''

Her voice was a sultry whisper. ''Demonstrate it again.''

''Not before you put this back on.'' He had the wedding ring with him and slipped it on her finger, sealing it with a kiss.

''I'm glad to have it back.''

''I'm glad to have *you* back.''

She ran her fingers through his hair. "Now?"
"Now."

His eyes piercing into hers, his mouth curved into that lazy smile she adored, he eased her thighs open and snuggled his hips between them. Her eyes closed when she felt his smooth warmth probing the portals of her womanhood. But there he paused, rubbing, softly, softly, prolonging the magic.

She caught a short, swift breath and held it.

"I love you, Caren. I have since I saw you on the beach with that surprised, endearingly innocent dazed expression on your face. You were so rare and sweet. Your breasts were beautiful." Dipping his head, his questing tongue found one rosy crest and laved it till it glistened.

"Derek," she sighed, lifting her hips toward his hardness. "Come into me, my beautiful, golden man, my husband...my love...."

She was filled, body, mind and soul, with the fiery splendor and tender loving of the Tiger Prince.